MW01384427

THEY SAY A JOURNEY of a thousand mile ___ know where you're going but only when ___ lands in a puddle, but it, and each step after that, takes him further from the pain and regret he's caused in the past. Along the way, he realizes two things—there is something to walk toward, and he doesn't need to walk alone.

Enough Grace to Make Things Right is a story of hope and redemption as one man seeks to repair a life that was broken and embrace the healing power of faith and forgiveness.

For anyone who has ever felt unloved or unloveable, Joe's journey reminds us that we are all fearfully and wonderfully made. Miracles happen every day as God's grace gently guides us toward the places we are meant to be.

—Shelley Divnich Haggert, Author, Editor, and Communications Professor, Windsor, Ontario

HAVE YOU EVER NOTICED that some paintings reveal considerably more to you about their subject than a photograph might? Although this novel is fiction, like a terrific painting it draws you in with each turn of the page. How wonderful it is to read a story that so effortlessly exposes the tireless work of God. This is not rainbows, sunshine, and unicorns. This is the Master Painter adding glorious strokes of grace, truth, and light to the dark canvas we call the weary soul. As an author, Janet Weiler invites you to a seemingly simple story about ordinary people. These people are from all walks of life. Some appear to have it all together, while others obviously don't. One is just getting by with a bit of help from above. When you're done, you can't get it out of your mind. And that's a good thing.

As a pastor, I feel like I know a lot of people just like the characters in this novel. (And I know you do too.) If this book does nothing else, I am sure it will help you wonder better. More specifically, it will help you wonder where God might be working next. I know it did that for me.

—Rev. David Bretzlaff (BRE, MDiv). Ontario Bible College, Tyndale University, Pastor, South Point Community Church, Leamington, Ontario

A BEAUTIFUL STORY OF God's unrelenting redeeming love in whatever stage we, or our loved ones, are in in life. It challenges the reader to remember that there is hope for those struggling with addictions. Well written, this book takes the reader on a journey with a troubled young man and shows how God uses people of all ages to mentor and draw to Himself. Truly a story that inspires and encourages us to never give up praying for our loved ones as God weaves their journey in His timing.

—Mary Journeau, Bachelor of Religious Education (BRE), Tyndale University College Seminary

Enough

GRACE

to Make Things

RIGHT

JANET WEILER

Printed in Canada

ISBN: 978-1-4866-2145-3
eBook ISBN: 978-1-4866-2146-0

Word Alive Press
119 De Baets Street Winnipeg, MB R2J 3R9
www.wordalivepress.ca

MIX
Paper from
responsible sources
FSC
www.fsc.org   FSC® C103567

WORD ALIVE
—P R E S S—

Cataloguing in Publication information can be obtained from Library and Archives Canada.

Acknowledgements

THE NOVEL IS FINISHED. LOOKING BACK, I REALIZE THAT I HAVE MANY PEOPLE TO acknowledge and who have been in my thoughts as I created this story. I've chosen not to name names, and it's my hope and prayer that every one of my readers will have amazing people like these in their lives. I thank:

My three sons: The oldest, who has told me countless stories over the years and even from a distance has blessed my heart. The youngest, who left this world far too soon. Contrary to the opinion of many, drugs and mental illness did not "win." It was not a game, and Jesus is "The Life." And my "middle" son, who rocks an extra chromosome. He can lighten my heart and make me laugh.

My daughters: All three of you inspire and challenge me; I really don't know what I'd do without you. I certainly wouldn't have written a book … or had a photo on the cover.

My husband: You aren't only an encourager, but you keep me steady and do most of the work that keeps this busy household functioning. That gives me time to write.

To the children, young people, and even some adults who have been part of our family for short or long periods of time. As you put up with me, you taught me so much about living and loving.

My niece, who is a writer: Thanks for your feedback and for encouraging me to "write what I know."

The "good cop" in my life who inspired me to make sure there were good cops in this book: He also gave me some tips about a police chase.

To my friends who have a farm that has been in the family for almost 150 years: At ninety plus, they're both active in the church and continue to pray for and pour into the lives of others.

And most of all, I thank Jesus for all He has done. We have a God who loves us and promises an abundant life in Him.

Prologue

JOE'S HEART RACED AS HE SAW THE FLASHING RED AND BLUE LIGHTS OF A COP CAR ahead. *It must be at the town line.* The cruiser chasing him was gaining quickly. He pressed harder on the accelerator, and the car surged ahead.

He knew this road. There was nowhere to turn. *I'm not stopping.* Joe made his decision but then noticed two sets of flashing lights ahead: a cruiser on each side of the road. *I can do this. Just keep going. I can do this.*

Seconds later, the car shuddered as Joe heard explosions and lost control. *They're shooting at me.* The car slid to the right and left the pavement. Sinking into soft gravel, it came to an abrupt stop in the shallow ditch beside the road. *I can still get out of here.* Joe tried to put the car in reverse. Nothing happened. Every light on the dashboard glared red. It was over.

He cursed as his clenched fists pounded on the steering wheel, and then he lifted his head and looked around. A cop stood a few feet behind the driver's door. He held a gun. It was pointed at Joe, who opened his hands and lifted them to where he knew they could be seen. He noticed movement to his right and slowly turned his head. Another cop. Another gun. The night lit up around him. There were cop cars everywhere.

"Driver. Keep your hands where they are. Do not move unless you are told to do so. Take your right hand and turn off your car. Remove your keys and hold them in the air." Somebody's voice was very loud.

Joe followed their step-by-step instructions. He had been in this place before but had never had guns drawn on him. He knew that he needed to comply. This was no place to put up a fight.

• • •

HANDCUFFED AND SHACKLED IN the back of a cruiser, Joe had two thoughts going through his head: *How could I be so stupid?* and, *Oh God, I need a fix so bad.* The windows were open, and he listened as the cops secured the car, shouting instructions to non-existent occupants, and checked the trunk. He watched them fold up the spike belt. No one had been shooting at him.

A sergeant arrived in a cage car thirty minutes later. Joe remembered this guy. He called him Sarge, but he pretended he didn't know him today. Actually, Sarge was one of the few cops who had ever treated him decently. Joe's eyes met his. He didn't see the anger and disdain that he'd seen in the eyes of the others.

Sarge shook his head and spoke. "Joseph Parker, I am arresting you on charges of arson, throwing an explosive, dangerous driving, and possession of a stolen vehicle."

Sarge read him his rights, and two officers escorted him to the cage car. He knew he was headed to the Coverton Police Services building downtown. By morning, he'd be back at the Coverton District Detention Centre.

• • •

FOUR MONTHS LATER ...

Joe looked around the courtroom at the Provincial Court Building in Coverton. He had pleaded guilty to all the charges. He had never intended not to. Now it was time for sentencing. He looked over at his lawyer. He had finally convinced the man to push for a court date. He'd had enough of this. His lawyer had been in no hurry and had tried to convince Joe to drag it out. *As if I don't know that my total time served before sentencing will count as time-and-a-half in the actual sentence. Just get this over with. I know I'll be in for a long time. This has got to stop.*

For an hour he watched the Crown attorney and his lawyer present their requests concerning his sentence. Joe's mind really wasn't on the sentencing, nor was he listening to the judge. He was recalling the horror of what he'd seen on the TV last night. He knew Brent had died in jail, but he didn't know the details. Understanding dawned as he stood with all the guys on the range watching the video of it happening. He recognized the NIDC range on the TV and had watched as a guard went along checking doors. How had he not looked through that window to see what was happening on the other side? Joe had glanced around him. From the looks on the faces of the other guys, he saw that they knew too. The camera from the opposite side of the range had shown it. A life snuffed out, witnessed by all of Canada on national news.

A graphic video of a tragic occurrence at the North Island Detention Centre was released today. Serge Smith, twenty-seven years old, changed his plea and was found guilty in the beating death of his cellmate, Brent Singer, twenty-four. The beating was described as an alcohol and drug induced frenzy as the men were locked together in their cell. Corrections workers from the facility are awaiting trial, as the Crown alleges they were negligent for not intervening in the incident.

Joe had been at NIDC that year, just before this all went down. Serge and Brent were friends, and they were his friends too. His attention was drawn to the front as he heard his name. "Joseph James Parker." He stood up. "Is there anything you would like to say before the sentence is passed?"

Joe looked at the judge. It seemed that he wanted an answer. "Well, sir, it looks like I might be put away for a long time. I've been in jail a lot. I suspect you know, Your Honour, that it's not hard to get drugs in jail."

Joe heard a gasp from his lawyer. He looked at him, thinking, *Oh give it up; we talked about this.* "Your Honour, I don't know if I'll be successful, but it's my intention to be drug-free when I leave this time."

The judge looked at Joe. He said, "I hope you can do that," and sentenced him to five-and-a-half years.

Chapter One

JOE PARKER OPENED THE CAR DOOR AND STEPPED INTO A PUDDLE. HE HARDLY NOTICED. His feet had been cold and wet when he climbed into the car less than an hour ago. It had been a long time since he took much interest in his comfort. *Will this rain never stop?* A chill April wind cut through his light spring jacket.

He was glad for the jacket and considered himself lucky that they had given it to him just before he'd walked through the gates yesterday morning. When he was discharged from the Coverton District Detention Centre, he wore the jeans and basketball shirt he had worn when he was arrested. That was in May … three years ago.

He looked at the small house before him and shook his head. When he'd stuck out his thumb to hitchhike from the city to this little hick town, he'd gotten a ride right away. The old guy who'd picked him up seemed to think he was on a divine mission, and it turned out that he knew Joe's grandfather. On top of that, he figured out who Joe was in the first two minutes of conversation, even though they had never met.

Joe stepped onto the covered porch, shook off as much water as he could, and rang the doorbell. The door opened almost immediately. Joe stared at the man standing in front of him. He looked into the clear grey eyes and after a moment said, "Gramps?" He wasn't sure where the name came from. He knew he had called this man that name before.

"Joey." The man closed his eyes and after a few seconds opened the door wider. He stepped aside and said, "Come in." Joe apologized for his wet clothes. "Just step in. Take your shoes off, and your socks if they're wet. I've got an extra pair you can wear."

Three hours earlier Joe had dialled 411 and asked for a listing for Wilkes in Souton. "I'll visit you sometime," he'd said to the man who answered the phone, the man who had assured him that he was indeed his grandfather.

The conversation had been short. He found out that his grandmother died four years ago. Joe decided two minutes into the conversation that he wasn't ready to reconnect with anyone. Leave the past in the past. He wasn't ready to meet Joseph Wilkes Senior from Souton. *But here I am.*

Stepping into a cramped entryway, Joe took off his coat and placed it over a hook just inside the door. He was glad for the old-fashioned shag carpet at his feet as he slipped off his shoes and socks. Without it, he'd be trailing wet footprints across the floor.

"Thanks, Gramps. I don't want to cause any trouble."

"I was just about to fix a sandwich for supper. Are you hungry?"

"Well, I ate a late lunch, but I can eat any time. I have some takeout here … even pie. The lady packed it up pretty good."

A smile came over his grandfather's face as he sniffed the air. "It's got to be roast beef." He motioned Joe further into the house. "Come on in. The bathroom's right there if you want to clean up. Towels are in the cupboard."

Joe took the offered pair of sports socks and entered a small bathroom off the little hallway beside the living room. He'd had a shower before he left the shelter this morning, but the wind and the rain made him feel dirtier than he probably was. *What was I thinking coming here? My grandfather … those eyes really are the same as mine. What does he know about me? I don't remember him at all. It must be twenty-six years.*

Ten minutes later, he was sitting across from his grandfather at a small kitchen table. "Gramps, there's something I need to tell you."

"We can talk after you eat."

"But, Gramps, I just got out of jail. I was in for three years this time."

"I know you were in jail, Joey. I read about you in the newspaper." He stopped as if trying to remember something. "Actually, a friend pointed out that it was you. I didn't recognize your new name. But let's just eat. There'll be plenty of time to talk later."

As they ate their roast beef dinners, complete with potatoes and carrots, neither said a word. Joe began wolfing down his piece of pie, then realized how he must look, shoving food into his mouth. He finished, smiled at his grandfather, and thanked him again for letting him in.

My grandfather. What am I going to tell this guy? That I'm homeless and have no money or possessions? That I shouldn't have left the city without notifying probation? That I've lost my place at the residence, because there is no way I'm going to get back there by 6:00 p.m.?

"I'll show you to your room."

Joe was shaken from his thoughts. He looked up to see his grandfather staring at him. "What?"

"I'll show you to your room. You plan to stay, don't you?"

"Gramps, we have to talk."

"Okay, we'll talk. And then I'll show you to your room. Let's sit in the living room."

Joe followed as his grandfather led the way. *More likely you'll show me to the door.* Settled in a chair across from his grandfather, Joe was the first to speak. "I don't know where to start. I've never been away for so long before." His grandfather said nothing. He waited for Joe to continue. "I hate being in jail, Gramps. I don't want to go back. I always have good intentions when I get out, but usually within a few months I'm back in."

"Are you a drug addict?"

This man didn't beat around the bush. "Yes." His grandfather's expression didn't change. "But I haven't had anything for almost three years. I think I've changed. I had a long time to think because most of my time was in segregation. I think maybe I can make it this time out, but I do know I need to be involved in some kind of treatment."

"Are you in danger of retaliation for the things you did to put you in jail?"

Joe paused as he thought back to an encounter four weeks previous. After being in protective custody for most of the past three years, it had been good to be free to roam the range. On his second day back at CDDC, he was sure things were going to end badly when he saw two members of Death Watch approaching him. Surprisingly, his adversaries listened as he apologized, and they believed him when he said he was finished with his old life. It seemed like they couldn't care less. He answered Gramps' question. "I don't think so. Some of their guys were with me this past month at CDDC. We worked things out." Joe could tell that his grandfather had read the details of his crime in the *Standard*. "The whole thing was pretty stupid, wasn't it?"

"Yes, it was." Again his grandfather answered frankly. "You could have killed yourself, or someone else. You got mixed up with some guys who aren't usually very forgiving. Are you sorry?"

Joe looked down, not answering the question. "I don't want to go back to jail. I don't want to do drugs. I want to have a quiet life without the police after me all the time. My life has never been normal. I just want to be normal, Gramps."

"Okay, so start. When did you get out? I want a detailed account of what you've done since then. I need you to be honest. I wouldn't worry about normal. I've been trying to figure out what that is all my life."

• • •

LARRY WATCHED THE YOUNG man climb the steps to the Wilkes' house. *Well, Lord, I think I played a big part in your plan today.* He often picked up hitchhikers and always took the opportunity to share his Christian experience with them.

His wife, Joyce, kept telling him to stop. "You could get hurt," she said. But he wasn't afraid. Today, as usual, he was sure he'd been prompted to pull over.

• • •

THE GUY HAD BEEN cold and wet, and there was something familiar about him. The younger man glanced at Larry as he slid into the passenger seat and thanked him for stopping. Then he looked straight ahead.

Larry took a close look. He recognized that face. "No problem, young man," Larry spoke as he waited for the traffic to clear so he could pull onto the road. "You were looking kind of cold. Hope you don't mind if I talk about the Lord to you … or with you? Your choice."

"No problem," came a quiet reply.

"Where are you headed?"

"Souton, I guess."

"That's where I'm going. Why Souton?"

"I hope to find my grandfather there. Haven't seen him for a long time."

"How long?"

"Since I was six years old."

"And how old are you now?"

"Thirty-two."

Larry paused. *This man looks like he could be in his mid forties. What kind of life has he lived?* "My name's Larry. And your name?"

"Joe."

"Joe Wilkes?"

Joe turned to look at him.

"No, Joe Parker. I guess Joe Wilkes would be my grandfather … or my dad."

"You're so much like both of them."

Joe raised his voice. "I am nothing like Joe Wilkes Junior."

With that retort, and the angry look on Joe's face, Larry backtracked. "I meant you look like them. I know your grandfather well, Joe. He's one of my best friends. I think he'll be glad to see you."

That was the end of that conversation. Larry knew that Joe had a lot on his mind. He turned on the stereo, and as usual a hymn from his favourite CD came blasting out of the system. He turned the volume down and was a little put out when he heard Joe start to laugh.

"God's faithfulness is nothing to laugh at, son."

Joe turned to face him and apologized quickly. "I don't think the hymn is funny. Of all the songs." He shook his head. "I know that song. I went to a Christian school in grade school, and we had a teacher who must have liked it too. We learned it by heart. All five verses. One of them in Dutch." He was smiling now, and so was Larry.

"Well, Joe, if you know the song, you better be joining in on the chorus."

And Joe did.

• • •

JOE RECOGNIZED MANY OF the hymns and songs on Larry's CD's as they travelled to Souton. Larry was okay. Joe was glad he didn't preach. It gave him time to think. He didn't know what to expect when he arrived at his destination. *Why did I change my mind and head out right away? What had Larry said? Your grandfather will be glad to see you. I don't know about this. Maybe I should ask him to drop me off as soon as we get into town. I'll check out the hotel, if there is one. That would give me a few options. Sure ... options. Like safe in a cell tonight.*

Joe had no idea how big the town was, but obviously Larry knew where his grandfather lived and thought that things would be okay. He tried to calm down. He could do this.

When they reached the town, Joe noted a few small stores. He saw a diner advertising its Wednesday special, *Fish and Chips $7.99,* and also a gas station, a doughnut shop, and two churches. There appeared to be about four square blocks of small older homes. There were newer, larger homes on the main street as they drove into town.

Larry signalled and turned into a gravel driveway. "Here we are."

Joe thanked Larry, opened the door, and stepped into a puddle. As he closed the door, he heard Larry say he would be praying for him.

• • •

"DO YOU WANT THE short or long form?" Joe asked his grandfather.

"Long form is good. It's early. I can hear about the three years in prison later. I need to know what you did yesterday and today. I think that might be a story in itself. Help me understand you a bit. What were your options? How did you feel? What brought you here?"

Joe hesitated, then relaxed and began to talk.

Chapter Two

THIS WASN'T THE FIRST TIME JOE WALKED THROUGH TWELVE-FOOT-HIGH GATES AND listened as they rattled shut behind him. Gates of at least a half dozen institutions across the province. The sound always filled him with hope and dread combined. This time—each time—there was the belief that it would be different. And this time—each time—came the fear that it wouldn't be long before he ended up inside again. Could he admit he was scared? For three long years he was told what to do almost every minute of every day. He was told when to get up in the morning and when to go to bed at night. Meals arrived on schedule. He wore an orange jumpsuit. There had been a few transfers, but basically, with the exception of an occasional visitor or phone call, his life on the inside was rock solid routine. All his choices were made for him. Today, after he had signed for them, he received his possessions in a plastic bag.

He'd been transferred back to the Coverton District Detention Centre a month ago. Right now, he planned to stay in the city. At discharge he was given the balance of his account, a total of $150.45. He didn't know how the money got into his account, but he was glad to have it. His only ID was his prison discharge paper. He headed for a small strip mall about a kilometre down the road and noted that April 3 was chilly this year. A sign for a dollar store drew his attention.

Stocked up on some personal items and snacks, Joe splurged and took a cab downtown. The chaplain at CDDC had said there were two beds open at Hope House; by noon he had arranged to be in one of them. There were rules at this men's residence. You had to be out of there between 8:30 a.m. and 6:00 p.m. each day. If you didn't check back in at 6:00, they gave your spot to someone else. It wasn't so bad. He got breakfast and supper, and the washrooms and beds were clean. He was expected to go to the evening chapel service. Most importantly, it would give him an address, which he needed to satisfy his probation order. The large two storey structure stood on a corner amid a number of small businesses, three blocks from the city core.

There had been a few changes downtown. Some stores had closed. New stores had taken their place. Coverton had always had an exciting downtown, and that hadn't changed. Joe was glad the Goodwill store still stood where he'd always known it to be. He strolled up and down the familiar aisles, purchasing two changes of clothes and a fair-sized duffle bag. Next, he picked up a coffee and six doughnuts at his favourite coffee shop and walked to the large park just past the middle of town. It was good to just sit on a bench and watch people go by. He stayed there until it was time to head back to Hope House.

Joe looked at his dollar-store watch. *It's 5:30. I better head back. I can take my time and still be there early.* He was a block away from his destination when a police car, its lights flashing, pulled to the curb beside him. An older officer, one he'd encountered many times before, got out of the car and walked toward him. "Mr. Parker. What are you up to these days?"

"Just trying to get to Hope House by curfew, Sarge."

"What's in the bag?"

Joe explained that he had just been released. He showed him the clothes along with the receipt. The whole time he was talking, Joe's stomach was in knots. This guy was usually fair, but too many of his fellow officers would have had him against the car. They'd frisk him, calling him a loser and far worse. Often they had found drugs or stolen property on him, so maybe he deserved their scrutiny. Finally, the officer walked back to his car. Joe was shocked when he said, "Good luck, Joe. I hope you can stay out this time."

• • •

BACK AT THE RESIDENCE, supper was good, and the chapel service went by quickly. Joe had no beef with God. He could take Him or leave Him. He just didn't need Him. He was completely capable of navigating this life alone. After a card game with one of the other guys, he had a snack and went to bed.

Joe shared a room with three others. He preferred a top bunk and had managed to get one. He was glad this place had lockers, complete with locks. He shook his head as he remembered the early days of living from shelter to shelter. It was unbelievable. He woke up the first morning to find all his possessions gone—stolen. Even his shoes were missing. No one thought to tell him he should sleep on his things if he expected to see them in the morning.

Joe woke up at 6:00 a.m., showered, and ate breakfast. At 8:30 a.m., he was out the door. The park he'd visited last evening was much less busy this morning. There were still a few people hurrying to get to work, but for the most part, it was quiet. He had picked up a coffee and now sat on a park bench, enjoying the breeze on his face. It was still a little cold, but the feeling of being free was intoxicating. Right now he thought he could handle being out. He had no desire for the drugs. After being away from it so long, even the smell of cigarette smoke was hard to tolerate. He wasn't going to fool himself, though. The past three years hadn't been easy. Contentment came and went, and any kind of uninvited feelings brought memories blasting into his mind.

He needed a place to live. Hope House was okay, but it wasn't a place to call home. He thought of three possibilities where he had friends and possible connections to something more permanent. Joe only hoped his old friends weren't still into drugs and the lifestyle that came with them.

He'd try Lilly first. She had a room she sometimes rented out. He walked ten blocks and stopped in front of a small house. The window shutters had once been bright yellow, but now the paint on them was faded and peeling. The porch sagged a little, and the screen on the aluminum door was ripped. He made his way across a cluttered yard and mounted the steps.

It took Lilly awhile to get to the door. She was only fifty-three years old but could have easily been mistaken for seventy. He greeted her with a smile. Her reaction was not what he expected.

"Joe Parker, get off my porch! I'll call the cops. I don't want you here."

"Lilly, what's the matter?" Joe tried to calm her, but she started yelling.

It took two minutes for the neighbours to start coming out to their porches. He couldn't understand much of what she said. He did hear her say that he had ripped her off. He had stolen her support cheque and her new phone, along with the free tablet it came with. Joe backed away with his hands open in front of him. She continued yelling and didn't hear him say, "Lilly, Lilly, I'm sorry" as he turned and quickly walked away. Three years ago, Joe's main goal in life was to stay high and support his habit. What had he been thinking to seek out one of his victims? *I don't even remember what I did to you, Lilly. Was I really that awful?* His pace slowed. *Maybe there's a spot at Steve's.*

The last place he lived before he was arrested, Steve's Place, wasn't far from here. It was a small townhouse housing four or five people who all chipped in toward expenses. When he'd lived there before there were four others: Carrie and her little boy, Evan, who Joe figured would be about eight now, a guy named Jack, and a younger girl named Shea. There was no Steve. It was a made-up name and always got a laugh when they turned someone away who was looking for Steve. As he approached the house he smiled. There was a sign hanging near the porch: "Steve's Place." Yes, this might work out. He was used to opening the door and walking in, but today he rang the doorbell.

Shea answered the door. "Oh Joe. You're out. Come on in."

"Hi, Shea," He greeted her with a big smile. "I'm looking for a room. Any vacancies here at Steve's Place?"

He noticed that Shea avoided his eyes. She replied that they were kind of full, with three adults and two kids. Jack had moved out.

Joe's next question was, "Did Carrie have another baby?"

Just then, a big guy came down the stairs carrying a toddler. Joe stared at the little boy, then looked from the guy to the boy to Shea. He closed his eyes as he heard Shea say, "This is my husband, Steve, and our son, Stevie."

Joe heard the name and would have laughed at the fact that Steve had landed at Steve's Place, but as he stared at the boy, he was speechless. He shook his head, turned, and was almost to the door when Shea said, "Wait, Joe, it's okay."

Joe stopped, turning to look at the three of them again. *It can't be. But look at those eyes.* "How old is he?"

"He'll be three in August." Shea paused. "Joe, yes, he's your son. But Steve and I were married before he was born. Steve is his dad."

Joe couldn't say a word. His face registered a look of shock and confusion. Emotions flooded Joe's thoughts as he tried to make sense of what was going on. *I said I'd never have kids. No kid deserves to have a guy like me for a dad. This can't have happened.* He looked at little Stevie, with the same face as Joe Wilkes Junior, the same eyes as his. He didn't understand the emotions boiling up inside him. He pulled his eyes away from his son, turned, and said, "Shea, I'm sorry that it came to this. I am so sorry." He was silent for a long time.

Little Stevie broke the silence with a grunt and wiggled to get out of Steve's arms. Joe looked at Steve and said, "Are you up for this, man?"

Steve seemed nervous as he spoke to Joe. He was big enough to pick Joe up and throw him out the door, but he spoke quietly. "Joe, Shea told me that you aren't a bad guy. We knew that you were in jail and might show up one day. Am I up for this? I love Shea, and I've loved your son since before he was born." He paused for a moment, looking at Shea and then Stevie. "I'm just finishing up a college diploma in radio broadcasting. I've got good leads on jobs. We can give Stevie what he needs—security, and two parents who love him." He paused again, and when Joe didn't comment, he asked him a question. "You know a man can love a kid who doesn't share his genes, don't you?"

Joe took a deep breath. "Yeah, Steve, I know that. A real man can do that. I'm adopted. My dad loves me." Joe felt like he had been sucker punched in the gut. He shook his head and realized that he needed to get out of that house fast. "Take care of him, Steve. And maybe when he gets old enough to understand, you can tell him that he has three parents who love him."

Shea's voice stopped him as he moved closer to the door. "Joe, Steve has never done drugs. And I stopped using as soon as I found out I was pregnant. We're going to raise him right, Joe. We're even involved in a church, the one on the corner of Main and Lewis."

"Good. Good," Joe said, with little emotion. He didn't know what to say. He didn't even tell Shea that he was clean too. He stepped closer to Stevie, who smiled a bright smile. Joe could tell that Stevie sensed that something was happening but had no idea what. "I'll keep moving on," Joe said quietly, but he didn't move. He couldn't take his eyes off Stevie.

Stevie looked from his mom to Joe and back again. Shea smiled at him. "How about a hug for Joe, Stevie?"

He reached out to Joe, who picked him up and gathered him in. Stevie hugged him back and then said, "Cookie, Daddy?" while looking at Steve.

"Sure, big guy," Steve replied with a smile. Joe put him down, and Stevie ran to the counter, where Steve gave him a cookie from a Cookie Monster cookie jar.

Joe could hardly breathe. He whispered a thank you to Shea and stepped outside. He took a deep breath of cool air and started walking. *Where now? What day is this? Thursday. The Drop Inn should be open*. Joe stopped for a moment, then headed toward a storefront on a narrow side street. He had to stop thinking about those grey eyes. At least he could find a coffee, and maybe a muffin, at the Please Drop Inn. *What a lame name for a place,* he thought, shaking his head as he went through the front door.

Conversation stopped as Joe entered a large room with a round table in the middle. There were six smaller square tables placed around it. In a back corner, three couches were arranged around a coffee table, and a tall bookcase nearby held a supply of games and books. He counted a dozen people seated at the tables. They were mostly addicts who were living on the streets, probably there for the warmth and free coffee.

"Joe, good to see you! Where have you been?"

Joe doubted anyone would wonder where he had been. His send-off was well publicized.

"Hi, Buzz. What's going on?" He sat down across from Buzz at one of the tables. A television up on the wall was set to a news channel.

A girl he knew, Callie, brought him a coffee and sat down with them. "Still double double?" she asked.

Joe nodded and thanked her. Looking around, he asked what everyone had been up to. Three years was a long time. There was a long list of stories about people he'd known—overdoses, suicides, a couple shootings. None of the stories had happy endings. Recently there had been a rash of deaths because of fentanyl. Joe remembered trying it before he was arrested. It had scared him back then, and now it was being mixed with other drugs and killing people.

As they talked, Joe watched Calvin, the volunteer that morning, leave the counter to go to the back room. Buzz was watching too and said in a low voice, "I can get you some good stuff; it'll be clean. In fact, I've got some oxycontin and coke on me right now."

Joe looked at Buzz. He shook his head and said, "No way, Buzz, I've been clean for three years. I even quit smoking this time."

"Well, you must be ready to celebrate. Let me fix you up." Buzz glanced toward the counter. There was no sign of Calvin. He reached into his pocket and pulled out his hand. There was no stopping him as he slipped a tiny pouch into Joe's jacket pocket.

Fingering the packet, Joe recognized what he was holding. It had been a long time. He would never forget the feeling. So much turmoil could be gone in a minute. He thought about going back to Hope House. It was only a step above jail. *I'm thirty-two years old. I don't need a babysitter. I can find a girl with her own place. I'll pour on the charm; that'll be that problem taken care of.* He sat thinking for a good ten minutes. Buzz and Callie were engaged in an animated discussion about American politics and seemed to have forgotten he was there. Joe looked around. He saw some smiles, but most of the people around him looked hollow-eyed and hungry. Some looked sick. Empty even. He wondered how they were doing. Were they on their way to dying young, like the ones he'd heard about today?

He grasped the pouch in his pocket. "Buzz." Buzz looked over at him. "I don't want to do it, man. I'm done. I don't know how, but I'm going to stay away from the drugs. They'll land me back in jail, and I hate it there. Everything I ever went to jail for was because of my habit. The stealing, the arsons, the money. An addict always needs money." Joe reached over and pressed the pouch into Buzz's hand. "I gotta try to beat this, and I've got a good start."

Joe left the Please Drop Inn feeling torn. *No worries. I can change. Yeah, right. No money, no hope for a job, no place to live.* Well, he had enough money for lunch. He'd try that little diner he used to take Evan to.

He'd gone a half block down the street and could see the sign, "Mary's Diner," hanging over the sidewalk. Suddenly, a police cruiser turned quickly into the alley in front of him. It stopped with its lights flashing. Two officers were at his side in seconds. One of them turned him toward the cruiser and said, "Hands on the car."

"Can you guys even do this to me?"

They frisked him and reached into his pockets. One officer held him there while the other checked his duffle bag and said, "Can we do this to you? We see you come out of a place where we see known dealers going in. We see you carrying a duffle bag, which is almost empty. Where were you going to hit today to fill it up? I have a good memory,

Parker. I was in the cruiser you almost hit when you were arrested. And let's not forget your little problem of a weapons history as well."

Joe was seething inside. *Calm down, Joe. Calm down. Don't let them get to you. You can get through this.* He gritted his teeth, clenched his fists, and tried to relax. "Can I talk now?"

"Talk."

"I got out yesterday. I've done nothing illegal. I was at the Drop Inn because I was cold, and I wanted a coffee. I was in for three years. Right now I'm clean and have been since I went in. Sergeant Waters stopped me yesterday, and he sent me on my way with a 'Good luck, Joe. I hope you can stay out this time.'" Joe saw the officer at his side glance at the one holding him. "My discharge paper is in the bag. I'm signed in at Hope House and plan to go back there tonight. What more should I be doing?"

"Maybe you should get out of town so we don't have to look at your ugly face." Joe felt the officer release him. Both men turned and climbed back into the car and watched him as he opened his bag and packed it again with the things they had dumped onto the ground. Anger boiled up inside of him. He couldn't trust himself to look at them as he turned and continued on his way.

Joe shook his head. *Not a great morning so far. What's the point in being clean if everyone keeps seeing me as dirty anyway?* Something from one of the books he'd read in jail came back to him—some inspirational garbage about counting your blessings to drown out your demons. Okay then.

There were a couple of good things. He had given Buzz the coke back. He wasn't thinking that his cop encounters would come so quickly, but he hadn't run away from them or lashed out at them as he sometimes had in the past. He wondered if his mention of the sergeant had made them stop harassing him. His thoughts went back to Steve's Place. *A son, I have a son.* Joe wasn't sure if it was good or bad, but he thought that it might be okay. He looked at the sign for the diner again. He had lost his appetite but decided to go there anyway.

Inside, he took a seat on a stool at the far end of the counter. Two older men sat at a table by the window. A middle-aged woman, whom Joe recognized as the owner, was busy clearing tables and taking the dishes behind the counter to the dishwasher. She stopped to ask him what he'd like, and he answered, "Fries with gravy and a coffee." He thought she looked frustrated.

"Okay, but it'll be a few minutes. I hope you aren't in a hurry."

Joe said he'd be fine, and she returned to what she'd been doing.

He watched her for a moment and then said, "Can I help you with that?"

She stopped to look more closely at him. "I remember you. Joe, right? You used to bring a little guy in here quite a bit."

Joe commented on her good memory.

"Have you got any experience with a dishwasher?"

Joe said, "Well, I worked the one at CDDC. The dishes went in one side and out the other. I worked in the kitchen there before I got fired."

Mary didn't pause at the mention of the detention centre.

"Yes, you can help. It'll only take a minute to catch on to the dishwasher. Looks like one in your kitchen at home but is actually easier. You just load the tray, open the door, and slide the tray in. Then pull it out when it stops. The soap goes in automatically. These are pretty fast. The trays are big. Three loads will probably do it. My waitress didn't show up, and the ladies from the walking club were late getting out of here. And my lunch crowd is coming through that door in fifteen minutes. It would be great if you could clear and wash down the tables and get the dishes through the dishwasher for me."

"I'm glad to help." Joe was also glad that he had purchased new clothes and had had a shower that morning.

Joe worked at clearing the tables. He sorted and piled the dishes as he went, making them easier to rinse before he put them through the dishwasher. He filled the sink with soapy water and found a cloth to wipe the tables. There were only ten tables in all. The counter was already clean and ready for customers. He picked up the change that had been left as tips and put it in the container beside the cash register.

As Joe headed to the dishwasher, he glanced over at Mary, who said, "I might run out of silverware, so run some through first. And then a tray of dinner plates." Joe was glad to be busy.

Mary usually had everything set out early for lunch, but today she'd been thrown off. Her mom, whom she had called in to help with the cooking, arrived at 11:20. In ten minutes there were two dozen hamburgers and a dozen hot dogs sizzling on the grill. Two baskets of fries sat ready to drop into the hot oil.

Joe pulled out the first load of dishes, sent another through, and watched as Mary and her mother set up lunch like a well-oiled machine. Later, Mary explained that kids from the high school walked ten minutes to the diner and ten minutes back to school on their forty-minute lunch break. Some got their burgers to go, and some sat at the tables and ate in a hurry. They were all cleared out of there by 12:10. Mary's regular customers knew that before 12:20, the diner would be a busy place. After that there would be great service and a meal worth waiting for.

Joe was amazed at how smoothly things went. He finished the dishes, all the while clearing the tables and wiping them off before he loaded the trays. The students cleared out on schedule. In the next two hours, at least twenty customers, some in groups of two or three, arrived and began to leave.

Joe paused and looked around. Only a few people were left in the diner. He had just emptied a tray, and the counters and tables were clean. Joe sat down as Mary put a plate of fries with gravy, and a burger, at his place at the end of the counter.

"I think Mom and I are fine from here. I do have a student who comes after school to help through supper. You were a lifesaver."

Joe smiled a real smile. His first in a very long time. "It was just what I needed."

Mary looked at Joe for a minute, then spoke. "You were gone a long time."

"Three years." He paused. "Time moved on while I was sitting there. I'm not sure what I'm going to do. I only know I don't want to go back."

Joe at his meal slowly. When he was finished, Mary was back at his side.

"More coffee?" she asked, and Joe shook his head. "So what's next for you, Joe?"

Joe gave a resigned sigh. "I should get out of town. I have a bed at Hope House downtown. Not a place I want to be at for long. This is the best thing that's happened to me in the last twenty-four hours."

"Well, drop by for a coffee if you're in the neighbourhood." Mary handed him $40.00, along with the change he had dropped into the cup beside the cash register.

"I wasn't expecting to get paid."

"I know you weren't. It's not much, but like I said, you were a lifesaver."

Joe looked around the diner. "Can you point me to a payphone? I've got lots of change, and I'd like to make a couple of phone calls."

Mary reached under the counter. "Here." She held out a cell phone. "Use my cell. I've free long distance. If you need directory assistance, they charge, but it isn't much, so don't worry about it."

"Thanks, Mary. I'll go outside to make the calls."

A few minutes later, Joe listened as the phone rang.

"Hello." Joe recognized Sam's voice. She was always happy. He loved that voice.

"Hi, Sam."

"Joe? Where are you? What are you up to?"

"I just got out. I'm trying to figure out what to do. What's happening on your end?"

Before Sam continued, Joe heard a baby crying in the background. He closed his eyes and shook his head as he listened.

"Oh Joe, what's it been? Four years? Well, that baby crying is Dillon. He's just over a year old, and he just woke up from his nap."

"I bet he's cute. And his dad?"

"Is my husband, John. We got married two-and-a-half years ago."

"Congratulations." Joe was not happy with Sam's news.

"Well, I've thought a lot about you, Joe. Heard you got lots of time for those arsons. Really, I had a hard time believing it was you."

Joe sighed. "It was me all right. Along with the extra year for trying to get past the cop cars. A five-and-a-half-year sentence. My longest ever. But of course I only had to serve two-thirds. I came out clean, and I hope to stay that way."

"That's great, Joe. Probably the best news I've had in months. Where are you going to live?"

"I'm in Coverton, staying at Hope House right now. I'm sure something will come up. It was good to talk to you. I'll keep in touch."

"Take care, Joe." The call ended. Joe had no idea what he should do next.

Three long years in jail. Joe was determined that he wasn't going back there. *Where can I go? I need to get out of this city. I can't call my folks yet. I have to show them I've changed. I'll call them when things are more settled.*

Joe had entered the system when he was six years old, and he was later adopted. He wanted nothing to do with his biological father, but in the past year he had started thinking about his grandparents. Joe believed that he was no longer a danger to others. He could stay away from the drugs and the self-centredness that went with that lifestyle. He knew his grandparents were from Souton, and he knew their last name was Wilkes. He pressed 411. A machine asked for the name of the city. Joe said Souton, and an operator came on the line.

"For what name please?"

"Wilkes."

"I have a J. Wilkes on Maple Street, and Joseph Senior on Main."

"Joseph Senior please."

"Please hold while the number is connected."

Joe listened as the phone began to ring. There was a click, and a man said "Hello"

Joe said nothing, his finger hovering over the *end call* button.

"Hello," came the voice again.

"I'm looking for Joe Wilkes."

"Well, you found him. What can I do for you?"

"It's … I'm Joe Parker. Are you my grandfather?"

There was silence, then the man spoke. There was a catch in his throat. "Joey? Joey, yes, I'm your grandfather. Oh Joey, it's been a long time."

Joe's thought was, *What was I thinking? I'm no good at this. Why did I even call?*

His grandfather continued. "Where are you, Joey? I can come and pick you up. Can I see you? I just would really like to see you."

"I'm in Coverton. I don't know what I'm going to do yet. I just thought I'd call and see how you and Grandma are doing."

There was silence on the other end of the phone. Then his grandfather spoke. "Your grandmother is gone, Joey. She died four years ago."

Joe could tell that his grandfather was struggling to talk. He closed his eyes, shaking his head. *What am I supposed to say after that?* Joe was silent. His grandfather finally continued.

"She prayed for this moment for so long. We always hoped you would call. She prayed for you kids all the time. Have you seen Lisa? Is she doing all right? Have you talked to your father at all?" His grandfather was rambling.

Joe's answer came quickly. "I'm not sure how Lisa is. If you're asking if I've talked to your son, Joe, I'll just say not lately. And I'll say my father is a man named Seth Parker. He lives about two hundred kilometres from here."

"But will you visit me? Please."

Joe sighed. "I will. I'm trying to make some decisions and figure my life out. I'll call you again and try to visit." His finger pressed the red button to end the call.

The wind had come up, and it was starting to rain. Joe went back into the diner and handed Mary her phone. He sat down at the end of the counter, and she brought him a coffee.

"Not good news?" Mary asked.

"Well, my grandfather, I haven't seen him in at least twenty-six years, would like me to visit. I guess my grandmother died four years ago. And my old girlfriend … that was a dead end. I won't be calling her again. I'm not sure what I'll do. I haven't even called my parents. My adoptive parents. They love me, but from a distance. I ripped them off pretty big time in the past." Joe sighed. "I'll call them another time. They might have some ideas for me."

"I guess I don't know your situation, but it seems to me it never hurts to make a grandpa happy."

"Maybe you're right." Joe sat quietly, thinking about the phone calls. Mary stopped in front of him thirty minutes later and refilled his coffee cup. Joe looked up. "What is that amazing smell?"

Mary smiled. "Today's dinner special, roast beef. Want some? It's ready."

Joe thought for a minute. "Well, I just had lunch at a great little diner. But how about two servings to go?"

Ten minutes later his order was packed into his duffle bag. He put the hood up on his jacket and hiked a kilometre down to the highway that would take him to Souton. He hoped he could find his grandfather's house. How long could Main Street be? He had no gloves, but that wasn't a bad thing when you hitchhiked in the cold. He wasn't above having people feel sorry for him. When he got to the highway, he crossed the street and stuck out his thumb. Within five minutes, an older Ford Focus pulled over. He hurried up to the passenger side, opened the door, and hopped in.

Chapter Three

JOE'S GRANDFATHER HAD LISTENED CAREFULLY AS JOE TALKED. THERE HAD BEEN NO prompting when Joe was silent for long periods of time. Joe looked at the clock on the wall. It had been two hours from the time he'd walked through the door. He looked at his grandfather, his gramps, and thought about the things he had said. He hadn't shared his thoughts and feelings with anyone for as long as he could remember. Today he had said only what was true and left nothing out of his narrative. Now his gramps knew about the way he had lived. He knew the seriousness of Joe's drug use and his crimes. He knew about the little boy with the same distinctive grey eyes as his own. Gramps knew that Joe was a loser and that he would never cut it as a father. He knew that today Joe's heart had broken as he hugged that little boy. But his gramps also could see that although he was weak, Joe had given the drugs back to Buzz. He had made an honest $40.00, and he had no desire to return to the lifestyle that had sent him to prison.

"Thanks, Joey, for catching me up. What do we need to do now? What's this about needing to be back at that place?"

"Well, Hope House won't let me in after six." They both glanced at the clock on the wall, which read 6:20. "If I'm not there, I'll be breaking the conditions of my probation."

"How do we remedy that?" Gramps looked concerned.

"Well, usually I don't worry about it. Before, I just avoided the police until they caught up with me. Then I'd get sent back to jail. It was never for very long."

"Would telling the police where you are now help?"

"Probably."

Gramps reached over and picked up the phone. He dialled a number. When someone answered, he started talking.

"Hi, Jerry … I'm good, thanks. And you? Well, tell her I'm thinking about her. Hope she's better soon … Well, yeah, I have a question for you. My grandson is here. JJ's boy. Well, not JJ's boy anymore. Never mind, it's a long story. His name is Joe, same as me … Yes, I know you know my name. Well, Joey just got out of jail … Is that important? … Well, he was in for three years … Well, no. I don't know what you have to do in Canada to get sent to jail that long. You probably read about it in the *Standard*. Arsons, in downtown Coverton …Yes, those ones … the gang places … No, he isn't in a motorcycle gang. He doesn't even have a motorcycle. Would you listen to me?.He did his time. He doesn't want to go back to jail. He came to see me, and we talked. Well, mostly he talked. He stayed at the Hope House in Coverton last night. Was stopped by the Coverton police twice since he got out, just for walking down the street … I don't know who they were. The first was a sergeant somebody. He wished Joey good luck. We just need to know what's the best way to report that he's staying with me … Of course I'm sure … What makes me so sure? Jerry, it's not the first time I've sat and talked to an addict and an ex-con … Yes, he's an addict, but he was clean the whole time in prison. He needs this chance, Jerry, and I plan to give it to him … I don't care what Jay says. What do we have to do? Thanks, Jerry. Take care now. Goodbye." Gramps hung up the phone. "That was easy."

Joe looked at him, and when Gramps didn't say anything, he said, "So what do I do, Gramps?"

"Well, Jerry is calling the detachment in Foxhill, just down the road. They'll send a car out. They just have to see you and talk to us. They'll notify the Coverton police that you're staying here."

"Gramps, who is Jerry?"

"Jerry Green. We've been friends for sixty years."

"And he can just call the detachment, and everything's fine?"

"Well, yes."

"And how can he do this?"

"Oh, that's what you're getting at. He used to be the chief of this department … you know, before things all went regional. He keeps up with the changes in policies and all that. They still think a lot of him over there."

Joe shook his head. "Okay, Gramps. If you say so."

A short time later, Joe heard a car pull into the driveway. "That'll be them now," Gramps announced. "And just to warn you, Joey, in a short while, unless your Uncle Jay is busy at the church tonight, he'll probably be close behind."

The doorbell rang.

The procedure for notifying the authorities that he had changed his address was easy. The officers had checked the terms of his release. They recorded Gramps' street address and telephone number. As they prepared to leave, one of them turned and spoke to Joe. "We're trusting you here, Joey. Your grandfather is a good man. He believes you're going to make it this time. You need to live up to that trust. AA meets at the Anglican church just down the road on Monday evenings and Saturday mornings. There's a social worker at the Health Centre in Foxhill who can point you to some solid supports."

Joe thanked them as they went out the door. As soon as the police cruiser pulled out of the driveway, another car pulled in. Uncle Jay had arrived.

• • •

JAY WILKES WASN'T USED to being out of the loop. He was enjoying a second cup of coffee after eating a late supper at the diner and wasn't in a hurry to go home. Michelle was working late, and the kids had gone into Coverton to a movie with some friends. He noticed his neighbours, Saul and his wife, entering the restaurant and waved. Saul smiled, then greeted him saying, "Hi, Jay. What's happening at your dad's house? There's a cruiser sitting in the driveway."

Jay immediately stood up, dropped a ten-dollar bill and four loonies on the table, and left. At the house he waited for a cruiser to back out of the driveway and then pulled up behind his father's car. He was out of the car, up the steps, and into the house in seconds. He stopped when he saw his father standing in the doorway of the living room.

"Are you all right? What were the police doing here? Why didn't you call me?"

Gramps sighed and stepped backwards into the living room. "I'm fine, Jay. Come on in and sit down. I've got company. I was going to call you tomorrow."

Joe had figured out that this was his uncle. Probably he was younger than Joe Junior. *They usually name the first son after the dad, don't they?* Joe believed that he was quite good at reading people, and the man in front of him was angry. Joe glanced at him, then looked away. He had no idea how to react.

His uncle spoke to him directly. "And who might you be?"

"Joe. Joe Parker."

"And why are you here in my father's living room? And why were the police here a few minutes ago?"

Joe took a step back as Gramps intervened.

"Now hold on, Jay. Joey is my guest, and if you can't calm down and treat him with respect, I'd like you to leave. You can come back in the morning, and we'll talk then."

Joe looked from Gramps to his uncle. He knew that his uncle had figured out who he was. His heart sank as he said, "It's okay, Gramps. I don't want to cause any trouble. I'll be on my way." Joe took a step toward the doorway but Gramps reached out, putting a hand on his arm.

"No, Joey. You're staying. I'm sorry, Jay. This all happened pretty quickly. Joey, your Uncle Jay knows we can talk this out. He's quite protective of his old man here. He probably thinks I'm going a little senile, but I'm only seventy-three years old. Jay, this is your nephew, Joey. Joey, this is your dad's, I mean my son JJ's, younger brother, Jay. Jay lives on the other side of town. Jay, please come in. Let's sit down."

● ● ●

JAY WASN'T SURE THAT he wanted to talk right now, but he was the one who'd come barging into the situation. Joey. Jay knew Joey had been involved in some serious crimes. When was that? It was years ago. He'd read about his nephew's initial arrest in the *Coverton Standard*. The publicity died down quickly, but he did recall hearing about a five-year prison term.

Jay sat down. He looked at his dad, whom he'd never seen so composed and sure of himself. *Obviously, Dad has heard Joey's story and isn't worried.* "I'm sorry, Joey. Your gramps is right. I do try to protect him. I am suspicious. I wonder what you're up to. But I shouldn't make any assumptions before I hear what you both have to say." Jay looked him straight in the eye and said, "Joey, I'm glad to meet you. Of course, I knew you when you were little. You visited us a few times a year. I watched my brother mess up, and when he lost you, we lost you, and Lisa too."

Jay paused, looking from his father to his nephew. "You were little. Do you remember us at all?"

Joe shook his head and avoided his uncle's eyes.

"Your grandparents were devastated. I think things have changed, but back then, they didn't seem to look for family for the kids to live with. At least they didn't consider us. I'm sorry. I came in here all upset. I had no right to be. But I do have to make sure we're safe around here. We need to talk."

"I see where you're coming from, Uncle Jay." Joe looked over to his grandfather. "Gramps, I don't think I can go through my whole story again."

"Do you want me to do the talking?"

"Please," was Joe's reply.

Joe listened as Gramps told a very shortened version of their previous conversation. He left out the parts where Joe had visited his friends that afternoon. Gramps ended by saying, "The police came because we had to tell them Joey is staying here. Something about his probation. Joey didn't know what to do, so I called Jerry. He told me he'd get them to send a cruiser out. They just had to confirm he's staying here and notify the guys in Coverton. Joey is going to stay here. We don't know for how long."

Jay was still concerned. He looked at Joe. "So why should we trust you, Joey?"

"Well, I guess you probably shouldn't trust me. I am an addict, even if I've been clean for almost three years. I've never been off drugs that long, but I have been in this position at least a dozen times. I always end up back in prison." Joe glanced at his grandfather, not able to read his feelings. His mind was racing. *This is where I usually tell people whatever I think they want to hear—that I'm misunderstood, that it's not always my fault.*

He shook that thought away and remembered an inspirational saying, mantra, or something he'd heard at a twelve-step meeting while he was locked up. Only this time it was like a whisper in his ear. Suddenly, it made sense. *If you want to BE different, then you have to DO different.* Joe wiggled his shoulders. *Tell the truth. Okay, then.*

"I've hurt people who love me, over and over again. But I am telling the truth. I want to change. I hate being in jail. I want to make it this time. I've never been able to walk away from the drugs ... and I did that today. I decided I couldn't handle being near my old friends. I just want to get as far away from them as possible."

"Why come here? Why not your mom or dad?" It was a fair question, and Joey thought for a minute before answering.

"I didn't know Grandma was gone. I really don't remember this place. But I ... I don't know. I thought maybe they would like to see me. I don't connect well. I have ... well, the shrinks call it attachment disorder. Apparently I have some other stuff too. But I want to ... to belong, I guess. I know families can be good, but I haven't had much experience with having them work for me. I knew the town, and his name, so I found Gramps by calling 411 today."

His eyes met his uncle's. "You ask why not my mom or dad, and I guess you mean my bio mom. She has her own set of problems, and I'm not good for her. A few years ago I stayed with your brother for a while. It was good for two weeks. I even started working with him. But then came Christmas, a week off work, the bottle, a fist fight." Joe shook his head. "He's sure got some issues. No, that didn't work out."

Gramps asked the next question. "What about the people who adopted you?"

Joe paused to gather his thoughts. "We've kept in touch. In reality, I only lived with them for seven years. They had younger kids, and I was doing some things that put the whole household in danger. I went back into care when I finished Grade Eight. Mostly into group homes, or special foster homes. Then I started breaking the law. First it was open custody, then closed custody. Most of my adult life I've been in jail. The Parkers are okay. They totally accept me as their son." He paused, shaking his head. "But the only time I visited them at their house, I stole some blank cheques and their credit card number. They lost a lot of money because of me.

"I'm really not welcome there, and for good reason. They still are foster parents and sometimes have younger kids. Children's Services' rules say I can't stay there because of my record. When I'm in jail, they accept my collect calls. Not many people do. They send

$20.00 once in a while for my account. When I'm not in jail, they try to visit, depending on where I live. If I'm close by, we go out for a meal. They give me money sometimes, but I never ask them for it." Joe paused, thinking about the Parkers, trying to explain them. "Once they offered to set me up in a rental house they own, but before we could work out any details, I was back in jail. They live just on the other side of Toronto. I need to call my mom. She'll be really happy to hear from me. My dad is a little laid back, but I know he'll be glad too."

• • •

JAY WAS STILL WARY of Joe being in the house with his dad. When Jay's mother died, Joe Senior lost interest in everything. He seemed to age very quickly. Jay looked across the room at the best dad a guy could have. He seemed different tonight; there was a calmness about him that Jay hadn't seen in years. Could Joey be an answer to prayer? Was his dad ready to start living again?

"Well, Joey, it seems your gramps has made a decision. I'm still not sure of this, not sure of you. But I'll trust his judgement here. And I'll help, as long as you work along with us. Your gramps and grandma prayed that you would someday find them, and here you are. They taught all us kids—your dad, your Aunt Marge, our brother Donny who passed away—about the Lord from the time we were little. That's what we learned growing up, and that's still what's important around here today." He looked at Joe, who didn't respond.

"Joey, I think you know that your former lifestyle, all that you've experienced, and most of all being incarcerated for the past three years, has affected every part of your life. It's going to be hard to stay off the drugs. There needs to be a definite plan to help you with that. I guess you know that it won't be easy to be back in society. You were gone a long time, and it's a whole new ball game." Jay paused as he looked over at his father. "Your gramps wants you here. We will all try to help you, but most of all, you have to help yourself. And no pretending. You need to be honest."

Joe understood what he was being told. *They'll help me turn my life around. I can't mess up. Strange that they're Christians.* He would never have pegged Joe Junior as being from a Christian family. Of course, no one who knew him now would think he was either.

Joe cleared his throat and answered, "I've got nothing against Jesus. Nothing against the church. My mom and dad are Christians. My sister tells me in every letter that I need to come to Jesus. She's a little younger than me and has Down syndrome. She says what she thinks, always gives it to me straight." Joe smiled as he thought about his sister Chandra.

"Gramps, Uncle Jay." Joe paused and looked at each of them, "I believe I've changed—no, that I'm changing. I don't want to lie, steal, and get wasted. I don't want to go back to jail. Ever. I know I'm safe here. I will try. But you need to give me time about the Jesus stuff. I'm not too interested in Him. I think I can do this by myself. I need to do it by myself."

After another half hour of discussion, Gramps showed Joe to his room. It was one of the back bedrooms, the one his father had once shared with his Uncle Jay. The bed was made up, complete with a nice bedspread and matching pillow shams. Gramps had turned down the covers. Joe had no doubt that he was welcome here. He made his way from there to the bathroom. After washing up and brushing his teeth, he returned to the room. He looked around and smiled. *So manly,* he thought as he took in the decor and noticed his grandmother's sewing machine in the farthest corner. This room was small, but he'd had smaller rooms in his life. He didn't have pyjamas. He slipped off his shirt and jeans, then climbed into bed. He should have called his mom, but he was tired. It had been a long day.

Joe could hear the muffled voices of his gramps and uncle talking in the living room. Joe usually had difficulty trusting people, but for some reason, he felt secure in this welcome from his grandfather, and he believed what his uncle had said. Sleep was not long in coming.

In the living room, Jay and his father were talking. "Are you sure about this, Dad?"

"I want to try. It'll give an old man something to do. There are lots of things that need to be done. It's all a little overwhelming."

"Why don't I take him out for lunch tomorrow? We'll go over everything. Sounds like he was just about living on the streets before he got arrested. He should see a doctor and dentist. I don't know what ID he has. Maybe we'll have to order things. Does he have a driver's license? Does he want to look for a job? Go to school? I can talk things over with him, and we'll make a list of things needing to be done."

"Jay, thank you. I feel like a part of me that was missing just came home. Your mom would have been so happy."

"Things will work out, Dad. The Lord is working here. You've been really hurting since Mom died, and we've watched you drop out of just about everything. I think this is a gift the Lord is giving you. Mom's prayers … our prayers … are being answered."

Jay looked at his father, who whispered a quiet "amen."

"I don't know where JJ is going to fit into all this, but let's give Joey a few days to settle in, then I'll give him a call. Joey needs you, Dad. You heard him say he doesn't need Jesus, but we know different, right?"

Joe Senior looked at his son and said, "Yes, Jay. You're right. I think there's going to be a lot of changes happening around here."

• • •

AS HE ENTERED HIS room for the night, Joe Senior looked at the picture of a beautiful bride on his dresser. He went over to it and picked it up. "Oh, can you believe this is happening, Kathy? Joey is here. All the years of hoping, of praying that we'd see the kids. He's really here. I think I've blown it since you left me. I wandered away from the Lord. But I'm back, Kath. When Joey called today, I knew the Lord was in it. I prayed. I prayed that Joey would find his way to our house, and a couple hours later, he was here." He looked over to the paper bookmark he kept clipped to the mirror on his dresser: *"And we know that in all things God works for the good of those who love him, who have been called according to his purpose"* (Romans 8:28). From the time he was in high school, he had claimed that verse as his life verse. He stood on that promise through all the joys and challenges of college and courtship, and his entire married life. There had been sorrow—Donny's death, JJ's rebellion, and losing Joey and Lisa—but when his wife of almost fifty years died, he was shaken. He had lost interest in everything. Today, he felt alive again. He sat in the recliner beside his bed for a long time, praying that the Lord would lead him. He prayed that his son and grandson would find what they did not think they needed.

Chapter Four

JOE WAS ACCUSTOMED TO WAKING UP AT 6:00 A.M. WHEN HE OPENED HIS EYES, HIS FIRST thought was, *I wonder if Gramps is up yet*. The smell of bacon wafted through the room. He sat up, stretched, and smiled. He liked his gramps. He never imagined experiencing a welcome like he had received last night. Joe felt settled—a rare sensation for him.

All his life he had wanted to be somewhere other than where he was. He always felt like he was running from something or trying to find something that was missing. He held no hope that things would ever be any different. What was he looking for? He didn't like to revisit his early years. He remembered being afraid, getting angry, and hurting people. Their stories, and the things that bothered them, were never his problem. He remembered not caring and never being sorry.

Over the past three years, he had slowly changed. It started because he hated his life and wanted a new one. He began to look closely at people, trying to figure out how they felt. When he did that, he started to connect, to actually care for others. He stopped using people for his own selfish purposes.

Of course, Gramps is pretty easy to like, Joe thought as he pulled on his shirt and made his way to the kitchen. Gramps was sitting at the table reading the newspaper. Joe looked around. Last night he had been so busy wondering what Gramps thought of him, he hadn't noticed the mess. The sink was full of dishes. There were things piled on the counter. The stove looked like it hadn't been cleaned in a long time.

"Pardon the mess," Gramps said when he noticed Joe surveying the kitchen from the doorway. "One of Jay's kids comes over every couple weeks and cleans up a bit. I haven't wanted to do much lately."

"Don't worry about it, Gramps." Joe smiled. "I'll be your dream come true. I'll clean her up. You won't recognize it this afternoon. I … um … I smell bacon."

Gramps smiled at him and said, "Help yourself. There's cereal or toaster waffles to go with the bacon. I guess with you here, we'll have to do some grocery shopping."

Joe worked on the kitchen, hallway, and living room for two hours that morning. It wasn't a difficult task. As he worked, he thought about his upcoming lunch date with his uncle. At first he had been taken aback that Gramps and Uncle Jay had made plans for him, but he could see their point. There were a lot of things that needed to be done.

Jay arrived a little before noon. Gramps had told Joe that his uncle was the manager at a car dealership down the road in Foxhill. That explained why his uncle had been dressed up both last evening and again this morning. It most likely explained the new car he drove as well. Jay was parked in Gramps' driveway. He announced that they would walk to the diner. The town seemed quiet as they walked along a sidewalk that was badly in need of repair.

Gwen's Kitchen was at the end of the block, on the same side of the street. The sign in the window read, "Home Cookin'. Just like your Momma's." The sandwich board out front, which he had noticed on the way into town yesterday, read "Thursday's Special: Shepherd's Pie."

Joe and his uncle entered the busy restaurant. Judging from the noisy crowd, Joe thought, *Gwen must serve good food*.

"The table in the back is open for you, Jay," called an older lady from the kitchen doorway.

Jay shouted back, "Thanks, Gwen." He then turned to Joe. "I called ahead. We should have a little more privacy back there."

As they made their way through the restaurant, most of the people greeted his uncle. Only once did Jay stop to talk. "Pastor Brad," he greeted a man sitting alone. "Good to see you. This here is my nephew, Joey. He's staying with my dad for a while."

Joe liked the man's calm reply. "Nice to meet you. Welcome to Souton."

They continued to their table at the back. Joe thought about telling his uncle that he really didn't like being called Joey. Of course, he understood his gramps calling him that, and maybe his uncle. They had known him when he was little, but it seemed quite childish. At the same time, he didn't want to be confused with Joe Junior. Maybe it wasn't so bad to go by a new name. He'd have to think about that.

Joe ordered a hamburger, fries with gravy, and a coffee. He could never get enough coffee. Jay ordered a corned beef on rye, which actually looked good. Joe wondered if he should try to change up his food choices a bit.

Jay had brought a clipboard. When they were finished eating, he opened it up. Joe saw titles going down pages, with spaces in between. This uncle of his was organized. Within the half hour, plans were in place for Joe to get his much-needed birth certificate.

With that, he would be able to get his health card. Joe brought up that he had to be in Coverton once a month to see his probation officer.

Jay asked Joe what his plans were in terms of a job or further education. At that point, Joe shut down. Looking down, he rubbed his forehead with his hand. He looked at his uncle, squinting his eyes. "Uncle Jay, this is just too much. You lost me back at the getting a job part. I know you're trying to help … and I appreciate it, but really, I have no idea what I should do. I kind of have been out of the loop for a while. Can we slow down a bit?"

Jay looked at Joe. He was about to contradict him, tell him that these are things that need to be done, but the look on Joe's face stopped him. Joe wasn't being angry or defiant. Jay thought he looked almost desperate.

"Oh Joey, you're right. I'm the one who told you how hard this stuff is going to be, and then I barge ahead with my own timeline. Are you okay with coming over to our house tonight? We'll get the birth certificate ordered."

"That sounds fine. And I'll call the probation office after I talk to Gramps. I guess he'll be the one driving me. I'll make that appointment." When they left the restaurant, Joe was still feeling overwhelmed, but he did have some direction. It felt good to know his uncle cared. When Joe walked through Gramps' door, he felt that he belonged somewhere for the first in a long time.

"Good lunch?" Gramps asked.

"Sure was, Gramps. Uncle Jay got some takeout for you. And some dessert. I wondered, but he said rice pudding is your favourite."

"Your uncle takes good care of me," was Gramps' reply. "Have you got plans for this afternoon?"

"Well, I'd like to call my mom. Nothing after that."

Joe dialled the first phone number he had ever learned and listened to it ring.

"Hello," said a familiar voice.

"Hi, Mom. It's me."

"No collect call, so it must mean good news."

"I got out the day before yesterday."

"Where are you?"

"Well, I was transferred back down to Coverton about a month ago. I wasn't sure what I was going to do, but I think something good has happened. I found my dad's family. It wasn't hard. I had their name and the town."

"I remember. Souton, wasn't it?"

"Yeah. My grandmother's gone, but my grandfather, my gramps, really wants me to stay."

"What's he like?"

"Mom, he's a Christian. He's really unbelievable. My uncle and his family live right here in town too. Mom, I want to stay out this time."

"I know, Joey. No drugs, right? How's that going?"

"So far, so good. I mean, really, I think I'm doing good. I feel a lot different. More settled than before I went in. I'm glad they let me go to AA this time. It helped. There's a meeting here in town. That should be good. My uncle was pretty upset when he found me here, but I think we're good now. Don't worry. I won't hurt any of these people."

"What about you? Are you safe? You were in protective custody through most of your sentence."

"I'm okay. I talked with some of the guys in that gang when I got back to CDDC. They said everything was good. Not like I'm some big threat to them. I was just the stupid pawn."

The conversation lasted five more minutes. Joe wrote down his health card number and his Social Insurance Number. When he was about to say goodbye, his mom broke in.

"Oh Joe, can I call you back at this number?"

"Sure, should be fine."

"And do you have an address? There are a few Christmas gifts and cards that have added up over the past couple years."

Joe asked Gramps for the address, and he relayed it to his mom.

"Oh, and Joe, are you going to talk to Sal? She's been wondering what's up with you."

Joe had never really figured out how his mom had kept up a relationship with his biological mom through the years. "Mom, I'm trying to get settled and really don't want to talk with her. Maybe later on. If you're talking to her, tell her I say hi and that I'm doing well." He knew his mom wouldn't mind being the go-between person here.

Gramps had been listening as Joe talked to his mother. He heard him say, "I love you too, Mom" and knew Joe had hung up the phone.

Gramps looked up at him and said, "Everything okay, Joey?"

Joe took a deep breath. He couldn't believe how emotional he was getting lately. "Gramps, that's the first time since I was eighteen years old that I could give my mom an address and telephone number. I was never sure I'd be staying in the same place long enough to get the things she sent." He looked at Gramps and shook his head, remembering the countless places he had stayed. "And I couldn't trust that one of my roommates wouldn't steal what was sent if I wasn't home when it arrived."

From the look on Gramps' face, Joe could tell that he couldn't fathom the life Joe had lived. Joe quirked his mouth into a half smile. "It's okay, Gramps. I'll … we'll … be fine."

Joe called the probation office and made an appointment to see his worker next Thursday. When he hung up the phone, Gramps suggested they go to Foxhill to go grocery shopping. Foxhill was much bigger than Souton. The grocery store was small, but it had everything they needed, including a big takeout pizza they could heat up for supper. Gramps was actually spoiling him. Up and down each aisle, he continued to ask, "Do you like this, Joey? How about this?"

"Gramps, I've been eating what they put in front of me for three years. I like everything."

"Oh! I should have shared my rice pudding with you," was Gramps' comeback.

Gramps smiled while they loaded up the car with groceries. It was a much easier task with some young muscles to help. He suggested that they go into the small department store just a few doors down on the main street. It had a good supply of men's clothes, and he insisted that Joe buy a few things. By the time they were finished, Joe was sure he had all the clothes he needed, and two pairs of shoes.

Gramps also insisted he buy a winter hat, gloves, and jacket that were on sale. "They're half price. You'll need them next year," Gramps argued when Joe said he didn't need them.

"I'll probably be gone by next year," Joe replied.

Gramps stopped and was quiet.

He hopes I'm going to stay. "Oh Gramps, I'm so sorry. We'll get the coat. And if I'm not living with you when winter comes, I won't be far away. I promise."

That evening, Joe spent time at his uncle's. He met his Aunt Michelle and his cousins, Jill and Kevin. Jill was in her last year of high school. Kevin had finished college and was working at the credit union in Foxhill. Using their family computer, Joe was able to check his Facebook. He decided to deactivate the two accounts he had and then open a new one, using a different name: Joey Parks. He set up his account so that his privacy settings would only allow a chosen few people to communicate with him. This would be his family and some friends he knew he could trust—friends who wouldn't pull him into his old lifestyle. His birth certificate was set to arrive within a week.

When Joe put his head on his pillow that night, he knew it had been a good day. It had been a long time since he had gone to sleep believing that things were getting better.

Chapter Five

A FEW PEOPLE TURNED TO LOOK AS JOE WALKED WITH GRAMPS UP THE AISLE IN CHURCH on Sunday morning. He hadn't planned to be there, but Gramps had actually begged him to come.

"Joey, I have a confession to make. I haven't been to church since your grandma died, except to be at a couple funerals. I need you for moral support."

Here they sat, halfway up on the right-hand side. Directly in front of them were his uncle, aunt, and cousins. The attendance sign at the front read "143." Joe thought that was a good-sized crowd for a small-town church. Some people were dressed up. Some were not. Most people seemed happy to be there. Joe wasn't uncomfortable. He really didn't mind being there. He had good memories of church as a kid.

Pastor Brad drew attention to Joe and Gramps during the announcements. "Welcome back, Joe Wilkes. We've missed you. Joe has his grandson, Joey, with him. Joey has decided to hang his hat in Souton for a while. We're glad you're here."

Joe enjoyed the singing but didn't know most of the songs. The sermon was familiar. He even remembered part of the scripture reference the pastor used.

Brad had dropped by the house yesterday to officially welcome Joe to town. He'd brought a half dozen doughnuts, and Gramps had put on a pot of coffee. Joe was surprised to find out that no one had told Brad that he was recently out of jail. He didn't seem worried about having an ex-con in town. His questions were genuine. When Joe told him he was an addict, Brad congratulated him for his three years of sobriety. He mentioned the AA meeting that the police officer had told him about.

The service ended, and Gramps greeted many of his friends as they made their way to the back of the church. They stopped when a familiar voice called out, "Joe, Joey, hold up."

"Hi, Larry," Gramps said as the man reached them. Joe nodded a greeting.

"Joyce told me to get over here and invite you two for dinner."

Gramps hesitated, and as he did, Larry spoke again. "Ham and scalloped potatoes?"

Joe and Gramps looked at each other and both laughed. Gramps' reply was quick. "Thanks, Larry. We'd be glad to come for dinner."

• • •

EVERY DAY THAT PASSED found Joe becoming more and more settled. Most of his time was spent with Gramps. Gramps liked to walk to the coffee shop, where he would sit for an hour and greet his friends as they came and went. Joe was content to spend the time listening and learning. He was becoming acquainted with what this town was all about. One of his goals was to get Gramps' house and yard cleaned up. He was able to get most of the outside work done. The weather was getting warmer, but rain sometimes stopped his plans.

Joe didn't have much job experience. He'd worked in a small factory for a few months when he left high school. One summer he worked for a pool and spa business, installing and servicing above ground pools. His last job was installing hardwood floors. None of the jobs had lasted long. He usually got in trouble and lost his job before he ended up back in jail. Joe realized that in any significant place he'd worked, he had been hired solely because he knew someone who worked there. Gramps had begun to tell people that Joe was looking for work. Today when they were at the coffee shop, an older fellow, Carl, asked Joe if he could drive a tractor.

"Well, no." Joe was hesitant.

"Would you like to learn?"

Joe thought for a moment and nodded his head. "Yeah, sure."

By the time they left the coffee shop, Joe had a possible job. He wasn't sure he'd make a good farmer, but tomorrow Gramps would drive him a few kilometres out of town to see the farm and meet Carl's son.

"It's my farm," Carl said, "but my boy takes care of most of it now. He told me yesterday to be on the lookout for a worker."

On the way home, Gramps told Joe that it was a big farm. "Carl told me it's about seven-hundred-and-fifty acres. They grow soybeans and winter wheat. I've been out there to buy apples, and they seem to have lots of produce by the end of the summer. They must have a big garden."

• • •

ON MONDAY NIGHT, JOE walked down to the Anglican church for the AA meeting. He knew that there were groups for drug addicts specifically, but there was no NA group in Souton. Joe had learned at his meetings in prison that his dependency problems started with alcohol when he was a teenager. Because the twelve-step principles were applicable to all kinds of addictions, Joe knew this meeting could meet his needs.

It was quite a large group, and as he entered the room, he saw a familiar face. He nodded at Brad, assuming he was there to support someone. When the introductions came, Brad introduced himself as an alcoholic. Joe was surprised but didn't show it. He'd been around long enough to know that all kinds of people have addictions. Seeing Brad there and hearing him say the same words as he did made Joe feel good. He couldn't figure why he felt that way, but he was glad Brad was there.

As Joe said goodbye to Brad in the parking lot and began walking home, he heard someone call "Parker." He stopped, looked around, and saw a guy who had been in the meeting. He was leaning against a nice car in the far corner of the lot. Joe walked toward him, trying to remember what he had said his name was. *Cavin? Calvin?* Joe forgot what he'd said. He took a closer look. *Oh, I know this guy.* In jail inmates often went by nicknames. Joe's name was Stretch, but he had left that name behind a few years ago.

"Raider?" Joe spoke as he moved to where Raider stood.

"Yes. It's been a while, Parker. Three years. They were shipping you out as I was coming in. I wasn't thinking I'd see you here."

Joe looked at the man, just a kid really, in front of him. "Yeah, they were shipping me out all right. Up to Kingston. But I'm out now. You from around here?"

"Not far. Need a ride?"

"No thanks."

"Need anything else?"

Joe stared at Raider. He looked a little wasted, which wasn't unusual for many of the guys Joe had once counted as friends. Even when they were off drugs, it seemed like they might be high. He knew sellers could show up at meetings, but he hadn't thought that would happen here in Souton.

"No, I'm good," Joe replied.

"So, Parker, are you serious about this stuff, or were you lying in there."

"Not lying. I haven't had anything for the past three years."

Raider smiled. "But you just got out, right?"

Joe just looked at him.

"Well, if I can help you out, let me know. I usually just come on Monday nights. Condition of my probation."

With that, Raider hopped into his fancy car and drove away. Joe walked quickly home. He was glad Raider had sped out of town in the opposite direction.

• • •

TUESDAY MORNING JOE WAS at the farm. He stared across acres and acres of farmland. Gramps had driven into the driveway of a nicely kept farmhouse. It was nestled on a treed lot in front of a large collection of barns and outbuildings. A middle-aged man approached from the driveway of a modern ranch-style house directly across the road. Joe was introduced to Jeff, Carl's son, who looked to be about fifty.

The morning went by quickly. Jeff showed him around. Joe marvelled at the sight of the machinery. Would he ever be able to drive the gigantic tractor, especially if it was pulling other equipment? The machine Jeff identified as a combine was massive. Joe was intimidated by the thought of operating any of the equipment in front of him. When he asked Jeff if he was planning for that, he was relieved by Jeff's reply.

"No. It's all pretty complicated for a newbie. You'll be a big help, though, when we're switching and hitching, loading and unloading. I try to maintain my own equipment, so there's lots to do." Jeff walked over to where two four wheelers were parked near the door of the building. He turned to Joe. "Ever use one of these?"

Joe smiled and said, "Yes. I loved it. When I was at a foster home in the country when I was sixteen, we used these all the time. Then a directive came from the agency saying we couldn't ride them. Too dangerous. We weren't impressed."

Jeff smiled. "Well, it was a skill learned that will come in handy. Our property is too big to walk around, and right now too many spots would bog us down in a vehicle. I'll give you a tour and stop in places where you'll be doing jobs. There will be grass to cut, lanes to fix, brush to clear. It'll give you an idea of what's to come if you stick around." He handed Joe a helmet. "Just stay behind me, and remember, you aren't a teenager anymore."

It was noon when the men returned to the buildings. Joe was excited at the prospect of having this job. He looked forward to working. He also knew that with the variety of things he'd be doing, he'd never be bored. As they walked toward the house and driveway, Joe asked, "How much work does your dad do around here?"

"Well, he's still putting time in here on the farm, almost full-time in planting and harvest season. He still drives the big tractor when I need him. His trouble is with the jobs where physical strength is needed. He's ninety, you know."

"No way." Joe couldn't believe it. "And he's still driving?

Jeff just laughed. "Sure is. Since he turned eighty, he's gone every two years to get checked out at the MTO office. Passes all the tests, all the time. He is slowing down a bit. That must be why he suggested that we might have a job for you, although maybe he thought he could help you out. My dad gives lots of guys chances."

"So how are you with that? Your dad told me you were the one looking for help."

"Oh, I trust my dad's judgement. And I'll be honest with you, I went to school with your dad. I didn't recognize your name, but you're the spitting image of him."

"So you know I've been in trouble?"

Jeff nodded. "It's a small town, Joe."

"And you're okay with that?"

"I think my dad is a good judge of character. Most likely he was figuring there would be some jobs you can't get with your record, so we'll see how you like it. It's hard work, but there's something about farming that gets under your skin."

• • •

"ENJOYED IT, DID YOU?" Gramps asked as they were pulling out of the driveway.

"How did you guess?"

"Well, you have this big smile on your face for one thing. And I know these people well. Anyone I know who has ever worked for them has been sorry when they had to move on."

Joe was amazed at how much his thinking had changed. He had a job. He wouldn't have to apply for government assistance. He could pay Gramps some money for rent. He liked the slow pace of Souton. People were being nice to him, even people who knew about his past. Less than a week in this place and it felt like home.

• • •

A 7:00 A.M. START time didn't bother Joe at all. He arrived at the farm, and Jeff met him in the driveway as Carl came out his door. "My dad's going to get you started in the garden this morning."

Yesterday, Jeff had told Joe that the first job for him, if he chose to work at the farm, would be to till the garden at the main house. His parents, especially his mother, would need more help with the garden this year than last.

Carl smiled at Joe. "Glad you decided to come on board. So you've never driven a tractor? You do drive, don't you?"

"I can drive, but I've never had a license."

"Well, that will limit you to driving only on our property, but that's okay."

Joe followed Carl to a smaller building that he hadn't entered the day before. Carl pointed to an old tractor sitting away from the other machinery. "This here is a Ford 8N. It's old, but it still does the job. Kind of like me."

Joe laughed. "How long have you had this farm, Carl?"

"Well, I was born on this farm, Joe. My grandfather started farming here in 1877." Carl smiled as he remembered his long life on the farm. Joe smiled in amazement as he thought of a place belonging to a family for almost a hundred and fifty years.

• • •

IT DIDN'T TAKE LONG for Joe to master driving the tractor. At the end of thirty minutes, he was able to shift gears and turn it in the direction he wanted it to go. It was more difficult to manoeuvre pulling the tiller, but under Carl's direction, he soon caught on.

The morning went by quickly. By noon, the garden was tilled. In the afternoon, Joe sat down with Carl and Annie at their kitchen table. Annie had taken an eleven-by-thirteen piece of paper and mapped out the plants already growing in the garden. It showed rows of raspberry and redcurrant bushes, a section of strawberries, and asparagus. There was a section of herbs, and Annie had neatly printed the names of each one. As Joe wrote down the names of the plants and seeds that had to be ordered, he was excited. He told Carl and Annie about his grandfather's garden up north. Rows of potatoes that lasted a large family a whole year. Carrots, squash, radishes a foot long. He'd never seen such a large garden with such a variety of things growing. He smiled as he realized that this garden was going to give Papa Parker's garden some competition.

• • •

THE DAY FLEW BY for Joe. Gramps arrived at 5:00, and Joe was tired. It was a good tired, though. As Joe told Gramps about his day, he mentioned a conversation he had with Jeff. He had just finished eating the lunch he'd packed that morning, when Jeff sat down at the picnic table across from him. Jeff told him about his son, Chad, who would soon be home from university. Chad was at medical school and had two more years before graduation. "I guess there's a group Jeff thought I might like to go to with his son. It's in Foxhill at some church."

Gramps was nodding. "They go to the Community Church in Foxhill. He's probably talking about a small group for younger folk your age. Or maybe a men's or a singles' group."

"Do you think I should go?"

"I think you should consider it. You might get tired of hanging out with old guys all the time."

"Fat chance, Gramps. You are amazing," Joe replied.

Chapter Six

JOE DIDN'T LIKE TO MISS WORK HIS SECOND DAY ON THE JOB, BUT JEFF ASSURED HIM that they understood he had things he was required to do. Today he would meet with his probation officer. He and Gramps had a leisurely breakfast and then left at 9:00 a.m. to get to his appointment.

Joe sat in front of the probation officer completely relaxed. He knew that the man was impressed as he reported all that had happened since he'd left CDDC. *Probably he's read my history and wonders how I can be the same guy. I'm impressed too. I have a great place to live, with lots of support. I went to the meeting; I've got a job. Things are looking good.*

"Joe, is this going to last?" The officer's question pulled him from his thoughts. For the first time in his memory, Joe looked sincerely at a probation officer. He hesitated and then spoke.

"Things are different this time. I'm different. I came through the gates saying I'm never going back, but after a week, I'm believing that. My grandfather is out in the waiting room. He's amazing. But he's not the only one who's rooting for me. There's this little town, and so many people are giving me a chance. Things are just really different."

● ● ●

AS JOE AND GRAMPS walked to the car, Joe recounted his conversation in the office. Before Gramps put the car in drive, Joe turned to him and said, "Thanks, Gramps. I couldn't do this without you." Gramps just smiled, and they were on their way.

Jay had mentioned the need for a computer, so he wasn't surprised when Gramps brought the subject up. "I'll pay for it, and you can pay back half when you get paid."

Joe knew of a small computer store that sold good used computers, so they headed farther into the city.

Trusting Joe's experience to pick out a system that would best suit their needs, Gramps was pleased when Joe announced he had found the perfect one. Gramps paid for it, and Joe easily carried the three boxes out of the store. As they made their way to the car, Gramps noticed a deli in the small strip mall. "How about I go over and order a couple of sandwiches? We can take them home for lunch."

"Sounds good, Gramps," Joe replied.

Gramps handed him the car keys and then headed for the deli. When Joe opened the trunk, he realized he needed to do some rearranging to fit the boxes in. He put the boxes on the ground. He had just moved a grocery tote and a lawn chair to the back of the trunk when he heard a sharp voice behind him.

"Parker! Back away from the car with your hands open and away from your body."

Joe closed his eyes, shook his head, and stepped backwards.

"I thought you were in jail," the officer said as he reached for Joe's wrists and handcuffed him. He pushed him toward the police car, with its flashers going. His partner had opened the back door.

"You are harassing me. I haven't done anything wrong."

"That's a nice computer you have there, and I doubt this is your car. Kind of a crime you're used to—not that you don't always get caught."

"It's my grandfather's car. We just got the computer."

"And you have a receipt?"

"He has it."

"Well, have a seat. We'll see what you've been up to."

Joe was roughly pushed into the back seat of the cruiser. *Why this again? Gramps, what's taking you so long? There must be a line up in there.* Joe saw the computer running in the front seat as the officers searched for something to pin on him. He'd been in this position countless times before, but this time he hadn't done anything wrong. The first officer opened the door. "What's your grandfather's name."

"Joe Wilkes." Joe knew that they already knew who the car belonged to.

"Where is he?"

"He went to get us a sandwich at the deli."

Joe couldn't see the deli from the position he was in. If he could have, he would have seen Gramps come out the door of the deli and walk slowly toward the car. When he arrived at the car, he stopped and looked at the open trunk. He had seen the police car and now made the connection. An officer looked up and saw him, closed the door of the cruiser, and slowly made his way over to where Gramps stood. Gramps spoke first.

"Where is my grandson?" He looked to the police car and then back to the officer. He shook his head, barely able to control his anger.

"Could I have your name, sir?"

"My name is Joseph Wilkes, and my grandson's name is Joseph Parker. And I have an awful feeling he's sitting in the back of that car."

"Is this your car, sir?"

"Yes, it is."

"Did you purchase a computer today?"

"My grandson and I did."

"Could I see your ID, car ownership and insurance, and the receipt for the computer."

"And you are allowed to ask me for all this?"

"Yes, sir, I am."

"Well, young man, I am not going to argue with you right now but be assured that I'll be checking this out. And if you're violating my rights, I will put in a complaint." After reaching into the car for the ownership, he handed the officer what he had asked for. "I think you should let my grandson out of your car."

"We usually run a record check when we see a known offender taking part in suspected illegal activity."

"And what was the suspected activity?"

"He was taking computer boxes out of this car."

"He was putting the computer boxes in the car. He had the keys. Is that a suspected illegal activity as well?"

"You have to realize, sir, that your grandson has been convicted of some serious crimes."

"I'm fully aware of my grandson's serious crimes. And I know he did his time. I also know that he's determined to stay out of jail. He's been off drugs for three years and is going to AA meetings. He got a job yesterday. Your officers stopped him twice in the first twenty-four hours he was out of jail. For nothing. He was just at the probation office, and the worker was pleased with his progress. Is this going to happen every time we come into Coverton? It's time for you guys to back off."

The officer didn't say another word. He slowly looked at each item and then returned them to Gramps. Then he went to the cruiser, opened the door, and motioned for Joe to get out. He unlocked the handcuffs and told Joe he was free to go. Joe slid into the passenger seat beside Gramps.

"Oh Gramps, I am so sorry. This is so embarrassing for you."

Gramps looked at him. "Joey, they put handcuffs on you."

"I can handle it. Don't worry about me. I'm just sorry you were involved."

"But you must have felt awful."

"You know what, Gramps? It wasn't so bad. I knew I hadn't done anything wrong. That's the first time I've ever been sure of that when they shoved me into a car. I haven't broken the law. And I knew you were close, Gramps, and that made all the difference in the world."

Joe continued to insist that he was fine as they drove away. He wanted to get out of the city fast. This wasn't a new experience. How many times had he sat in the back of the police car and listened as the officers told him what a useless piece of crap he was? Sometimes they'd let him go with jeers and warnings. Most times they had arrested him because something showed up on the computer.

For the first time since Joe had walked through the gates of the detention centre, he let anger take root. *Things are never going to be any different. Why can't they just leave me alone?* He doubted himself and wondered if he'd really be able to stay away from the drugs. He fluctuated between anger and a sickening feeling that things were not going to be different after all. His mother once told him that anger was a term that was hard to define. In his mind, he heard her words: *I know you're angry, Joe, but what are you feeling? There are so many possibilities. Fear? Despair? Hopelessness?* Well, right now Joe would go with the latter two. He would never admit he was afraid. Gramps glanced over at him.

"If it helps, I'm angry too. But we can't let that defeat us, Joey. You're doing great, and you're going to be okay." He knew something was going on with Joey but decided not to say anything else. He knew that Joey would talk it out when he wanted to or, more likely, when he was able to.

• • •

JOE WAS GLAD TO be back on the job the next day. He worked hard and was pleased that he was learning new things. He felt that Jeff trusted him, and he hoped that he could live up to that trust. No matter how hard he tried to forget it, the incident from yesterday weighed heavy on him. Some things would just never change.

When Joe came home from work, he was physically tired. He thought he'd go to bed early, but he knew that Gramps was in the mood for visiting. After supper, they watched a movie together, and at 9:00 p.m. Joe stood up. "Gramps, do you mind if I head off to bed?"

"All that fresh air catching up to you, Joey?"

"Probably, Gramps. But that fresh air is so good. I'm never going to forget that cramped cell, and the days we went without any yard time. Sometimes months. You won't find me complaining. The work is great, and I love my job."

Gramps laughed and said, "Says the man who has worked at a job for two days."

Joe laughed too.

As Joe made his way to the bedroom, the phone rang. He stopped and listened while Gramps picked it up.

"Hi, JJ. How are you doing? Yes, he said he was going to call you … Joe Junior, what's your problem? Just settle down."

Joe turned around and went back into the living room. He knew who was on the phone, and his voice was so loud he could hear what he was saying from across the room: "Let me talk to him."

Gramps looked at Joe and saw the look on his face. Anger? No. It was fear.

"I don't think so," Gramps spoke into the phone.

Joe closed his eyes, shaking his head, as the man he used to call *Daddy* shouted obscenities into the phone. He heard the threat clearly: "Tell him if he doesn't get out of your house, I'm coming down there to." The voice stopped. Joey looked up. Gramps had hung up the phone. There were tears in his eyes as he looked at Joe.

Joe hurried to the bathroom. He stayed in the shower until all the hot water was gone. When he was finished, he went straight to his bedroom, not even looking to see if a light was still on in the living room. He climbed into bed. Of course, he couldn't sleep. He hated the feelings inside him. How could hearing his father spew such hatred affect him so much? *I'm safe here. My gramps loves me. I'm going to make something of myself.* Why the feeling of hopelessness? Why the thought that one joint would settle him down … or a glass of wine … really anything along that line. He felt as helpless as he had as a little boy when his dad picked up the belt.

An hour later there was a soft knock on the bedroom door. "Joey, can I come in?"

"Gramps, I have to get some sleep."

"Please, Joey. I need to get some sleep too, but that won't happen if I can't talk to you." "Okay," Joe sighed. "Come on in."

Gramps sat on the side chair in the corner, next to the sewing machine. They both spoke at once.

"Gramps, I'm sorry."

"Joey, I'm so sorry."

"Well," Gramps continued, "I don't know why you would be sorry. But I'm sorry that he called here. Your uncle and I had talked about calling him when you were settled in. I guess Jay called him, and I guess he doesn't like the idea of you being here. But that's his problem, not ours."

"I know that's how you feel, Gramps, but it's my fault too. Look at me … total loser … wasted life. I don't know if I can do this, Gramps. Uncle Jay said I have to be honest. You want honest? I don't think I can do this. Right now what I want is to get drunk or high."

"Joey."

Joe looked at his grandfather.

"What did he do to you?"

Joe was silent for a whole minute. "Gramps, I was only six years old when Children's Services took us. By then he and Sal had split up, but he came and went. And other guys came and went. What do I remember about my dad? Mostly nothing. But when I hear his voice screaming like that, I see glimpses of pain. I feel the pain, and … and I don't know. I remember seeing him hurt Sal. Once the stove was on, and, somehow, he hurt her. She screamed and screamed. I guess he beat me. That's what the court papers said. I read them when I read my file. The agency let me read it when I turned sixteen. I don't think he ever hit Lisa. Thank God he didn't hurt her. It was a long time ago. It was scary—I remember that. I guess he was a drinker. I don't know. Sal says that he used to tie my arms to the beam in the basement and hit me." Joe shook his head, trying to remember. "I don't think that happened. I don't remember that. I just remember him telling me … lots of times … to be a man and stop crying."

Gramps thought for a moment, trying to fathom what Joe had said. *All this before he was six years old.* "Joey, you've got lots on your plate. Things happened to you that should never happen to any kid. I don't know how to help you through that, Joey, but I want you here with me. Right now, I need you here with me. You've had two things in two days shake you up and remind you of your past. I know that's got something to do with your wanting to escape. I'm sorry about that. What can I do to help?"

"Believe me, Gramps, you're already helping. I should be able to get past this. I learned a lot in the meetings in jail. AA will help. I don't know what else to do." Joe looked at Gramps, shaking his head.

"We'll find a counsellor, or someone who can help. Joey, I think you can do it. You can get through this. I'm not going to give up on you, and I don't want you to give up on yourself. We'll talk again tomorrow and try to figure some things out."

After Gramps left, Joey tossed and turned for a long time. The last time he looked at the clock, it read 3:05. He kept going back to Gramps' words: *I'm not going to give up on you, Joey.* Finally, he drifted off to sleep.

Chapter Seven

THE WEEKEND PASSED QUICKLY FOR JOE. HE WORKED AT THE FARM ON SATURDAY morning. Joe felt good as he worked outdoors. He never tired of the openness and fresh air, and the weather was getting warmer daily.

Saturday evening he spent some time with his cousin, Kevin. Kevin seemed to like Joe and invited him to go with him to a friend's house to hang out. At first Joe was hesitant. His cousin was much younger than he was, but Kevin pressed him. "It's not a party. We just hang out. Play pool and video games. Eat. It'll be fun."

They arrived at a house located about eight kilometres from Souton, on the highway going toward Foxhill. It was a large ranch house, set back from the road. Joe noticed a big building a little farther down the driveway. "That's what they call the arena. They have horses. Actually, they're pretty rich," Kevin explained.

The house was impressive. They walked through a long hallway into a big family room. Joe was surprised to see about twenty young adults gathered in the room. Some played pool, but most of them were gathered around a large TV, watching a hockey game. An impressive bar, with bottles of alcohol grouped on the end of it, stretched for twenty feet across the back wall of the room. Joe could see cases of beer stacked into a commercial style fridge behind the bar. He shook his head and thought, *I didn't know I'd be facing this temptation tonight.*

Joe was introduced and felt very out of place. He went to the pool table, and when a game ended, he was invited to take on the winner. Joe played pool well. He remained playing for three games, soundly beating his opponents. He was glad to stop playing when he lost a game. He was content to watch the group as they interacted. Joe noticed that many of those present were drinking quite seriously. Kevin wasn't drinking, but Joe became concerned when he left the room with two other guys. When he returned, he approached Joe, who wasn't surprised that he smelled like pot. "What are you thinking?" Joe asked Kevin.

Kevin's reply came quickly. "It's no big deal. I can get you something stronger here if you need it." Kevin moved on to a group of his friends.

Joe hadn't seen this coming. *So much for just hanging out.*

Joe made a decision. He didn't want to be at this party. It wasn't likely the police would come to the house, and it wasn't likely that he'd give in to the urge to drink or smoke pot; but there was no way he could even entertain the possibility of those things happening. He walked over to Kevin, who turned when he tapped him on the shoulder. "I'm headed out, Kevin. I'll get home on my own."

"Okay, Joe. I'll see you later," Kevin replied nonchalantly.

It was a beautiful night. Joe wasn't used to seeing the sky covered in stars, but already, at 10:00 p.m., it was absolutely beautiful. He could hear frogs peeping, and there was a slight breeze. Eight kilometres wasn't far, and he had a while to do it. He walked on the shoulder of the road, facing the traffic. A few cars drove past as he walked. After about twenty minutes, a car slowed down on the opposite side of the road. As it stopped across from him, he noticed that it was a cruiser. The officer rolled down the window and said, "Joey, what are you doing walking out in the middle of nowhere at this time of night?"

Joe recognized him as one of the officers who had arrived at Gramps' house on that first night.

"Well, I found myself at a party that wasn't supposed to be a party, and the temptations were a little too much for me. I decided I better get home to my gramps."

The officer laughed. "Kind of like Joseph and Potiphar's wife?"

"Well, not quite that temptation, but a couple of things I didn't want to get back into."

"Well, good for you. How do you know about Potiphar's wife?"

"Six years of Bible stories at church and home, along with a private Christian school. I do have a good memory. I guess I should have let the lessons sink in a bit better."

"Lots of us don't let the lessons sink in enough. Do you want a ride the rest of the way home?"

"No thanks, it's a beautiful night."

"Hey, Joey, on Tuesday nights I go to a men's group up at the Community Church in Foxhill. We have dinner and then do a Bible study, usually with a video. I'd be glad to pick you up if you want to go."

"Is that the same one Jeff's son goes to?"

"It is. He's one of the younger guys. The rest are old men like you and me."

Joe laughed, and after he thought for a moment, he made a decision he hoped he wouldn't regret.

"Okay. It sounds good. It's been a long time … but it sounds good. And by the way, my name is Joe."

"Great. I'll get you at 6:30."

As the cruiser drove away, Joe realized that he didn't even know his new buddy's name.

When Joe got home, he talked to Gramps for a while. "I wasn't very comfortable with that young crowd. It's a beautiful night. I enjoyed the walk." He mentioned a few things about the gathering, not telling Gramps about the drinking and drugs. Gramps was glad to hear he had talked to the cop.

Joe told him he had agreed to go to the church meeting, the same one he and Jeff had discussed. Gramps wasn't surprised. "Oh, Rob. That must have been Rob. He's Warren Schroeder's boy. Got married a couple years ago. He and his wife just had a baby a couple months ago." Every day it became plainer to Joe that everyone knew everyone in this corner of the county.

Joe told his gramps that he wasn't going to church in the morning. Gramps didn't ask why, and if he was disappointed, he didn't show it. He did thank Joe for going with him last Sunday and said he was glad that he had been welcomed back. Joe smiled as he went to his room when Gramps yelled out, "But don't you be crying when I come home telling you about the great dinner I had, because someone invited me over."

Joe woke with a start on Sunday morning. His alarm had gone off. He reached over, fumbling for the button to turn it off. He'd slept through the internal alarm he had woken to for years. That had to be a good sign. Today he smelled sausages and smiled. Gramps was just finishing up his breakfast when Joe sauntered into the kitchen and saw a pan on the stove. There were lots of sausages left. He noticed another pan that Gramps must have cooked an egg or two in. The eggs were still on the counter. In no time, he cooked two eggs and had them on his plate, along with lots of meat and two pieces of toast. His first thought as he sat down was that his life was starting to look a little more normal.

Gramps was still sitting at the table. He smiled as Joe sat down across from him. "Jay called this morning. He plans to come over and talk to you before church."

"Did he say why?" Joe's first thought was *Oh no, Kevin got loaded and they're going to blame me.*

Gramps was talking. "Just asked what time you got home and if you were drunk."

"And you told him?

"The time, and no, and what you told me."

Just as he was finishing up breakfast, Joe heard his uncle arrive. Jay came into the kitchen, poured a coffee from the pot, and sat down on a chair set back against the wall. He looked at Joe.

"So should I be mad at you?"

"I don't know, Uncle Jay. What's up?"

"My son arrived home at about 2:00 a.m. The time wasn't a problem. He's almost twenty-one years old. Frankly, I've never thought to make a rule about coming home drunk, but that's what he was. Or high. Or something."

Joe didn't say anything. Jay continued talking. "Dad says you'd walked home earlier and that you weren't drunk. Can you tell me anything about how Kev ended up in that condition?"

Joe hesitated, not knowing what to say. *I couldn't have done anything differently. What's my responsibility here? Kevin's an adult. But look at Uncle Jay. Kevin lives at home. His dad loves him, and he's really hurting here. I owe it to them both to try to help.* His uncle waited patiently.

"Kevin had told me when he invited me that it wasn't a party. I was surprised that there was a crowd, about twenty kids around his age. Some were playing pool, some watching the game, some just sitting around. There was lots of drinking going on. Uncle Jay, I knew right then I had to get out of there. I can't be around alcohol." Joe stopped. *How do I say this?*

"And?" his uncle prompted.

"Kevin wasn't drinking at that point. I wasn't too concerned, but I'd seen people leaving a couple at a time and coming back in soon after. Kevin left, and when he came back, he came up to me." He paused again.

"There's more." His uncle knew Joe was trying to find the words.

"Yes." Joe sighed and went on. "He reeked of pot. I said something like, 'Why on earth would you do that?' You know, Uncle Jay, I wasn't all that concerned at that point. Well, I was, because there I was in the middle of that, and it wasn't okay for me to be there. I really believe pot can lead to doing harder drugs. But what Kevin said next concerned me. He said, 'It's no big deal. I can get you something stronger here if you need it.' I'm sorry I didn't press Kevin further, but at that point I knew I couldn't stay. Walking home was my best alternative."

Jay was quiet. He looked over at his dad and then back at Joe and said, "I don't know what to do." Joe noticed that there were tears in his uncle's eyes.

"What did you say last night?" Gramps asked the question.

"I told him to get his butt to bed and we'd talk this morning. He was so …"

Jay paused and looked at Joe, who whispered, "wasted."

"He was so wasted that he probably doesn't remember."

"Does he know about my past, Uncle Jay?"

"A little of it. And he's seen your dad in action. He watched your grandma and gramps, I guess all of us, hurting for him all these years." His uncle shook his head.

"Uncle Jay, you just need to talk to him. You love him. Tell him how you feel. That you're afraid for him. Ask him how you can help him. I don't know. You never know what's going on in someone's head." Joe paused, knowing he had his uncle's total attention. "He could be thinking anything. Maybe it's just a new thing. Maybe just the wrong crowd. Talk to him and remind him that you love him. That's a start. I can tell him what I know of drugs and give him a hundred examples of lives wrecked from them. But hearing doesn't convince a person as much as knowing they're loved and cherished. I'm convinced that Gramps and you, and my mom and dad and sisters, along with all of your prayers, are the only reason I didn't stay at that party last night."

Jay sighed and looked from Joe to his dad. "That's lots to think about. Thanks, Joey. Thanks, Dad." Jay stopped on the way to the door to give his dad a hug. "I have to run, so I'll see you later. Michelle put a roast in the oven. Plan to come for dinner."

It was quiet in the kitchen.

"Gramps, what do you think?"

"I think Kevin is going to be okay. And Joey, I think you belong here with me."

Joe looked at his grandfather. "Gramps, what went wrong with my dad? How could he turn out like he did?"

"Oh Joey, if we could answer that question, we could help every addict everywhere. But I can tell you we're not a perfect family, and different things in families affect people in different ways. Grandma and I weren't twenty yet when we got married, and JJ was on the way. We were madly in love and loved him, but we were young. I'm sure we made lots of mistakes. Your dad was a bright little guy, but from the time he was a baby, he was very strong willed. We probably should have done a lot of things differently. When your dad was two, Donny was born. You said your sister has Down syndrome, and that's what Donny had. We just brought him home and loved him, and JJ loved him too.

"Back then there weren't all the special programmes and medical interventions there are now. Donny had a heart defect. The doctors told us he should be put in an institution, but we kept him at home. Your dad was so gentle and kind with him. He was his personal trainer from the time they were small. He taught Donny to say words and copy actions. Donny was able to do lots. We understood his speech, and he could dance and sing. He was always happy and could put you in a good mood at any given time. We all loved him so much. Your Aunt Marge and Uncle Jay arrived two and four years after him." Gramps paused, smiling at his thoughts. Joe watched and noticed his expression change.

"When Donny was ten, he started getting sick. He had lung problems, and with his heart defect, he got less and less able to do things. He required a lot of care. Your grandma and I and JJ gave him lots of attention. Here was this twelve-year-old boy acting like a man. When Donny was eleven, he developed pneumonia, and after three weeks in the hospital, he died.

"We were all devastated. Your grandma went into a deep depression, and I fumbled around trying to keep things normal. I think it was a crucial time in your dad's life. His brother was gone, and he'd tried hard to save him. JJ should have been safe and secure, but neither your grandma nor I were there for him.

"In hindsight, that's what I think happened. He started doing things in a reckless way very soon after Donny died. He pretty much did as he pleased. The day he turned sixteen, he quit school and moved out of the house. He was in quite a bit of trouble in his late teen years. Spent time in detention and then jail. By the time he was twenty, he was with Sal and had you. He seemed settled, and he's been able to keep a job. He still has a temper, though, and he's very unpredictable."

"He did some time for beating me. I read that in the court papers," Joe commented in a low voice.

"We hadn't heard that. I'm sorry, Joey. When you visited here, things seemed fine. We lost track of him for a few years, and we didn't know you and Lisa were in foster care until your adoptions were being finalized."

"Well, I'm here now … right, Gramps?"

"For sure, Joey. I'm so glad you are." He looked at the clock. "And I better get out the door before I'm late for church."

Gramps left with instructions that Joe should be at his aunt and uncle's for dinner at 1:00 p.m.

Joe was sitting on the couch in the living room, watching the news, when his cousin came in through the front door. He glanced at the clock. It was 12:10.

"I think I'm in big trouble." Kevin looked at Joe as if he held an answer for his troubles. He sat down in the chair across the room.

"What kind of trouble?" Joe said.

"Last night, Joe. Where did you go? I remember talking to you, and you saying you were leaving. Then I must have started drinking. I must have been really drunk, because I don't know how I got home."

"And you're here because?"

"I woke up just when they were going out the door for church. I'm surprised my dad didn't make me get up … not that he's had to make me get up before. All he said was 'Joey's at home. When you wake up a bit, go see him.' So a shower and two coffees later, here I am." Kevin paused, grimacing. "Does Gramps have any Tylenol? My head feels like it's going to explode."

What's Uncle Jay thinking? Am I supposed to play counsellor here? Well, he's expecting me to say something, so I better give it a shot. He couldn't resist a sarcastic reply. "I don't know, Kev. Where would Gramps keep the Tylenol?"

Kevin went down the hall to the bathroom. Joe heard him go to the kitchen to get a glass of water. He came back to the living room and sat down again. He looked over at Joe, who spoke first. "Do you know that I'm a drug addict?"

"I figured you might be, but you don't seem like a drug addict to me."

"Well, I am. Every day my mind tells me just one drink … just one joint … just one line of coke, or even one little pill, will take away all my stress, all my troubles, and make everything all right. Some people can control their drinking and pot use, but I can't. So I can't drink or use any kind of drugs." Joe paused, looking at his cousin. He didn't know him well and wasn't sure how to word what he wanted to say. Kevin just sat watching him.

"I was in jail, without drugs or alcohol, for three years. My body doesn't usually tell me I need them anymore, but sometimes it does. It's a horrible life to have those substances controlling you. I treated people I love terribly. Can you imagine waking up all the time wondering what you did the night before? You know now what a terrible feeling that is. Three years, Kevin—no drugs, no alcohol. I've changed. I control myself, and I don't plan to use people or hurt them the way I used to, but every day it's a choice for me. I'm still an alcoholic, and I'm still a drug addict.

"Do you remember what you said to me after I confronted you about the stink of pot on you?"

As Joe studied him, waiting for an answer, Kevin just shrugged his shoulders.

"You said, 'It's no big deal. I can get you something stronger if you need it.' I had no choice but to leave. It was such a big deal. If the cops had dropped in on your party, if they stopped your car on the way home and found drugs, I would have been on my way back to jail. And if I'd been weaker, God knows I've had some rough days lately, I would have given in and taken you up on your offer.

"You know the people who you're getting the drugs from, even the pot. I used to be one of those people. No dealer is doing you a favour. Do you know all the people who were there? Is it that guy … what's his name? Pete? Is it his house?"

"It's Pete's parents' house. They've been down south for the past month. They're coming home this week. That's why Pete invited us out last night."

Joe shook his head and sighed. "So how deep are you into this stuff?"

Kevin was quiet for a minute. "My last year of college I drank a lot and smoked up a lot. I worked at a restaurant in the city three hours a night, three nights a week, and then one shift on the weekend. I lived with four other guys in a house near the college. Sometimes during the week I'd get high, and always after my weekend shift some of my buddies and I would party. I don't think it was a problem. I kept my grades up and graduated with honours.

"Since then it's really just the weekends. Last night was a little extreme. I've never been in that bad shape before." Kevin stopped and looked at Joe. "There were pills being passed around. I think I must have taken something. I was so out of it that I don't know what I said to my dad. He asked me where my car is, and I don't even know. How on earth did I get home?"

"Your dad didn't mention it, so he can't be too worried about that. He was pretty surprised that you came home in such bad shape. He wasn't mad, just confused. More like he couldn't believe it had happened. He had called Gramps early to see what time I came home and if I'd been drinking. Then he showed up here before church. He was just trying to figure it out. All I saw was a dad who loves his son so much he can't bear the thought of him getting into a life of drugs. He watched it happen to his brother, and he knows my struggle. He asked, and I told him what you had said to me, and that you had smoked up while I was there. He's really upset, Kev, but only because he loves you. He'll talk it out with you. Gramps too. Whatever they can do to help you, they'll do it."

Kevin looked at Joe and after a moment spoke. "Joe, I don't think I'm into it that deep. It's only on the weekends. It's fun. You may not have noticed, but life isn't too exciting around here. Last night was a little scary, though … at least looking back at it, it was."

"Kevin, maybe you can handle a lifestyle like that. But maybe you can't. In your words: 'Last night was a little extreme.' You've got some decisions to make, and there's one other thing. Right now there are drugs on the street so lethal that if you take them, you will die. They're in pills and mixed with other things. Kev, you just can't go there."

The cousins stopped talking. Joe turned up the news and they watched it. When Joe noticed it was 12:50, he turned off the TV. "Well, we've got a lunch date, so we better get moving."

"Where are we going?" Kevin was confused.

"I was told to be at your house at 1:00 because your mom has put a roast in the oven."

Kevin shook his head and said, "Oh no. My headache is gone, but my stomach isn't ready. You haven't tasted my mom's roast. How could I have been so stupid?"

Joe laughed at him. "There are some real good benefits to staying sober."

Kevin was smiling as Joe locked up the house, and they were on their way.

Chapter Eight

JOE WAS MORE COMFORTABLE WALKING INTO HIS MEETING THE SECOND TIME AROUND. In fact, he'd met Brad when he walked by the coffee shop, and they walked to the church together.

"Missed you yesterday," Brad said as they walked along.

"I make no promises when it comes to church and stuff."

"So I've heard. But I also heard you have a background in church and stuff."

"Brad, that was a long time ago. I hadn't been to church for almost twenty years when I went last week. I actually thought the roof might fall in. Oh, I forgot, I did do an Alpha course when I was up north in a prison, about five years ago. A bunch of us went. You know they usually have a meal with Alpha, right? Well, we didn't have a meal, but we got coffee and donuts. Not saying that's why I went or anything." Joe laughed and was surprised that Brad laughed too. Joe looked around as he entered the meeting room. Raider gave him a nod as their eyes met.

Joe didn't like going to the meetings, but he knew he had to. It wasn't a condition of his probation, but he knew he couldn't stay off the drugs on his own. He sat through the meeting, not saying much, and was glad when it was over. Raider called to him as he got to the parking lot. He'd been walking with Brad, and when he stopped to talk to Raider, Brad kept going.

"Hey, Brad, I'll just be a minute."

Raider looked at Brad and then said to Joe, "Hey, you got something going on with that preacher?"

"I think he's a good guy. Don't know him too well. What can I do for you, Raider?"

"I'm thinking more it's what I can do for you."

"Look, man, I'm not going there."

Raider just laughed. "I'm here, Parker. See you next week." Once again, he got into his fancy car and sped away.

Joe walked to where Brad was waiting. "I take it you know Cavin."

Joe answered, "I was in CDDC with him when I got arrested three years ago. I did some travelling to different centres in the three years."

"I think he's still using."

"Oh, he's doing more than using," Joe replied.

"The coffee shop's open for another hour. I'll treat," Brad offered.

"Okay," Joe replied. "You can buy me a piece of their chocolate layer cake if there's one left."

There was no chocolate cake left, but Joe settled into the booth across from Brad with a big cinnamon roll. Brad was easy to talk to. He told Joe a little about his past. In some ways, it was like his own. Brad had spent a few years in foster care after his father died and his mother had a nervous breakdown. Eventually he went back to his mother, but he struggled with his own anxiety and depression. He started drinking as an older teen and kept with it until he was in his mid-twenties. He'd gone to a Christian residential treatment program for a year and then graduated from seminary five years later. At forty years old, Brad seemed to have it together. As they talked, Brad made it clear that he knew little of Joe's background. His uncle apparently had not shared Joe's story, and Joe was glad for that—not that he had anything to hide. He was just glad that Jay knew it was his story to tell.

Brad was surprised that Joe was only thirty-two. "I'd have pegged you closer to my age," he commented. For Joe, it was just another reminder that his body had taken a big hit from his lifestyle. Joe told him a little about his past. He told him about the Parkers and also about his recent incarceration and what he'd done to get there. At that point, Brad went back to their earlier conversation. "What about the Lord, Joe?"

Joe didn't have an answer except to say, "The jury is still out on Him. I did agree to go to some men's meeting tomorrow night at a church in Foxhill. I prayed *the prayer* at camp when I was ten. But I've been determined to do things my way as far back as I can remember. As you can see, my way hasn't worked out too well."

"Well, you know He loves you, Joe. And He has a—"

Joe put up his hand to say stop. "Yes, I know all that."

Brad wasn't offended. He said he hoped they could be friends. Joe figured they already were.

• • •

EASTER. JOE HADN'T THOUGHT much about Easter in a long time. He had dodged church his second Sunday in Souton, but he had to give Gramps an answer. Gramps had almost begged as he told Joe all the reasons he should be in church on Easter Sunday. It was the pleading in his eyes that made Joe give in. His Aunt Marge and her family would be at church this morning. Marge and her husband, Dave, and his cousin Faith had stayed at Uncle Jay's. His cousin Kathy, her husband, and their two little girls were with friends who owned a bed and breakfast in Coverton. After church, everyone was expected for dinner at Uncle Jay's. Gramps was excited.

This morning Joe was ready for church early. He and Gramps arrived with fifteen minutes to spare. Joe saw Kevin and went over to greet him. Not much had been said about last week's incident. Joe was glad to see a smile on Kevin's face and sensed that things had calmed down for him. As he went back to find Gramps, he overheard him say, "Yeah, I'm excited. The whole gang will be here for dinner. Since Marge moved to Kitchener, that doesn't happen much." In the back of his mind, Joe hoped that Gramps didn't mean that *all* his kids would be there.

Joe enjoyed the service. He sang the songs and listened as Brad spoke about the hope that comes with the risen Christ. It made so much sense sitting there in church. But as soon as he went out the doors, reality hit him. How could that story be true? He thought about the sermon as he walked with Kevin to his house. As they neared the house, he heard Kevin say softly, "Oh no."

"What's wrong?" Joe asked, and then he looked toward the house. JJ stood there, leaning on a late model truck, watching them approach. Joe stopped. He didn't know what to do.

JJ spoke. "I thought I told you to get away from my dad."

Joe made his decision. He turned and walked back toward the church. Back toward Gramps' house. JJ covered the short distance between them in seconds. Joe jerked to a stop as JJ grabbed his shirt and pulled him backwards. At that second, Joe was filled with a rage that scared him. In an instant, he felt every punch and heard every vile thing this man had ever said to him. He exploded. He turned, and his fist plowed into JJ's face. As JJ's hands went to his head, Joe punched him in the stomach. He pummelled him again and again and then pushed him to the ground.

Joe had begun screaming obscenities at JJ the moment he threw his first punch. He stopped and looked at the man who had done all those same things to him many years ago. He turned away and continued walking. Behind him he heard JJ say, "You filthy little pig. You good for nothing …"

Then he heard Kevin's voice. "Oh, give it up, Uncle JJ. Look who's talking." And then his cousin was walking beside him, and they walked to their grandfather's house.

• • •

WHEN THE REST OF the family arrived at Jay's, they found JJ sitting in a lounge chair on the front porch. Joe Senior took one look at him, looked around for Kevin and Joe, and said to JJ, "What happened here? Where are the boys?"

"I asked that kid why he was still here, and he flipped out on me. Dad, he shouldn't be here. He's dangerous." JJ looked over at Jay. "Your boy was mouthing off at me too."

Joe Senior turned to get back in his car. "Where are you going, Dad?" JJ asked.

"I'm going to get the boys. It's almost time to eat. And if you aren't going to settle down and act like you belong in this family, you can go now. Joey only gave you what you gave him. But there's a big difference between you at your age and a six-year-old boy."

"He's a liar!"

"No, Joe Junior, he's not a liar. He doesn't even remember what happened. But he read the court papers when he was sixteen. You beat him. You beat him so bad, you went to jail. He read about his injuries. The abuse stops now, Joe Junior. We want you in our family, but you have to let it go. Now." Joe Senior got in the car and drove off.

When Gramps entered the house, he found Joe sitting on the couch, with Kevin sitting in the chair beside him. "You two okay?"

Joe said nothing, but Kevin looked at his grandfather. "Gramps, it was awful. Uncle JJ was awful. I was scared for Joey because Uncle JJ went after him when he turned and walked away. But Joey was so mad. And the things Uncle JJ said! How could a man treat his own son that way?" Kevin started to cry.

Joe spoke, "It's all right, Kev. I'm not his son. I'll be fine. Gramps … I lost it. I hope I didn't hurt him. But in those moments, I hated him. I'm sorry. I know you were excited to have him here for dinner."

Gramps sat down beside Joe. He was taking a chance, but he was going to do it anyway. He reached over and pulled Joe into a hug. He felt Joe stiffen, but he didn't let go. And then his thirty-two-year-old grandson, who hadn't cried in twenty-two years, relaxed in his arms and sobbed. After ten minutes, Joe settled. Gramps shifted and Joe sat up. Gramps stood up, went to the bathroom, and came back with a box of Kleenex. He took a couple of tissues and passed the box to Kevin, who passed it to Joe.

"Well, now that we men have bonded," Gramps said, "we aren't going to let this spoil our Easter dinner." He blew his nose, and his grandsons followed suit with smiles beneath their tears.

They all laughed when Joe said, "You should have got man-size Kleenex, Gramps."

Gramps looked at his grandsons and asked, "Do you think you can handle going back?"

Kevin spoke first. "Is he still going to be there?"

Gramps looked at Joe as he answered. "I'm not sure. But if he is, there won't be any trouble. I had a few words with him. He knows if he stays, he has to stop the abuse. I hope he's there. It's time for some changes in this family. But if he isn't, that's okay too."

• • •

JJ WATCHED HIS FATHER drive away. After a moment, he got up from the chair and started down the steps to get to his truck. He was halfway there when he heard Marge's voice. "JJ, wait."

He turned to see his brother and sister watching him. Jay spoke. "Things can change today, JJ. How many years has anger, and even hatred, been part of our family? Stay. If you aren't ready to talk, just be with us."

"Look what he did to me, Jay."

"We can see what he did to you. And I've gotten to know him, JJ. I'm sure he's sorry for what he did … kind of the same way you're sorry for what you did to him when he was little. He wants to start over. He's trying really hard." Jay paused to look at his brother. "He's been clean for three years, and he wants to stay that way. And he's been good for Dad. Dad's been praying for you to come home for years. He doesn't mean just drop in and leave in a hurry. He's longed for you to be back in his life. And then a few weeks ago, Joey called, and made no promise to come here. Dad begged God to bring him here, and three hours later, he was at the door. This could be a new start for all of us. There's enough grace in this family to make things right."

He heard his younger sister say, "We love you, JJ. Please don't leave."

After a moment, JJ walked back toward the house, went up the steps, and sat down again in the lounge chair. He was still sitting there when Gramps, Joe, and Kevin arrived twenty minutes later. The rest of the family had gone in for dinner. He looked at Joe Senior and said, "I'll try to let it go, Dad. I want to stay for dinner." He turned to Kevin and said, "I'm sorry, Kevin, for messing up your day." Then his grey eyes met the grey eyes of his son.

Joe was the first to speak. "I'm sorry for going ballistic on you. It wasn't in my plan for the day."

JJ looked away. "I'm sorry too. I know how you feel. I guess the problem is I stopped worrying about the outcome of my blow-ups a long time ago. When I was your age, Joe, I hated myself for what I did to you. To your mother. But through the years, I buried that."

Joe knew exactly what JJ was saying. Maybe he hadn't set out to physically hurt people, but his actions had hurt people in very real ways too. He looked at JJ once again and said. "I forgive you. For it all."

• • •

MICHELLE AND JAY HAD a large dining room table, and they had set it with Grandma Wilkes' china. It was a tight fit, but thirteen place settings graced the table. There was a high chair for Kathy's youngest at the corner, beside her mom. Joe heard the noisy conversation as soon as he entered the house, but everyone stopped talking as the four men entered the dining room. Joe chose to sit beside Jay, and Kevin sat beside his mother. Gramps took the empty chair at the end of the table, and JJ slid into the seat beside him.

Gramps looked around. "Did you say grace?" he asked.

"Of course we did, Dad," Jay replied. "But maybe you'd like to pray again, now that we're all here." Jay put an emphasis on *all*.

Joe kept his eyes open and looked around as Gramps prayed.

"Father God, we know that you have blessed the food, so I won't pray for that. But we do want to thank you, Lord, for all your blessings. Thank you for bringing Joey here. And thank you that JJ is here today. Thank you that we know you finish what you start, and we pray that we will bury our hurts and sorrows deep in your love. Amen."

Joe had been introduced to his Aunt Marge and her family right after church. He didn't talk much during the meal but listened as different conversations went on around him. He heard Gramps say, "We haven't talked about that." He looked up to find Gramps and JJ looking at him. There was a lull in the conversation, and Gramps said, "JJ is asking about Lisa, Joey." Joe looked around and realized everyone was waiting for an answer. They probably had been wondering about his sister for the past twenty-five years.

"Well, I never lost track of Lisa. My mom and dad fostered her before I went to live with them. After the first place I went kicked me out, I went to their house. They adopted us both at the same time. I know they wanted me. I really made it difficult for them, though. I'm sure they were sorry more than once, but they kept me till I was thirteen. Of course, I never thought so at the time, but my behaviour was right out of control. They still love me, though, and consider me theirs.

"Lisa is amazing. Happily married to a guy who's a teacher, with five sweet little kids and a labradoodle. I've got pictures in my things if you want to see them."

"Will she want to meet us?" The question came from his cousin Jill.

"I'll ask my mom to talk to her about it. Lisa has a hard time initiating things like that. I'm sure both of us came out of our pasts with more than our fair share of insecurities. We're not close. She's really protective of the kids, and probably herself too. She doesn't want people coming into their lives who are going to leave just as quickly.

Joe was done. He had never talked about his past like this. His feelings were spinning around, like the turmoil his life had been. He looked at Gramps, who seemed to understand and turned the conversation away from Joe by asking Dave, his aunt's husband, about his new job.

The conversation flowed as everyone relaxed and enjoyed the family dinner. Joe stayed for an hour after the dishes had been cleared. His aunt insisted it was the girls' turn to do the dishes and had shooed him out of the kitchen when he offered to help. He asked Kevin about this, and Kevin answered, "This is totally serious. Just you wait for Thanksgiving. We'll be in that kitchen." Joe laughed. His new family was growing on him.

Joe didn't mind the quiet of the empty house when he got back to his grandfather's. He made some coffee, sat down in the living room, and went over the things that had happened that day. He looked down at his hand, which was bruised from when he hit JJ. Colour was forming around the prison tattoo on his fingers: P A I N. He'd had it done to show that he was a tough guy. Now the word mocked him as he flexed his hand. Could he be losing the pain inside him? He lifted up the phone and in three rings his dad picked up. "Christ is risen." He greeted his dad the way they had always greeted each other on Easter morning.

His dad replied, "Christ is risen indeed."

"So did you hide an Easter basket for me?" Joe was smiling, remembering the good times he had growing up.

"Well, no. But if you give me your address, we'll send you some candy. Your mom still goes overboard with the half price sales after a holiday. Now that there are dollar stores, what do I hear? 'Seth, they were five for a dollar.'"

Joe laughed. "Mom has the address, Dad."

"Oh, I remember. You're with your grandfather. How's that going?"

"Really good. No drugs, Dad. Nothing."

His dad was silent for a bit. "That's great, Joe. So your grandfather's a Christian. Did that have anything to do with your greeting?"

"No, that was pure nostalgia, from when I was at home."

"You know it's true … right, Joe?"

"I'm thinking more so every day, Dad. I just don't know where I'm going with it. Is Mom around?"

"Yeah. Actually, you're on speaker phone. The whole gang is here. I'll let her do the talking."

"Hi, Joe. I took the speaker off. How are you doing?"

"Well, it was quite a day. My aunt had everyone over for dinner after church. My dad showed up."

"Oh Joey, are you okay?"

"Well, my knuckles hurt."

He heard his mother's "No, Joey," and kept talking.

"But It turned out okay. Gramps said something to him, and he really changed his attitude. I think it's going to be okay. They call him JJ. He lives up your way, so he doesn't come around much. The rest are asking about Lisa, though, and Gramps especially would like to see her. Do you think you could ask her?"

"She's here right now. You can ask her. Maybe when we come to take you out for dinner, Lisa could come too and meet him then. Probably just her. No kids. Her experience with Sal has left her a little wary of having people come and go in their lives. She's pretty sensitive to that stuff. I'll put her on when we're done. The others will want to say hi too."

"Okay, I'll ask her, and you can talk to her about it too. When do you plan to come down?"

"Well, I'm not sure. I retired last year, and when Dad was sick again, he decided not to go back to work. Except for kids coming for respite once in a while, we don't do much fostering. We should be able to come soon."

"I'm working, so a Saturday or Sunday would be good."

"I'll talk to Dad about it and get back to you. And I'll mail off that package. I haven't sent it yet. I might as well put some candy in before I send it. I'll hit the sales tomorrow morning. I'll get the others so you can say hi."

Joe smiled as he waited for one of his siblings to come on the phone. His mom always was going to send things off right away, and sometimes that took awhile. Joe smiled again as he hung up the phone. He had even talked to his oldest niece and nephew. To top it off, Gramps would be ecstatic. Lisa said she would visit.

Chapter Nine

JOE LOVED WORKING AT THE FARM. EVERY DAY WAS A NEW EXPERIENCE. BOTH CARL
and Jeff constantly encouraged him, letting him know that he was appreciated. He felt
like he was part of a team, and when Joe got his first paycheque, he felt a satisfaction
he never had before. He wasn't making much more than minimum wage, but he was
happy—much happier than he'd been when he held a wad of money from selling drugs
in his hand. A highlight of Joe's day was spending time with Annie. She thought he was
the sweetest boy she'd ever met. He listened to her stories and tried extra hard to get
her garden just the way she wanted it.

● ● ●

JOE FAITHFULLY ATTENDED HIS meeting on Monday nights, and he and Brad always had
coffee together afterward. Their discussions usually went along with the topic discussed
in the group. Joe felt that Brad was on his journey of recovery with him. He trusted Brad
and considered him a friend.

Brad surprised him one evening by saying he was planning to get married.

"Whoa, man! Where did this come from?" Joe replied.

Brad explained that he had known Jennifer for a long time and that they'd been good
friends. He had hesitated to make a commitment to her, but she had waited patiently for
him to come to his senses. "She's just your age, Joe. We met on a mission trip to Haiti
ten years ago. Then she went out on the mission field for five years. She's from Ottawa,
which is where I'm from. We've written back and forth quite a bit over the past five years.
I guess you could say we've had a long-distance romance. When I visited my mom just
before Easter, we decided we were ready. She thinks being a pastor's wife sounds good,
and she knows about my past mental health issues and addiction."

"So when is this happening?"

"By the end of May, I'll be a married man."

Marriage was never something Joe had thought about. Not that it mattered. With his track record, there wouldn't be anyone looking to marry him.

• • •

JOE FAITHFULLY ATTENDED THE men's group at the church in Foxhill. As promised, Rob Schroeder picked him up on Tuesdays. The meal was always good, the video interesting, and the discussion genuine. The guys shared their struggles and prayed together earnestly. They welcomed Joe into their circle but never made demands on him. He felt comfortable and almost secure in their midst.

Joe had visited Rob in his home and met his wife and new baby boy. He and Rob were the same age, and although they didn't have much in common, Joe liked being around him. He never imagined that he'd be friends with a cop, but Rob was different. When he said as much to Rob, he replied, "And I never thought I'd be friends with an ex-con, self confessed drug addict, but I am." Rob had been smiling as he said it. Then he added, "Joe, whether you're willing to admit it or not, the Lord is working in your life. You need to let Him have His way. Without the Lord, Joe, I don't want to think about where I'd be."

Joe just shook his head. He wasn't going to argue with a friend.

• • •

JOE WASN'T LOOKING FORWARD to his upcoming trip to Coverton. It was time again to see his probation officer. He wasn't worried about the meeting. He just hoped he didn't have a run-in with any Coverton cops. There was one other thing on his agenda for the day. He and Gramps would go to the MTO office, and he would write the test for his G1 license. He'd been studying the handbook and was confident he would pass. The men left Souton early and arrived at the license bureau shortly after it opened.

Gramps waited in the car when Joe went in to write the test. Twenty minutes later, with a license in his pocket, he came out of the office. His photo license would arrive in the mail within the next fourteen days.

Why is this place always so crowded? Joe wondered as he entered the probation office with Gramps at his side. After giving his name, he left the counter. When he turned around to look for Gramps, he ran into a big guy wearing a leather jacket. Gramps was watching from across the room, and Joe noticed he was instantly on the alert.

Joe looked up, and the guy quietly said, "Parker, I'll see you outside after you're finished here." With that, he turned around and left the office.

Joe sat down beside Gramps. "I take it you know that fellow, Joey?"

"Yes, that's Am."

"Am?" Gramps replied.

"Yeah, short for Amoeba. He's so small, you know."

Gramps smiled. "What did he say to you?"

"Just that he'll see me outside after I'm finished here. I'd like you to go out first and wait in the car."

"We'll see," Gramps replied. They waited an hour and then Joe's name was called. He hoped that Am had moved on, but as he glanced through the window, he saw him casually sitting on his motorcycle in front of the building. Joe's appointment didn't take long. Once again, the probation officer was pleased with Joe's situation.

Aware that Gramps was right beside him, Joe wished that he had taken his suggestion to wait in the car. They walked to where Am was now standing.

"Parker, it's been a while."

"Three years and a bit," Joe answered.

"Who's this. Your bodyguard?" Joe was surprised when Gramps laughed.

"No. He's my new sidekick. Am, this is my gramps. Gramps, this is Am." Am looked at Gramps and back to Joe. "I told Gramps he should wait in the car, but he never listens to me. Don't worry. I have no secrets from him. What's up?"

"Are you available?"

Joe paused. It wasn't like he was at a job interview, but he felt he had to choose his words wisely. He looked directly at Am. "No, Am. I'm out of jail and drug free. I don't plan on going back to that life."

"Aren't you afraid they'll track you down?"

"I think I worked it out with those guys. Three of them were at CDDC when I went back at the beginning of March. We talked it out. They regrouped and are back in business somewhere else. I told them I did it for drug money, which is the truth, except that I never got paid. I was stupid to get involved with that. I don't want to live that way anymore. No more drugs for me. I even have a job."

"What happened? You get Jesus or something?"

Joe heard Gramps say "I wish" under his breath.

Joe said, "No. I just want to live without the hassle. I have to keep this old guy in line." Joe smiled at Gramps, and Am looked away.

Gramps surprised both young men by saying, "It's lunch time. Am, would you like to join us? My treat."

Am stammered and replied, "No. No. Not today. Maybe another time." He turned away and climbed onto his motorcycle, stopping for a moment before he turned the key. Seeing Joe with his grandfather had made him think of his own grandparents. He decided at that moment that he would drop in and visit them today.

Joe watched as Am rode away. At the car he hopped into the passenger's seat and turned to Gramps. "So let's go for lunch, but I'll treat. We can celebrate getting a license at thirty-two years old!" It was 12:30. Joe knew that the high school kids had just left Mary's Diner.

"Sure you don't want to drive?" asked Gramps before he started the car.

"Never thought of that," Joe replied. "How about I just drive home so I don't have to manoeuvre through the traffic in town. It's been a while, and I never did practise safe driving. Remember, this is the first time I've had a license."

Gramps followed Joe's directions to the diner. As he pulled into the small lot beside Mary's Diner, both he and Joe noticed a police car parked on the road in front.

"How about we go somewhere else, Gramps?"

Gramps shook his head. "Hey, I've tasted this lady's cooking. I'm a goin' in there right now."

Joe smiled, but for the second time today, he wished Gramps had taken his suggestion.

Joe headed for a table in the back corner, away from the lone officer sitting at a table near the door. As he walked past, he heard his name: "Joe." He stopped as he recognized Sergeant Waters.

"Oh, hello." He had no idea what else to say.

"So you've found this gem of a place too. Best food in town."

"Yeah, I used to come here a lot when I lived in Coverton."

"Where are you now?"

"Over in Souton." He nodded at Gramps. "With my grandfather."

Kyle Waters looked at Gramps, who put out his hand. "Nice to meet you. My name is Joe Wilkes."

"Related to Jay at the car dealership over that way?"

"Yes. That's my son."

"Well, it's good to meet you too. My name's Kyle Waters. I know Jay well. We sit on a committee for the regional churches together." He paused. "Well, I better let you men get to your lunch."

"Hi, Joe," Mary called from behind the counter.

"Hi, Mary. This here's my gramps, Joe Wilkes."

"So my suggestion was a good one after your phone call that day."

"No, Mary, it wasn't good. It was genius. Thanks."

Gramps looked at Joe, wondering what he was talking about. Before he asked, Joe continued. "Remember, Gramps? She lent me her phone. She's the one who said that it could never be a bad thing to make a grandpa happy."

"Oh!" said Gramps. "Thanks, Mary. And by the way, your roast beef dinner was fantastic."

"Well, that was your grandson's idea," Mary replied.

"Smart boy I have here."

Joe loved to hear Gramps talk like that about him.

"Normal," Joe said as they sat down.

"What do you mean, Joey?"

"I even had a normal conversation with a Coverton cop."

"You're doing great, Joey. But I did want to ask you about Am."

Joe thought for a moment before he spoke. "That turned out much better than I expected. Am is capable of some real all-out violence. He beat me up once. I had messed up a deal, and he wasn't pleased. But he gave me another chance, because he knew I was deep in the drugs and he shouldn't have given me that job in the first place. He's one of the leaders of a group I was involved with sometimes. They aren't a gang. They have a loose affiliation with the Dark Riders, the DRs. It was the DRs who hired me. They have an ongoing feud with Death Watch, whose businesses I torched. Am was really laid back today. Maybe because you were there."

Mary was at the table to take their order. Joe ordered a burger and fries, and Gramps ordered the same.

"Lots of help today, Mary?"

Mary laughed as she answered. "Yes. My waiter just left a bit ago. I won't coerce you into dishes this time, Joe."

"You wouldn't need to coerce me. I'm glad to help. Can you believe I have money from a real job? And Gramps and I are celebrating one of my biggest accomplishments in thirty-two years." Joe paused and then laughed as he said, "I got my beginner's license."

"Excellent," Mary replied. "Maybe we'll see you in here a little more often."

"I don't think so. Not all the cops in Coverton are as good as Sarge over there. I plan to stay away from town as much as I can."

"Did you know that Sarge over there keeps asking me out?" Mary turned to look at Kyle as she spoke loud enough for him to hear.

Kyle answered back, "And she keeps saying no. She's told me all she has at home is her cat to keep her company. She prefers her cat to me. You'd think a date with me would make her life a little more exciting."

"Listen to this guy. Every Wednesday he stops here for the lunch special after his visit to the high school. Every Wednesday he asks me to go with him to some adult fellowship at his church. He won't stop."

Kyle just shook his head and said loudly back, "No, he won't stop."

Joe couldn't resist. "Oh Mary, I'm sure his intentions are honourable. You are an amazing woman, good and kind. A successful businesswoman. And on top of that, what single man wouldn't appreciate a woman who can cook like you?"

To Joe's surprise, Mary blushed, and then Gramps spoke up. "I think you should go."

Joe just laughed. "That would make Gramps happy, Mary, and you know it never hurts to make a grandpa happy."

"I'm a grandpa too," Kyle said loudly.

Mary just smiled and went to get their order. Kyle left while Joe and Gramps were still eating.

They finished up and paid for their meal. At the counter, Mary handed them a bag that obviously contained food. "Here you go. Supper's on me, guys. Congrats, Joe. I'm so glad you're doing well."

Both men saw the notice on the blackboard behind her: "Supper special: Hot Beef Sandwich."

As they made their way to the car, Joe said, "Isn't she something?"

"She sure is," came Gramps' reply. "I hope she goes to the fellowship with Kyle."

• • •

INSIDE THE DINER, MARY watched them leave. She was glad that young man was doing well. Her younger brother was struggling with drugs, and she didn't know how to help him. She smiled as she thought about Kyle. He had been flirting with her for the past two months. It had taken awhile, but now she was glad to see him come in. She enjoyed their conversations. She'd learned that Kyle was a widower. His wife had died seven years ago, and he was planning to retire in five years at fifty-five. He was nine years older than her. He had a daughter who was married with two little kids. The only thing Kyle knew about Mary was that she lived with her cat and that her mother sometimes helped out at the diner.

Mary hadn't been much for going to church. It hadn't been important to her, or anyone else in her family. She had never been married but had been in three long-term relationships. When the third guy left her for someone younger and prettier, she decided that *three strikes and you're out* applied. She would never put her heart on the line again. At thirty-five, she had gone back to school. When she graduated with a chef's license, she worked at a fancy restaurant for four years and then struck out on her own. After gaining a reputation for serving great home cooking, business was booming. She'd even been written up in a local business magazine. She didn't need the attention of a religious cop. What did he really see in her anyway? Mary went over to the tables and began to clear. Kyle had left her a note. Again. She read it and smiled: "No, he won't stop. See you next week." Mary slipped the note into her pocket.

• • •

KYLE WAS BACK AT the precinct waiting for a meeting to start. He couldn't get Mary out of his mind. The conversation back and forth at the diner had been fun. He had developed a plan on his way back to work. Every time he left the diner, he left her a note saying, "I'll see you next week." This week he was going to change things up a bit. "I think I'll go see her tomorrow," he said to himself. At least he thought he had said it to himself.

He was surprised when the district chief, who was also waiting for the meeting to start, turned to him and said, "Pardon?"

Kyle looked at him and said, "Oh. Nothing. I was just thinking out loud." He noticed that the district chief was smiling as he turned back to his papers.

• • •

HE WATCHED AS THE video played, and he thought about his past relationships. Tim, the group's leader, turned and looked at the ten men seated around the table. This Tuesday's meeting was becoming a little too intense for Joe. The banter around the meal had been fun, but as soon as Joe heard the evening's topic, he was on guard: *Loving Your Wife.* He looked at the door wondering if he should leave and catch up to Rob later. He looked over at Rob and saw that he was watching him. Rob raised his eyebrows; it seemed that he was issuing a challenge.

Joe cleared his throat. "I think I'll go for a coffee. I'm not married. You guys will have a better discussion without me." He looked around as he stood up. The others were all smiling at him. He knew that two of the other guys were single too.

"Oh, sit down, Joe. This might come in handy someday."

Joe sat back down.

Joe knew what a good relationship looked like. He'd watched his parents' marriage, and his Uncle Jay's, and Carl and Annie's. As he watched the video play, he thought about his past relationships. He'd never beaten a woman the way JJ had. He'd never considered himself an abuser, but he knew he had mistreated his past girlfriends. The things he'd seen in the video hit him hard: the many Bible passages the speaker shared that stressed how a man was to treat a woman and love his wife. If Joe hadn't seen those things happening with some of the couples he knew well, he would have shrugged them off, thinking the whole meeting was a joke. Instead, he felt remorse for his own use of casual sex and his callous treatment of the many girls who had wanted to be with him.

Everyone was quiet when the video ended. "So, Joe, it wasn't too painful, was it?" As Tim spoke, Joe looked up to see all eyes turned on him.

"Well," Joe answered slowly, "yeah, it was pretty painful."

Tim backtracked. "Oh Joe, I'm sorry. I didn't mean to put you on the spot." He stopped as if unsure that he should keep speaking. "Do you want to talk about it?"

Joe had never actively taken part in the discussion around this table. His mind was in turmoil. *What should I say? Just say you don't want to talk about it. These guys won't mind. But I do want to talk about it. These guys really care about me. Just look at what some of them have shared before. Some pretty heavy stuff.*

He started talking. "No worries, Tim. I do want to talk. The video hit me pretty hard. I'm a total failure in this stuff. I don't have a wife, but I knew right from wrong from the start—not as deep as the stuff we just saw, but I knew how I should be acting. I completely ignored that and did what I pleased when it came to girls. From the time I was really young, I used girls who cared about me. And I hurt them. I never once thought of getting married. Why bother? I was fine with the way things were. I've always said I will never get married and definitely never be a father. I was afraid of what kind of dad I would be. No," Joe shook his head, "marriage is not an option for me."

The others were quiet for a minute, and then one of the younger guys spoke. "Joe, you aren't alone here. It sounds like you were awful. But we all are. We've watched you over the past month, and we don't see that Joe you describe. If that was you, you need to repent and ask Jesus to forgive you. He is so full of love and grace, Joe."

Another guy spoke up. "Joe, I've been married six years, and I still mess up. It's hard to love like we're supposed to. Ephesians 5:25 says, *"Husbands, love your wives, just as Christ loved the church and gave himself up for her."* That sounds impossible, and it is impossible unless the Lord helps us do that."

Joe interrupted. "But you don't know what I've done … over and over again. Most of you know I just got out of jail. The first day out, do you know what I found out? I just knocked on the door of a place I used to live, and one of the girls I'd shared the house with came to the door. I thought I could move right back in there. I hadn't even thought twice about the fact that I'd slept with her. I wanted to, and she was the kind of girl who would do what I wanted. But then a guy came down the stairs carrying a little boy—two-and-a-half years old. I looked at him and"—Joe paused, shaking his head—"and I knew he was my son."

Joe kept talking. He wasn't aware that there were tears in his eyes and in Rob's eyes as he came to stand behind him. "Some other guy is going to raise my son. I never wanted to have kids. Never. But now I think about a little boy named Stevie all the time, and I love him. But I won't see him again. I'm glad he has a dad who loves him and who loves his mom, because no sweet little kid deserves a dad like me."

When Joe stopped talking, everyone was silent. He felt Rob's hand on his shoulder and saw Tim stand and come to him too. The older man beside him also stood. Joe had seen this happen a few times in the group and felt himself calm down as Rob began to pray.

"Father, thank you for loving us and that you know us. We bring Joe before you, Lord, and ask that you work in his life in a mighty way. He carries so many burdens. We pray that he might simply give them to you and that even today he might give his life to you. We pray that you will show Joe clearly that you love him with your pure and perfect love. Remind him that you are his father. Please be with little Stevie and his mom and dad, and give Joe peace about this whole situation. We pray this in the mighty name of Jesus. Amen."

The rest of the men said "Amen," and Joe heard himself saying it too. He wasn't embarrassed or self conscious. He knew something good had just taken place.

Tim asked if anyone else needed prayer, and many of the others spoke out requests. The meeting went a little longer than usual, but the guys weren't in a hurry to leave.

Driving home, Rob turned to Joe. "It's a hard thing, this situation with Stevie."

Joe thought for a moment. "I think one of the hardest things I've ever experienced. But his dad, Steve, is a good guy, and his mom will do fine. I find it hard to believe I could mess up so badly, but I'm glad Stevie was born."

"Reminds me of a Bible verse," Rob said.

"No kidding," Joe said sarcastically, but he was smiling. "Which one?"

"Well, since you asked," Rob smiled as he replied, "Romans 8:28. *'And we know—'*"

Joe interrupted him. *"That in all things God works for the good of those that love him, who have been called according to his purpose."* Joe paused. "Rob, do you think I'm called according to His purpose?"

"I'm sure of it, Joe."

• • •

GRAMPS WAS WAITING UP for Joe when he arrived home. "Gramps, why aren't you in bed?"

"Couldn't sleep again. Something exciting happen tonight? I was praying."

Joe thought for a moment. "Gramps, the guys prayed over me. It was a pretty deep topic, and I told them about Stevie."

"It's good you have friends you can pray with. I'm glad for you, Joey."

Joe left Gramps in the hallway. He was tired after working all day, and the emotion of the meeting had drained him. He climbed into bed, but rather than switch off the lamp, he reached over and picked up the leather Bible that sat on his nightstand. His sister had bought the Bible for him for Christmas, five years ago. His mother had just sent it with his Easter candy last week. She had once tried to send it to him in jail, but it was one of the things he wasn't allowed to have. He ran his finger over the engraving in the lower right corner: *Joseph James Parker*. He turned to the presentation page: *To brother Joe from your sister* and then looked at the reference underneath: *Proverbs 3:5–6*. He thought of his sister Chandra. She never missed sending a card on his birthday, Christmas, or Valentine's Day. With every one came a reminder that he needed Jesus. Joe turned to the passage in his Bible: *"Trust in the Lord with all your heart and lean not on your own* understanding; in all your ways submit to him, and he will make your paths straight." He remembered the verse from his grade school days. Joe stopped and considered all that had happened in the last weeks. He went over the events of the evening and remembered Rob's prayer that he might have peace. *Oh Lord, how can I deny you any longer.*

He prayed out loud, "Well, Lord, what can I say? I've blown it big time. But I believe you, Lord. I trust you. I ask that you forgive me for my sins and teach me your way. Thank you. Amen."

Joe fell asleep quickly. He woke up eager to start a new day. When Joe entered the kitchen, he saw that Gramps was eating raisin bran. Joe grabbed a bowl, poured out some cereal, and then poured himself a coffee.

"So how did you sleep, Joey?" Gramps asked.

"I slept like a log. How about you?"

"It took awhile for me to get there, but I did sleep well."

Joe sat and looked for a minute at this amazing man. Every morning Gramps drove him to work and picked him up at four o'clock. He took him to appointments. He loved him. "Guess what, Gramps." Gramps met Joe's eyes as he silently thanked God for what he knew Joey was going to say. "I gave my heart to Jesus last night. It's so real. It's like I'm walking out those prison gates again. But I'm not afraid I'm going to blow it, like I always did before. All I feel is peace."

Jesus, thank you. Thank you for bringing this boy home to you. Gramps stood up and went to Joe. He didn't say a word, but he squeezed Joe's shoulder. After a minute, he said, "I don't think Jeff will mind if you're a bit late. Why don't you call your folks?"

The phone rang at the Parker house and his mom answered it.

"Hi, Mom."

"Joey, is everything all right?"

"Everything is fine, Mom. Just have something to tell you."

"What's up?"

"I accepted the Lord last night. I know He is who He said He is. Who you and Dad say He is. I know it's all true."

"Oh Joey! Here, talk to your dad." Seth Parker came on the phone.

"Hi, Dad."

"Hey, Joe. What did you say to your mom to have her crying and smiling at the same time?"

"Oh … just that last night, the Lord answered the prayers you two have been praying for me for the last twenty-six years. He stopped me in my tracks. Dad, I'm His."

Seth's heart felt like it was going to explode. He kept saying over and over, "Thank you, Jesus" and "Oh Joey."

Joe was smiling as he said, "Well, Dad, I just wanted you two to know. Tell the other kids for me. I gotta get out the door here. I'm late for work."

When Joe pressed the end button, Gramps said, "So it sounded like that went well."

"Oh Gramps, it is so good to have people who love me."

• • •

JOE LOOKED AROUND AS he got out of the car at the farm. Everything was green and bright. The winter wheat, eight inches high, was blowing in the wind in the field to the left. Annie's garden was starting to sprout. The seedlings Joe had planted three weeks ago looked strong and healthy. The fruit trees that stretched across the yard at the back of the house were in full bloom. Joe was struck by the beauty of it all and pleased that he had become a part of the team that was making it happen. He watched Jeff walk from across the street.

When he reached Joe, his first words were, "Chad said you guys had an amazing time last night."

Joe smiled and answered, "Did he tell you what happened?"

"No details. He said what is said in the meeting, stays in the meeting. I guess he meant you men have to be sure your concerns don't get spread around."

"Well, I can tell you it was amazing. The topic was about loving your wife, and I tried to get out of there, but they made me stay. The Lord did a whole lot of healing of me and lots of the other guys. I told them about some things from my past, and, Jeff, they prayed for me. I felt so much peace. And then I went home, and I gave it all to Jesus—my sorrow, my despair, my sin. I asked Him to forgive me, and I gave myself to Him. I'm still wondering how I rate Christ living in me, and then I remember it's only because of His love and grace that it can happen.

"That's fantastic, Joe." Jeff was celebrating with him. "I'll be praying for you. Make sure you tell my mom and dad. They'll be so pleased."

Jeff told Joe that he'd be working with him today. "That north field needs to be seeded, and I want you to ride along in the big tractor. There's a lot of work before that, though." Joe had a great day.

Chapter Ten

VICTORIA DAY WEEKEND ARRIVED. MAY TWO-FOUR, JOE SMILED TO HIMSELF. *NO WILD parties for me this weekend.* On Sunday, Joe was in church. He was excited and had decided he was going to stand up during the prayer and praise time. He planned to tell the whole congregation what had happened to him. Brad was still away. Yesterday he had married Jennifer in front of a small group of people at her home church in Ottawa. This afternoon he would be leaving on his honeymoon. Joe was happy for him. Brad had been so excited. There would be a reception next Saturday afternoon in the fellowship hall here at the church.

Joe set his thoughts back to the service when the music started. He closed his eyes and listened as the congregation sang a couple of the newer worship songs and then a beautiful old hymn. His hand was the first to go up when the visiting preacher asked if anyone had anything to share.

Joe took the mic that was handed to him and started talking. "I just want to thank all of you folks who have been praying for me since I arrived in Souton. Thanks for welcoming me to town. I think most of you know I've lived a pretty messed up life. I came here because I didn't want to go back to my old life. You folks trusted me, gave me a chance when you really had no reason to. Last Tuesday night at a men's meeting in Foxhill, the Lord broke my heart in a good way. When I got home, I prayed ... I guess they call it the sinner's prayer. I know that's what I was ... I am. But now I am His." Joe choked up and couldn't say another word, but no one noticed. The whole congregation started clapping. He heard shouts of "Praise the Lord."

Joe listened as the visiting preacher gave his sermon and shared his thoughts on the Parable of the Prodigal Son. Joe remembered this story, but he had never considered himself the prodigal. *Quite the lesson after my week. Thanks, Lord, that I'm not a prodigal anymore.* He smiled as he remembered his parents' reaction when he called them.

The preacher ended his sermon by saying, "We heard this young man today talk about God's amazing grace and love. I don't know him, or anything about his background, but from your response, I think there must be a story there. It's important for each of you to realize you all have a story, and if you haven't yet come to Christ as Saviour and Lord, your story is broken. If you are a prodigal, you need to come home. Pray along with me as I close. If you want to pray personally with someone, I invite you to come to the front. No matter how young or old you are, Jesus is waiting to welcome you home."

Joe looked back as he was about to exit the sanctuary. Six people were at the front, ready to pray with the preacher. His uncle Jay was there with his arm around Kevin.

● ● ●

JOE MISSED BRAD AS he walked alone into his Monday night meeting. When one of the guys asked where Brad was, Joe replied that he was honeymooning. Everyone seemed happy for Brad. There were some good people in this group, people who really cared about each other. Then there was Raider, who had become a constant annoyance to Joe. Every week he smugly offered Joe drugs. Last week he had told Joe to come prepared because he was bringing *something special* next time.

Today Raider seemed different. Usually he presented himself well in the meetings. He greeted people and interacted. Tonight when he arrived, he sat down as the meeting was about to start. He was fidgety, and he hadn't said anything to anybody when he came in. He sat in the last row of seats. As the meeting was starting, he slumped over in his seat and fell forward. When people realized what had happened, they scrambled back to him, moving chairs out of the way. A younger girl, who identified herself as a nurse, instructed two guys to lay him on his side. She held his wrist for about thirty seconds while checking her watch. "His pulse is really slow." She looked at the leader. "Call 911. We need an ambulance."

The leader told everyone they were free to leave, but most people stayed out of concern for Raider and to see if they were needed to help. An older man, Joe recognized him as a man named John, identified himself as Raider's sponsor. He had already been on the phone trying to reach Raider's mother.

The ambulance arrived in seven minutes, and as the paramedics began to work on Raider, they asked the others to step back. "Does anyone know this guy well?"

John answered, "His name is Cavin Shields. He's twenty-four and has come away from some hard drugs. He's been doing well, though."

Joe looked around and then began to speak. "Actually, he's still using. He's had lots of different drugs available lately. Last week he told me he was going to have something special today. I think he was talking about meth."

The paramedics hooked Raider up to a heart monitor and slipped an oxygen mask over his face. As they worked, one of them said to Joe, "So you were going to get drugs from him today?"

"No way," Joe said. "I've been clean for three years. We were at CDDC together, and he won't believe I'm done with that life."

The paramedics strapped Raider onto the stretcher and quickly left the building.

Joe could hear the siren blaring as they left town. John approached Joe and asked if he'd like to go to the hospital with him. Joe knew that the people in the group were committed to helping each other.

"I really don't know him very well. We aren't friends, but I can go if you want the company. I only have my G1, so I'll need to ride with you."

John said he would appreciate the company. On the way out of town, they stopped at Gramps' long enough for Joe to run in and tell him what was going on.

In the car, John told Joe that he hadn't been able to reach Raider's mother but had left a message. They talked about Raider, and both realized that they didn't know him well. John shook his head. "He sure had me fooled."

Joe thought for a moment before he spoke. "Speaking from my experience, I think it's easy to put on a good show. Often when I was high, people didn't know it. It was when I was coming down that I reacted. I felt awful and acted accordingly. You come to a point where the drugs take over. I don't know what happened to Raider tonight. I think he may have taken something right before he came in. He told me he had some high-grade stuff coming this week. I'm just thankful I'm clean. When I got out of jail a couple of months ago, I counted twelve old friends who'd died in the past three years. All because of drugs."

They continued talking, and at one point John looked at him and said, "You're JJ's boy, aren't you? I just put it together, because Cavin said your name is Parker. But you look so much like JJ and his dad."

Joe wasn't smiling as he answered. "JJ is my bio dad. My parents are a couple up near Toronto. I went to live with them when I was six, and in spite of what I've been through, what I've done, they still love me. I'm theirs. But my gramps is back in my life. I saw JJ at Easter. He started a fight with me, and I got so mad I hit him. Hard."

"I remember him from his younger days." John shook his head as he thought about JJ. "He was quite a wild one. Sorry to hear there's still trouble."

"Well, somehow my gramps got things settled out. JJ even stayed for dinner. I think some healing is going on in our family. Going on in me. Most importantly, I came to the

Lord a week ago. I know I need to reconcile with a lot of folks … and I have to care about Raider. I never thought I'd be hurrying off to be at the hospital with him. And you know what? I've been praying for him, since I first saw him slump over in his chair."

They arrived at the hospital half an hour behind the ambulance. As they walked through the ER doors, John's cell phone rang. Joe heard him tell Raider's mom what had happened. He said they were just going into St. Joe's. She must have said she was on her way because John said he would see her soon. Inside, John spoke to the attendant at the desk. Assured that they would be called when Raider was settled into a cubicle, they sat down to wait in the waiting room.

Forty minutes later, Raider's mother arrived. She looked frantically toward them when the receptionist pointed in their direction. John stood up and greeted her as she came over to them.

"Thank you for being here with him. My name is Elise, Elise Shields."

John explained in detail what had happened in the meeting. When he introduced Joe, she said, "Is he a friend of yours?"

Joe told her that he knew Raider from CDDC, but they weren't really friends.

She sat down in the chair between John and Joe. "I was afraid I was going to get a call like this." She started to cry. "We just don't know how to help him."

John had some words of wisdom "Let's just see what the doctor has to say. He'll be able to give some direction."

She looked over at Joe.

"Do you love him?" he asked quietly.

"More than you could imagine," she replied.

"That's a good start." Joe thought of a time he'd been Raider's position. He'd woken up, handcuffed to a hospital bed, after a five day cocaine binge. He had decided then and there: *no more drugs.* He shook his head at the memory. *I hope he sticks close to his family. He won't make it if he cuts himself loose like I did.*

"Mrs. Shields." Elise stood when the nurse called her name. "You can bring one other person in with you." John said that Joe should go in. They followed the nurse to the far end of the area and entered a small cubicle.

They introduced themselves to the doctor who was with Raider.

"Are you the one who said he must be on something?" the doctor asked, looking at Joe.

Joe replied to the affirmative and then explained. "He said he was bringing something special. I have the feeling it was meth. He's never offered me that before."

Nodding his head, the doctor explained that there were drugs in Raider's pocket, which they suspected were meth. He added, "We saw three guys in here over the weekend who almost died. Two are still in ICU. We're thinking there's a bad batch of something going round. This young man is lucky he was where he was and that the paramedics started working on him right away. He's going to be okay.

He turned to Raider's mother, who had not taken her eyes off of her son. "Mrs. Shields?"

"Yes."

"There are some things we can do to help Cavin if he's willing. We'll keep him in a room upstairs for a few days to give you time to make some plans. Maybe he could go to detox here at the hospital. They'd keep him for ten days to get all the drugs out of his system. You could make some plans for treatment from there. We'll get him settled upstairs, and you can wait there with him till he wakes up. He'll be groggy. If he agrees, the social worker can meet with you in the morning."

Elise took a deep breath. "Thank you so much. So he's going to be okay?"

"From the way he has responded, I believe he will be. His vitals are good. His cardiogram shows a healthy heart. We'll do some more tests in the morning. Let's get him rested up and the drugs out of his system. We'll see what tomorrow brings."

A nurse entered the room and asked Elise to have a seat so that she could answer some medical questions about Cavin. Elise turned to Joe, "You might as well leave, Joe. Thanks so much for all you and John did tonight."

"Are you sure you're going to be okay?"

"I'll be fine. My husband should be home by now. He'll come when I call him. He had a meeting in Toronto this evening and was on his way home at 10:00. He'll take tomorrow off to be with us."

Joe could see that Elise was more settled than she had been when she arrived at the hospital. "I guess I'll be on my way then. Do you mind letting me know how Cavin does? I don't have a cell phone, but I can give you my home number."

"Sure, Joe." She seemed pleased with his concern. "I'll just put your number in my phone and give you a call when things settle. Can I give it to Cavin if he wants to call you?"

After Joe had assured her that Cavin was welcome to contact him, he made his way back to the waiting room. John was reading a newspaper when he got there. When he saw Joe coming, he tossed the paper onto a side table, and they left.

The clock on John's dashboard read 2:00 a.m. when they arrived at Gramps'. There hadn't been much conversation on the way home. Joe got out of the car and climbed the stairs to the porch. The porch light came on, and Gramps opened the door. "Everything all right, Joey?"

"Gramps, what are you doing up?"

"I fell asleep on the couch and heard the car door shut."

"Well, you should have gone to bed."

"Why? I want to know how your friend made out."

"They say he's going to be okay. It's not going to be easy for him, though. Pray he gets his head on straight and stays away from the drugs."

"I'll do that."

"Thanks, Gramps."

Joe was tired. He decided that he wouldn't be in any shape to go to work in the morning. He hoped Jeff would understand.

Chapter Eleven

THE SUN WAS STREAMING THROUGH JOE'S WINDOW WHEN HE OPENED HIS EYES. HE turned to look at his clock: 9:29. "Oh no!" he said out loud. He had forgotten to set his alarm, and he had to call Jeff. He got out of bed and made his way to the kitchen. It was empty. "Gramps," he called.

"In here, Joey," Gramps called from the back storage room.

Joe walked back to see Gramps on his hands and knees, looking at the dial on the hot water heater. "There's no hot water this morning. I'll have to call the gas company." Joe looked at the wall beside the tank. He was going to be a hero here.

He smiled. "Gramps, reach over and unplug that cord in the wall."

"Joe, it's a gas hot water heater."

"Just try it, Gramps."

Gramps pulled out the plug and looked at Joe.

"Just give it a minute and then plug it back in."

Gramps muttered under his breath for a full minute. He reached across and put the plug back in the socket. Right away, the heater started up. Gramps looked at Joe.

"Magic," Joe said as he started laughing.

Gramps laughed too, and when they both stopped laughing, he turned to Joe. "How did you know that?"

Joe started to say "Ma—" but Gramps interrupted.

"How did you know that?"

"Well, that happened at Steve's Place. At first just once in a while and then quite often. The landlord eventually had the hot water heater replaced. The new one didn't have a plug. It was something about an igniter." Joe suddenly remembered what time it was. "Oh no! Gramps, I'm supposed to be at work. I have to call Jeff."

"I called Carl and explained what went on last night. He said I should take you out for breakfast." Gramps was smiling.

"He did?"

"No. Carl said to stay home. He's glad the kid is okay. I decided I would take you out."

• • •

AFTER A DAY OFF, Joe thought he should work twice as hard at the farm. It was time for lunch, and Jeff was about to walk over to his house when Annie called to him from the porch. She came down the steps with a tray. "I made you a sandwich, Jeff, and I thought you'd both enjoy some iced tea and a piece of pie."

Joe was glad when Jeff joined him at the picnic table under the tree. It had been a great morning. It was a sunny warm day, but there was enough breeze that Joe was comfortable. He had been on the tractor cutting grass around the main fields. He and Jeff talked about the garden. Carl and Annie had worked closely with Joe, and he was amazed at what he had learned and was pleased to see it growing so well. It was big. Tomorrow he would start picking strawberries.

They finished eating, but Jeff didn't seem to be in a hurry to get back to work. "I hear there are some pretty exciting things going on at Souton Baptist these days."

Joe wasn't sure what Jeff had heard. "Well," he began, "Pastor Brad got married, and they had his reception last week. Jen seems like a nice girl. Brad sure is flying high."

Jeff smiled. "Well, I had heard that, but other things too. My mother-in-law goes to your church. She called me very excited after the service … I guess it was the Sunday after your men's meeting. She didn't know that you work here. She started in about the young man who stood up and testified that the Lord had saved him that week. Joe, she said that Sunday was the start of a change at the church. She even used the word "revival." Do you realize the Lord is using you?"

Joe was a little embarrassed. He really hadn't noticed anything different, but he had noticed that Kevin was different. He and Kevin had talked since then, and Kevin told him that he was done with drugs. He said he wanted to live for Christ. Kevin had mentioned that he had asked Brad about getting baptized and wondered if Joe should consider it too. In fact, later they had talked to Brad together about it, and now they were both going to be baptized.

"Well, honestly, I didn't know. Kevin and I talked to Brad about being baptized. That's going to happen in two weeks."

Jeff smiled as he looked at Joe. "Did you know that a bunch of others are going to be baptized that day too?"

"Well, no. That's got something to do with me?"

"It sure does, Joe. After hearing your testimony, my mother-in-law said she was touched. She knows it's the Holy Spirit working in you and in the church. I'm talking about a rather staunch, eighty-year-old lady who doesn't ever mention what happens in church."

Joe thought back to that morning. He remembered the men's meeting and what happened there. "Well, I guess it's good then. I don't doubt that the Lord is working in my life. It seems like a bonus that others are coming to Him too."

Jeff looked at Joe. He had come to love this young man. Joe was real, honest, and humble. When Chad told him what had happened at the men's meeting, he knew the Lord was working. When Joe related what he experienced that night, Jeff was convinced God was going to use Joe Parker in an extraordinary way.

Joe looked up at Jeff. "Jeff, I've never met your wife."

Jeff could see that Joe was wondering. He smiled and said, "Well, Joe, my Rose was …" He paused. "Everything I could have hoped for in a wife."

"Was?" Joe questioned.

"She passed away when Chad was seventeen. She had quite a battle. ALS. Over the course of her last two years, she went downhill quickly but was still able to be here at home. Her mom is a nurse, and she moved in with us. I don't know what we would have done without her."

Joe thought for a moment. "I'm so sorry." He paused. "That's why Chad wants to be a doctor." Jeff just smiled and nodded.

Joe went back to the field thinking about all the things they had talked about.

● ● ●

JOE WOKE WITH HIS alarm. It was 7:00 a.m. He paused for a moment and thanked God for who He is and for giving him a second chance at life … well, really, for giving him a whole new life. Sometimes Joe couldn't believe how much he had changed. He knew in his heart that it was not him who was changing. It was the Lord in him. And today was Sunday. Today Pastor Brad was going to baptize him. This was not a bid for acceptance or attention. Kevin and eight other people were being baptized too. His mom and dad would arrive with their gang, and Lisa would see Gramps for the first time since she was little. It was going to be a great day.

Joe waited outside the church for his family to arrive. It was going to be crowded today. He saw a big van enter the parking lot, and he quickly made his way to where it stopped. He had not seen his dad in four years, and he was engulfed in a big hug.

"Joey. I can hardly believe this is happening." Seth just looked at his son.

"It's real, Dad. I promise you it is."

"I know it is. And I'm so glad."

Joe turned to his mom and gave her a hug. "It's good to see you, Mom." He had seen his mom more than his dad over the years. She had picked him up sometimes when he was getting discharged and had sometimes visited him at CDDC.

"Oh Joey, this is one of the best days of my life."

"Mine too," Joe replied. He greeted his siblings as they got out of the van and then paused for a moment. "Where's Lisa?"

"Oh … they'll be here in a bit."

Joe couldn't hide his excitement. "They're all coming?"

"Yes, the whole gang. She's taking a chance here, Joe. We're thinking it's the real deal. She doesn't want new relatives coming into the kids' lives and then leaving."

Joe smiled. "Don't worry, Mom. This is the real deal. Gramps and my Uncle Jay's family won't let her down. And neither will I." He looked at his watch. "Okay guys, I'll see you after the service."

Joe was nervous as he waited to go to the front. He would be the first of ten. He wore jeans and a t-shirt. A couple of people had chosen to wear a baptismal gown. Pastor Brad had said either was fine. The church was packed. At the beginning of the service, he had turned to see Lisa and her family sitting in front of his mom and dad. Joe listened as Pastor Brad welcomed everyone and led the call to worship.

Instead of introducing a song, he sat down as a song began to play through the sound system. Joe knew the song, and as the music played, he listened again to the words. He praised God that he had found the "Chain Breaker." Then Pastor Brad was talking. He looked out at the people. "Do you know how long it's been since someone was baptized here at Souton Baptist Church?"

Someone yelled out "too long," and everyone laughed.

Pastor Brad continued. "You're right, Max. Way too long. It's been over three years. In the past year, many of us have prayed earnestly, alone and in groups, that the Lord would use our church. We don't want to be a social club. We want to share the gospel. We want people to come to Jesus because He is the way, the truth, and the life. Over the past few weeks, we've seen some changes in our church. People are getting serious about the Lord. I'm excited, and I know many of you are too.

"Today we have ten people being baptized. Joe Parker is going first. I want to tell you a little about Joe. Most of you were here when he stood up at church a few weeks ago. The Lord had touched Joe in a very real way that week at a men's group over in Foxhill. I talked to other guys who were at that meeting, and they said they knew something special had happened during their prayer time. Joe accepted the Lord when he got home to his grandfather's that night. And he was here the next Sunday, testifying about what the Lord had done. When I was off getting married, hearts were being touched here at Souton Baptist Church. I am still thanking God for that. Are you?"

There was a chorus of "yeses" and "amens."

"So Joe is going to come up first."

Joe made his way up the stairs and across the platform. Pastor Brad went down into the baptistry, and Joe followed. They turned to face the congregation. All the candidates had been asked if they would like to share a few words before they were baptized. Joe eagerly started to talk.

"I want to thank you people for having this place. You welcomed me. Most of you know that I was pretty messed up, but you were willing to give me a chance. I want to thank my gramps, who welcomed me back, kind of like a prodigal son. He told me that he and my grandma had been praying for me all of my life, even though they hadn't seen me for twenty-six years. And my mom and dad out there, along with my sisters and brother—thank you for your prayers. Thank you for never ceasing to love me. But most of all, I have to thank Jesus. Somehow, He broke through the darkness and despair of my life. I have sinned grievously, but His relentless love tracked me down. I praise Him for taking my sin away through the power of His blood shed on the cross."

Pastor Brad addressed him. "Joseph James Parker, have you trusted Jesus Christ as your Lord and Saviour?"

"Yes, I have."

Brad couldn't stop smiling. "I now, in obedience to the Lord's command, baptize you in the name of the Father, Son, and Holy Ghost."

When Joe came up out of the water, he was overcome with emotion. He had never experienced such joy.

Joe left the baptistry, exited through the side door of the sanctuary, and went into the men's room. He quickly dried off. Wearing the dry clothes he had stashed there, he made his way down the hall and into the sanctuary within minutes. He stood at the back of the sanctuary and watched each person go into the baptistry, be baptized, and exit out the other side. Some of those people joined him as he watched the proceedings. Joe listened carefully as Pastor Brad talked to each person. This was no assembly line. Pastor Brad personalized each one's baptism. He encouraged them, rejoicing in their testimonies and the whole experience.

Kevin was the last person. When he entered the tank, Pastor Brad looked to where Gramps was sitting and then over at Jay and Michelle. "Joe Wilkes, it's only a few months since you came back to us. I know that you're rejoicing in your Saviour these days. I'm sure today that you're feeling doubly blest, as you see your two grandsons following the Lord in baptism."

It had been a long service. Before getting out of the tank, Pastor Brad looked at the congregation and reminded them of God's great love. He challenged each one to consider their own lives. "Today you've seen ten people testify to the saving grace of

Jesus Christ. Maybe you've sat in this church for years and never answered the call of Christ on your life. Maybe you just came to see one of these people baptized today, and this is all very new to you. Do you know what the Word of God says? *Now is the accepted time. Now is the day of salvation.*

"If you don't know Him, or if you are far from Him, I entreat you to take in the words of this well-known Bible verse and remember why Jesus came: *'For God so loved the world he gave his one and only Son, that whoever believes in him shall not perish but have eternal life'* (John 3:16). Many of you have known that verse all of your lives. Talk to Him today. Talk about Him with someone who knows Him. We're going to sing a song, and if you need prayer, we'll have people here at the front to pray with you."

Joe recognized the song as the congregation stood and started to sing. The words were up on the screen at the front. A few people immediately made their way forward. Joe glanced back and forth between his parents and his grandfather. He saw Gramps staring over to his right and then looked over to see what he was staring at. JJ was walking down the side aisle to the front of the church. Joe hadn't known he was there, and he didn't think Gramps had known either. He looked again at Gramps and saw that his head was bowed and there were tears streaming down his face. Joe didn't think twice. He walked down the middle aisle until he was even with Gramps. Gramps looked up and saw him standing there. He stood up, and the two of them went to the front of the church and stood, one on each side of JJ.

Twenty minutes later, Joe set off to find his family. Kevin pointed to the fellowship room. "My mom took everyone back there. She has things set up for a barbeque at our house, so we're going over there. We're just waiting for you, my dad, and Gramps ... and I guess JJ. It's weird that he showed up."

"Probably Gramps or your dad invited him. He gave his heart to the Lord in there." Joe pointed behind him at the sanctuary and shook his head. "Can you believe all the things that are happening? Good things."

Kevin nodded. "It's pretty amazing. Some other couple my dad knows is back there too. I'm headed over to the house. A bunch of people are on their way there now."

Joe entered the fellowship room and saw his Aunt Michelle talking to his mom. His dad was talking to a couple who had their backs to him. Joe recognized the woman when she turned her head to speak to the man. *Mary?* And the man was Sergeant Waters.

Joe walked over to the table where they sat. As soon as Sarge saw him, he got up and shook his hand. "Joe, this is amazing. I'm so happy for you. I've never seen the Lord work on a man like He's working on you."

Joe was a little confused. He didn't like the emphasis being put on him. He thought for a moment. Today was quite overwhelming. Joe looked around and saw so many people who cared about him. "You know, now I realize that the Lord has been working. I didn't know it, and I didn't help Him. A few years back, something happened that made me stop running. It made me stop fighting Him. I don't even know what that was. The shrink I saw in detention thought it must have been all the drugs I'd taken … that somehow they had affected my brain. I don't think so. I think the Lord was doing something even back then. I just hope all of you realize how thankful I am to have you in my life." Joe looked at Mary. "How did you end up here this morning?"

Mary seemed a little embarrassed as she looked at Sarge. She paused before speaking. "Well, this guy here"—she pointed at Sarge—"came back to the diner the day after you and your grandfather were there. He convinced me to go to the adult fellowship night at his church, and I've been going ever since. He was right … it is fun. I even went alone the night he had to work late. When your grandfather called the diner and invited me to your baptism, I said yes. Then he hinted that probably Kyle would like to come too. So here we are."

Joe was smiling as he went to sit beside Lisa. "How's it going, sis?"

She stood up, hugged him, and he hugged her back.

"I don't know when I've been happier, Joey. Right now you and I have something that we've never had before. It's hard to believe we aren't just brother and sister here on earth. We're brother and sister in the Lord."

"Oh Lise, I'm sorry for all the hurt I caused you. By God's grace, things are going to be different." Lisa sat back down, and Joe sat beside her. "You know JJ is here?"

Lisa bit her bottom lip and said, "I saw him. What's he like?"

"Well, he can be awful. He wants to see you. On Easter, after I punched him hard enough to knock him over, Gramps told him to straighten up. I think that helped. We hadn't seen him since then. He came to the Lord today."

"I saw him go up. Oh Joey, I'm scared. All these feelings are rushing back at me."

Joe sighed. He knew exactly what she was saying. "I think it's going to be okay, Lise. We've got mom and dad here. They certainly aren't threatened by JJ. I remember how they helped us pray for him and Sal when we were small. Watch, Dad will have his arm around JJ's shoulder in no time. Aunt Michelle and Uncle Jay have a big yard. The kids can run around. You can hide in the house if you want. It will be okay."

• • •

JAY WILKES LOOKED OUT across the back yard at the many people gathered there. *When have there ever been so many here? This nephew of mine brought together such a variety of people: Carl, Annie, Jeff with his mother-in-law, and Chad. Kyle Waters … I'll have to find out how he's connected with Joey. He brought a lady friend. Pastor Brad and his new wife. Larry and Joyce. Rob Schroeder and his wife and baby. And the kids' family ... their mom, Joy, is into a serious conversation with the woman Kyle came with ... Lisa. It's so good to see her again, sitting beside her mom, talking to my Jill. Jill's holding the baby.*

Jay watched his father, who sat in a lawn chair close to Lisa's husband, and the other four kids. They sat at the Little Tykes picnic table he had pulled out of the garage when he got home from the church. *That Matt has everything under control. Lisa found a good man. Seth Parker talking with JJ. I wonder what JJ thinks of Andrew. Joey told us about his sister with Down syndrome but didn't mention that his brother has it too.*

Jay watched as JJ looked at Andrew and said something to him. All three men laughed. *Is JJ thinking about Donny?* He watched Andrew open up his arms as he gave JJ a hug. Jay silently thanked the Lord for the scenes unfolding before him. Imagine ... a crowd that big with no conflict, and Joseph Wilkes Junior and his two kids together at a family gathering. He wished Marge had been able to come. It was a sight to behold. Jay turned off the valve on the barbeque and went to join the party.

The barbeque wound down at 3:30. The Parkers, Lisa and her family, Gramps and JJ all gathered in the family room with Jay and his family. Gramps loved having the little ones around. He made sure Kevin took at least a dozen pictures on his cell phone. JJ snapped a few too and then asked that Kevin use his cell phone to take a picture of him with all the kids. When the kids tired of the picture taking, Jill sat with them around the big TV at the end of the room. *Veggie Tales* was a hit with them from the start. Gramps requested a picture with Lisa and Joe. Then he wanted one with JJ, Joe, and Kevin so that they would have a visual reminder of all that had happened on this amazing day. Joy had taken her pictures earlier. She had one of her oldest son between his mom and dad and one of all her kids together, which didn't happen very often.

Lisa had talked to JJ. When he looked at her and said, "Oh Princess," she started to cry. She remembered the nickname. "I'm so sorry. For everything," JJ had whispered.

Lisa had not come back with "It's okay." She looked at him and said, "I forgive you." She looked over and saw that Seth and Joy had stopped what they were doing and were watching her. Those two had taught and showed them from the time they were very little that God's love and grace were boundless. Their smiles were wide as they took in the scene.

• • •

JOE FELT GOOD AS he said goodnight to Gramps and went down the hall to his room. It had been a long day, and so much had happened. It was good to see Lisa again and to meet her kids. They were all sweet, and Matt was really a great guy. When they had met eight years ago, they hadn't hit it off too well. Matt had taken great offence at Joe's macho man approach. Joe had warned Matt that he better be good to his sister, or he would answer to him.

Joe would never forget Matt's reply: "I plan to love and cherish Lisa. How dare you suggest I would ever hurt her. She's had enough hurt from men in her life, both you and your biological father." Joe had backed off, almost ashamed. He was glad Lisa hadn't heard what was said. Today it was as if that conversation had never happened. He felt loved and welcomed by Lisa, Matt, and their kids. *Yes*, Joe thought, *it was an amazing day.* The only sad point for him was when he had watched Lisa's three-year-old for a long time and felt a longing in his heart for Stevie.

• • •

AS GRAMPS ENTERED HIS room at bedtime, his eyes went to the picture on his dresser. He went over and picked it up. "Well, what do you think, Kathy? JJ came home. The Lord is using Joey in an amazing way. He and Kev were baptized. And Lisa … she reminds me of you. So beautiful and so in love with the Lord too. He's blessed us so much." Gramps' heart was full as he climbed into bed. He fell asleep quickly after he thanked the Lord for the day and all the blessings it had brought.

Chapter Twelve

JOE LOOKED OUT ACROSS THE FIELDS. THE WINTER WHEAT WAS ALMOST READY. IN TWO weeks, 230 acres of soft red winter wheat would be combined, loaded into transport trucks, and taken to a nearby river port. From there it would travel to a number of possible places in North or South America, destined to become pastry flour. He watched the soybeans blowing green in the breeze. "A forgiving crop," Carl called them. They didn't have a delicate timeline to be planted and harvested.

Joe hadn't enjoyed his experience with hay. Carl had a two-acre field between two woodlots. Three times in a good year, one with lots of rain and sunshine, a farmer from down the road arrived with his equipment. After the hay was cut, raked, and dried, Joe manned the wagon and piled the bales as they came out of the baler.

"Lots of folks use the smaller rectangular bales rather than the big rolls," Carl had told him. It was hard, itchy work. Jeff lent Joe to the other farmer. Joe strongly suspected Jeff considered that this was character building work, specifically for him. Carl had sold off his equipment when they sold the last of their livestock. Now, for the most part, he was doing his neighbour a favour. The farmer gave them a small percentage of the bales, and Carl put a "Hay for Sale" sign out at the road.

Joe's biggest satisfaction at the farm was Annie's garden. He had done the physical work, and she was the brains behind the operation. The garden was bigger this year than it had ever been. Early in the summer, Joe asked, "Annie, why don't you have a fruit stand like other folks around here?"

She had thought for a moment. "That's a good idea, Joe, but it would be a lot of work."

Joe talked to Carl about it. Annie was thrilled the morning she looked out her front window to see a ten-by-four-foot covered stand. It was painted bright red, and across the front Joe had stencilled "Annie's Garden." Carl and Jeff had patiently worked with Chad and Joe, who with their "git 'er done" attitude would never have completed such a beautifully crafted stand. It had taken two days to build.

The surprise came complete with a promise from Carl: "I'm not doing near as much work on the farm, Annie. Between the two of us, I'm sure we'll keep up with the selling. Joe can get the things harvested and do the setting up each morning."

Now Joe looked at the little stand with a smile. *The rhubarb and asparagus are finished. Look at that variety! We are looking at an amazing yield of sweet corn. There's lettuce, radishes, carrots, beans, and peas ... that early apple is too sour for me, but people are buying them up. Strawberries are winding down, but raspberries and blackberries are almost ready to pick. And that small patch of herbs is really a hit with the Generation Xers. Tomatoes, cucumbers, and peppers will be ready soon.* Annie and Carl didn't ask him to sell. If they weren't available, they asked people to leave the money for their purchase in a locked box with a slot in it. It was screwed onto the stand. They suspected that sometimes the produce was taken without payment, but that seldom happened.

Joe felt that he couldn't have a better job. It gave him satisfaction and a sense of accomplishment. Most importantly, it had given him contact with people who recognized his worth. Their encouragement and trust made Joe extremely committed and determined to do his best.

At the end of the day, Jeff told Joe that he needed to talk to him about something.

"What's up?" Joe asked.

"We have a men's breakfast at our church once a month."

Joe knew this because his friends from the men's group had invited him every time it came up. "Yes?" Joe wondered what was coming next.

Jeff continued. "We'd like you to do the talk after breakfast for the July meeting."

Joe looked at him and stated flatly, "I can't preach."

"But you can share, Joe. Every time you talk about the Lord, there's excitement in your voice. All you have to do is share what you see Him doing in your life. It's time, Joe, that you recognize that God is using you in very specific ways. We see it, and I know you do too. The best thing about this is that you don't brag on your past. Some people think it's great that they were such bad sinners. We listen to testimonies and hear all about the person instead of what the Lord has done in their life. Joe, your humility draws people to you, and you can point them to Christ. You can do this."

"Well, when you say it that way, I guess I can't say no. I've been praying that the Lord will use me. Maybe this is a start."

When Joe told Gramps about his conversation with Jeff, Gramps just smiled. "Joe, the first time I held you when you were a baby, I prayed that you would grow up big and strong in the Lord and that He would use you."

"Thank you, Gramps. I hope that's what's happening."

Gramps had an idea. "How about we ask Jay and Kevin to come along? And JJ too. It can be a Wilkes men thing. The people at the church won't mind. Jay and I have been to their men's breakfasts before.

"*Wilkes* men, Gramps?"

"Oh, I forgot. You're a Parker. Well, ask Seth. He and JJ can drive down together. It'll be a Wilkes/Parker men thing."

"Okay, Gramps. You talk to JJ. I'll talk to my dad."

• • •

TWO WEEKS LATER, JOE found himself at Foxhill Community Church. He was seated at a round table with the men from both his families and Pastor Brad. The breakfast started at 8:00 a.m., and he noticed that most of the guys from his men's group were there. His dad and Andrew had arrived with JJ at Gramps' house at 7:00 a.m. They had all driven together to the church.

After eating, the group was welcomed. They sang a song, and Jeff introduced Joe. He was nervous, but he knew nobody would mind. He clutched the small podium, looked out at the large group of men, and sent up his own silent prayer. He saw Carl sitting with Chad and Jeff, who gave him a thumbs up. He looked at his dad and smiled at him. He lost his nervousness the minute he started to speak. He talked about his past. He had decided not to give any details about his early days, or about JJ's abuse. He talked about his fear and his confusion and his behaviour that caused foster placements to break down. He talked about his initial separation from Lisa, and how he eventually came to live with her at the Parkers'.

"My dad says that when I came to his house at six years old, I seriously believed that I could live on my own. And that's how I lived my life—a little boy thinking he was an adult. Pushing everyone away. Not needing anybody."

Joe told them about reaching adolescence and how his behaviour disrupted the family. "I was doing things that were dangerous. I did as I pleased, and I didn't care who I hurt. I started running away, and I got in trouble with the law. My mom and dad signed me back into care when I was done Grade Eight, but they never lost touch with me. All the other foster homes, group homes, youth facilities tried to help me, but I wouldn't let anyone into my life."

Joe gave a brief account of his addictions and imprisonment. "But am I ever glad the story doesn't end there. Some of you may know about the last time I was in jail. It was a horrible crime, and I was in for three years. I'm not going to tell you that I had a Jesus moment and lost my desire for drugs. I didn't even consider Him. In that regard, though, I want to make something clear. If you're here today thinking you want nothing to do with

Jesus ... if you have decided that you want Him out of your life, you need to understand something: Jesus wants you. He's not going to leave. You can step away, or try to push Him away, but He is relentlessly chasing you. If you stop, you'll see that He's doing all kinds of things to keep you safe and bring you to Himself. Only you and your stubborn will can stop His plan, because He wants you to come willingly.

"When I went into prison this last time, I decided that I would change. For many years I'd watched a lot of my friends, both guys and girls, die because of drugs and the perils that come with them. In prison, I was surrounded by anger, destruction, and despair. Three years, most of it in protective custody, which meant segregation for me, gave me lots of time to think. One of the things I was allowed to do was attend AA meetings. I learned some things about myself that I needed to learn. I stopped using drugs, and I stopped being angry." Joe looked at JJ and smiled, gritting his teeth. "Well, mostly I stopped being angry.

"You'll notice that I just took a lot of credit for what has happened over the past three years. Looking back, I see clearly that it wasn't me making the changes. I know now that it was only through God's grace that it happened. My whole life, even when I was doing things my way, the Lord was working. He kept me safe from violence on the streets and in our prison system. He kept me safe from the dangerous drugs I poured into my body. He never stopped working. Then I got out of jail, and He brought me to my grandfather's house.

"In the last few months, I've had some great examples of godly men in my life. God used those men, many of you are sitting here right now, to teach me and reach me. You know how? By loving me and accepting me. They called me out on my sin and still loved me. They were Christ to me. The precious Holy Spirit of God did a work in my heart and brought me to Himself. I asked for forgiveness, and Jesus forgave. I was born again. You need to be born again too." Joe stopped talking.

JJ was standing up. "Joey, can I say something?"

Joe nodded and stepped away from the podium as JJ came forward. He started to speak.

"A lot of you guys know me, and you know what I've been up to lately. I'm looking here at my son. When I saw Joey this past April, he refused to acknowledge me as his father. I certainly don't deserve that title. I've been living with a lot of anger for a lot of years. Joey didn't tell you that I abused him when he was little. I hurt his mom in front of him. I didn't let him be a little boy. When I reunited with Joey a few years back, we started out as friends, but then I went on a drunk and we ended up in a fist fight. So when I heard he was at my dad's, I was irate. On Easter I went to my dad's, and I started a fight with Joey. That was before he came to the Lord. He won the fight. He was so angry. By the end of that day, thanks to my dad's intervention, I knew that Joey's anger was because of me. I finally started looking at myself and looking for a solution. A few weeks ago, I watched Joey and my nephew Kevin get baptized. I know Joey says it too. All the teaching, all the caring, all the love we had pushed away came rushing at us. I came to Jesus that day."

Joe saw tears in JJ's eyes. He remembered back to when he was six and JJ had mocked him for crying. But that thought didn't hurt him anymore.

Carl's pastor came up to close off in prayer. He said "amen," and looked at the men in front of him.

"You men have heard a powerful testimony this morning … actually, two powerful testimonies. Have you been pushing God away? I won't ask if you're a sinner, as we're all sinful men. But God is rich in grace and mercy. We men don't want to talk about our hurts, but we have them. Do we know despair? Abandonment? Are we angry at someone, or at ourselves? Are you ready to let Him wash away your sin and take care of all the things that keep you imprisoned and powerless? A loving Saviour wants you to give all of that to Him. He has not moved. He is waiting for you. Let's sing our closing song together."

Joey smiled as he looked up to the words on the wall behind him. He recognized the song, "Chain Breaker." It was becoming his favourite. After the song, Joe joined the other men at his table. No one was surprised that many of the men around them were in deep conversations, apparently about the message they had just heard.

• • •

JOE HAD NEVER FELT time go by so quickly. Summer was almost over, and he would never forget those years spent in and out of prison cells. He didn't want to forget all of that. He needed to be reminded of where the Lord had brought him from. He loved the feel of fresh air, the sunshine, and even rain on his face. He loved being around family and friends. He loved singing in church, with the radio, and as he went about his work. He had come to realize that his life would never be normal. He didn't think that, when it came to a person's life, there was any such thing. But he was satisfied and was learning new things every day.

To be honest, there were still times Joe thought about drugs. Why was it easy to forget the pain they had brought into his life, and even easier to remember the euphoria, the feeling that everything was fine and he didn't have to worry about anything? Joe considered himself blessed to have support to get through those times. He could pray. That was the biggest help. He remembered his conversation with Gramps on the night of the phone call from JJ. Gramps had said they would find a counsellor. Joe felt that he had found wise counsel and a friend in his relationship with Brad. He had many other friends who stood beside him and encouraged him.

Joe had been able to talk to a few young people who were beginning to experiment with drugs. Some heard his story and came to him to talk. Some parents asked him to talk to their kids. Joe never claimed to be a counsellor. He would simply tell his story and answer questions. If he thought that someone had a serious problem, he would encourage them to seek further help and offer to go with them.

• • •

RAIDER'S MOTHER, ELISE, HAD called Joe a month after the incident at the meeting. She said that Raider was living at home, and she was quite sure he was still using drugs. He was attending a different AA meeting and had a court date scheduled to address the charges stemming from the night of his overdose. If convicted, he would most likely return to detention. Joe was sorry that he couldn't give Elise much encouragement. He'd been in that position countless times and returned to jail time and time again.

Elise gave Joe her son's phone number, and Joe called him. When Raider answered his phone, Joe identified himself. Raider's response was to laugh, swear at him, and say, "You've got to be kidding" before hanging up. In a subsequent call to Elise, Joe stressed the importance of finding a support group for herself. He also asked her to tell Raider that he'd be glad to meet with him if he ever wanted to talk.

• • •

JOE STILL DIDN'T HAVE his full driver's licence. Because of the province's graduated licensing process, he had taken driver's training and could try for his G2 license in two months. He was confident that he would pass the road test. Gramps had been generous in driving with him to all his appointments in Coverton, but he was looking forward to passing the test and being able to drive alone.

Joe knew he had to make some plans for his future. He loved working on the farm. Up to now, it had been what he needed. This week Jeff had given him a large cheque. At Joe's look of surprise, Jeff explained, "Well, Joe, you've done an excellent job this summer. Dad and I talked, and so far my mom's fruit stand has brought in $4,000.00. She is determined that you have it. They don't need the money, and they want to give you a head start toward your future. The rest of the money is your pay. You've gone far beyond what a normal employee would have given us work-wise. We're headed for a really good harvest."

"So you just more than double my earnings? I'm not sure I can accept that."

"Joe, it's all about the yield of the farm. It's your share. You're right, we never promised that to you. You're worth every penny of it, Joe. Maybe we won't be able to do it again, but we want you to have this. You've blessed us so much by being here this summer. My mom has never been happier. They've seen you grow along with the crops, and they're proud of you, Joe. And I've gained a friend and brother. Let us do this."

Joe thought for a moment. His future. What did that look like? He did want to get married and maybe have a family someday, but he was hesitant to even date. He had such a messed-up past. Any relationship he'd ever been in had ended in turmoil. He knew he had a lot to learn. If he married, he believed he could be a good husband. And if he had kids? He hoped he could be a good dad. "I don't know at all what my future holds." He looked at Jeff.

Jeff was quiet for a minute, then spoke. "Joe, you really are just starting your life. The Lord's going to show you."

"But I've messed up so badly." Sometimes the shame of his old life came blasting back.

"Joe, I think you know the Bible verse. *"Forgetting what is behind ..."*

Joe finished the verse, *"and straining toward what is ahead."*

Jeff challenged him. "Well, you should know the next verse too."

Joe thought for a minute, then said slowly, *"I press on toward the goal."* He stopped and looked at Jeff.

Jeff smiled and finished the verse, *"To win the prize for which God called me heavenward in Christ Jesus."* Joe suddenly felt that things might be starting to work out.

"By the way," Jeff was smiling, "my dad and your grandfather have been talking. They think you should go to Bible school for a year."

"And how's that going to happen?"

Jeff started another verse: *"With man this is impossible, but with God ..."*

"All things are possible. What is this? Making sure Joe knows his verses day?"

Joe and Jeff both laughed.

Chapter Thirteen

JOE WOKE UP TO A DREARY DAY. HE HEARD RAIN BEATING AGAINST THE WINDOW, AND HIS first thought was to roll over and go back to sleep, but he got out of bed and got dressed. His cell phone rang. Joe had bought a cell phone a few weeks before. Because he was trying to save money, he bought a cheaper phone. It had texting and a small amount of calling, but no data. He could use the internet when he was connected to Wi-Fi.

"Hi, Jeff," Joe answered on the first ring. "Sounds good to me. Are you sure there isn't something inside we need to do? Okay. I'll see you tomorrow." Joe ended the call. A day off. A rainy day off. Joe made his way to the kitchen. "Morning, Gramps."

"Was that Jeff?"

"It was. No work today."

Joe sat down to have a coffee with Gramps. When he finished, he put on a windbreaker and hurried down to the donut shop. He liked the atmosphere there at this time of day and wasn't able to get there often. The early morning, with the hustle of folks coming in and out, would lend some excitement to this rainy day. Only a couple of regulars were sitting at the tables. Three people were lined up to order. His turn came and he ordered a coffee and a bagel. Picking up a newspaper, he headed to a corner table. He ate his bagel and then picked up his coffee. He glanced at the headline on the front page of the *Coverton Standard*: "Young Father killed in Downtown Accident."

He began to read: "A twenty-six-year-old Coverton man was killed early Monday when the 2008 Cobalt he was driving was broadsided by a late model Ford F 150. Steven Findlay was pronounced dead at the scene. His three-year-old son is in the PICU at St. Joseph's Hospital, having sustained life-threatening injuries."

At that point Joe stopped reading. He cried out loud, "No, please no!" He didn't notice that everyone in the shop had looked his way. All of a sudden, Pastor Brad was by his side. His hand was on his shoulder and he shook Joe, saying his name so that he'd look at him. Joe looked up and focused on who was speaking to him.

"Brad? Where did you come from? Look." He pointed to the paper, with pain and confusion written on his face.

Brad read as far as Joe had read and stopped long enough to say, "Oh Lord Jesus, help us here." He sat down in the chair beside Joe.

Joe looked up with tears streaming down his face. "What can I do?"

Brad thought for a few seconds. "I can get you to Coverton, Joe. Maybe we should call the hospital. Stevie's mom might be there. You said they were involved in that little church downtown. I can try to reach the pastor there."

Joe knew he had to see his son. He believed that Shea would be okay with that. "I want to go."

"Okay. We'll stop at your house so you can tell your grandfather."

Joe stood up and looked around him. He knew most of these people. "It's my son. He was in a car accident. He's in ICU. Please pray for him." He and Brad went out the door.

Gramps looked up as Brad and Joe came into the living room. "Oh Joey, what's wrong? What happened?"

Brad told Gramps what was going on, and Gramps went to Joe and hugged him. "We'll be praying, Joe."

"Gramps, please call my mom. They don't even know about Stevie. She'll put a request on their prayer chain, and Brad says you'll call ours. Call JJ too."

• • •

THE DRIVE TO COVERTON seemed to take hours. In forty-five minutes, Brad parked the car, and they went straight to the front desk of the hospital. Joe asked about Stevie, and the clerk seemed to know who he was talking about. "And your name, sir?"

"Joe Parker. I'm Stevie's biological father."

"Is Mrs. Findlay expecting you?"

"No, I just read it in the paper. I live in Souton. I don't think she'll mind."

The clerk could see that Joe was distraught. She said, "Joe, if you'll have a seat in that waiting area to the left, I'll call up to PICU and see what they say."

Joe and Brad sat down to wait. A few minutes later, the clerk walked over to them. "You can go up to the PICU waiting room on the fourth floor. You'll find Mrs. Findlay there."

"Thank you," Joe said with relief. He was silent as they went to the elevator. Brad pressed the button. As the elevator door opened, Joe saw the sign, "Pediatric Intensive

Care Waiting Room," on a door straight ahead. Joe walked through the door, and Brad followed. Shea was sitting with a blanket around her on one of the chairs. She looked up when Joe came in and greeted him. Joe sat down beside her and put his hand on her arm. "Shea, I am so sorry. Steve was an amazing guy."

Shea answered softly, "He was. I don't know what I'm going to do without him."

Joe leaned back in the chair and looked around the room. He noticed an older woman sitting across the room watching them, and he remembered that Brad was with him.

"Shea, this is my pastor. He's also my friend. His name is Brad."

"This is Mrs. Griffin. I think I told you about her. Maybe not. She's from our church … she kind of adopted us. We call her Grandma."

"How is he?" Joe's tears started again.

"He's holding his own. I can … we can go in for five minutes once an hour. The doctor should be here to speak to me, I mean speak to us, soon. I don't know if they'll let us go in together."

They both looked up when a nurse spoke from the door. "Shea, I understand this is Stevie's father."

Joe spoke up. "I'm his bio father. Steve was his father. But I love him and want to see him."

The nurse smiled "One visitor at a time. You can come in now."

"Thanks, Shea," Joe said as he left. He washed up just inside the door of the PICU unit, and the nurse led him to a room at the end of the hall. There were four cribs in the room, each one in its own cubicle. Only two were occupied. Even with the dressings and multiple tubes, Joe recognized his son. "How is he?" He turned to ask the nurse.

"He has a lot of injuries. He's holding his own, though. He had a collapsed lung that appears to be resolving. He has a broken arm and a broken leg, along with some broken ribs. He has a head injury, but the latest CT scan shows that the bleeding has stopped, and that's good. He's sedated so that his brain and body can rest." She stopped as Joe took all that in. "I'm curious. Do you mind if I ask? Do you get to see him often?"

"No," Joe answered. "I didn't know he existed till five months ago. Steve was his dad, and that was fine. But I can tell you I loved him the minute I laid eyes on him." Joe stood and looked at Stevie. He whispered a prayer. "Lord Jesus, please heal him." Before he knew it, his five minutes were up.

When he entered the waiting room, Shea stood up to go back to see Stevie. Joe sat down on a chair and looked at Brad. "He's so little. There are so many tubes. Brad, I'm so scared. What if he dies?"

Brad searched for an answer, and Mrs. Griffin spoke. "If he dies, Joe, your heart will be broken. You'll think about him probably every day of your life. You'll never forget him, but the pain subsides. Remember, if Stevie dies, he will be brought *into His glorious presence, with mighty shouts of everlasting joy*. It says that in the Bible. Heaven is real, Joe, and death for the believer is really just like coming home."

Brad looked at her. "The voice of experience?" he said softly.

"My son died of meningitis when he was nine. But you know what, Joe? I think Stevie will be okay. Last night the doctor said he is holding his own. The nurse was more positive than that this morning. There are hundreds of people praying for him as we speak. Pastor, how about we pray right now."

Brad prayed, thanking God for the fact that even though Steve was gone, they could be assured he was in Heaven, and that in reality he was rejoicing with his Saviour. He asked the Lord to touch little Stevie and heal him, and to bring peace to Shea and Joe and everyone who loved this little boy. As Brad finished, Joe looked up to see Shea standing at the door. She sat down, and Mrs. Griffin put her arm around her. Everyone sat in silence.

After what seemed like a long time, but was actually only ten minutes, Mrs. Griffin told Shea she'd be on her way. She had been with Shea for most of the past twenty-eight hours. Joe assured her he was staying for the rest of the day. Shea hadn't left the hospital. She'd checked into Ronald McDonald House last evening but preferred to spend the night in the waiting room. She napped in a recliner in between the visits to Stevie's bedside. Shea yawned. She was exhausted.

It was Brad who asked her if she had things that needed to be done.

"Well, Steve's parents are taking care of the funeral. I guess he had an insurance policy that named his mom as the beneficiary. It's kind of a mess. You see, his parents didn't like me much. They very reluctantly came to our wedding. Steve argued with them after Stevie was born. From the beginning, they knew Stevie was his by choice, but they just couldn't accept him as their grandson. I don't know what to do about all that. I want to write his obituary, and I'd like our pastor to have some part in the funeral." Shea shook her head. "They sure are making this hard for me."

Brad spoke softly. "Shea, you need to get some rest. But if you can come with me for an hour, we can go over to the funeral home to see what has been done there. Maybe I can talk to Steve's parents, or their minister can, if they have one doing the service. Hopefully we can work something out." He paused and looked from Shea to Joe. "Joe, you'll stay here?" Joe nodded his head.

Shea stood up and straightened her clothes. "I'm wiped, but I can handle a couple more hours. I have a room at Ronald McDonald House. It's right here in the hospital. I'll check in on Stevie when I get back, then head off to sleep for a while."

Joe left the waiting room to go downstairs to pick up a coffee, a sandwich, and a magazine. On his return, he settled into a chair in the corner. A young couple had arrived in his absence. Joe nodded to them and then put his head in his hands and prayed. An hour later, just as Joe had settled back into his corner after seeing Stevie, he looked up to see his mom.

"Hi, Joe."

"Hi, Mom," he answered. They looked at each other, then he stood up and gathered her into a big hug.

"Thanks for having your gramps call me."

"What can I say? Sometimes a guy needs his mom."

"How's Stevie?"

"I don't know, Mom. He's hooked up to all kinds of things. I just came back from seeing him. The nurse thinks the doctor is going to give us some good news. She's due in soon. Shea and my pastor took off to try to settle some things about Steve. They'll be back soon."

Joy sat down in a chair across from Joe. They sat quietly, neither knowing what to say. After ten minutes, the other couple stood up. The man asked if either of them would like a coffee from the cafeteria. Both Joe and Joy put in an order. After they left, Joy spoke. "I was surprised that I have another grandson."

"When I got out this time, I was surprised that I had a son. Shea and I lived in the same house. We weren't even in a relationship. It just happened. Mom, I can't believe I was such a ..." He stopped and shook his head.

"You know what one of my favourite verses is, Joe?"

Joe smiled. "Hit me with it, Mom."

"'*Therefore, if anyone is in Christ, the new creation has come. The old has gone, the new is here!*'" (2 Corinthians 5:17).

"Thank God for that. When I first saw Stevie, Steve was holding him. They made it very clear that Steve was Stevie's dad, and I agreed. I would never have interfered. But today I knew I had to be here. I think Shea will let me be in his life."

"Joey, I think some amazing things are going to happen."

Joe hoped his mom was right.

● ● ●

BRAD AND SHEA WERE quiet as they left the funeral home. Brad shook his head as he contemplated the things that Steve's parents had done to take control in the situation. The funeral director had shown them the obituary that would appear in tomorrow's newspaper. He was surprised when Shea asked if she, as Steve's wife, could change it. The man looked embarrassed and admitted that he had questioned the Findlays when he saw what they had written. There had been no mention of Shea or Stevie, and that didn't line up with the news article he had seen in the *Standard*. When Steve's mother said, "No, he was not married, and he does not have a child," he hadn't pressed the issue further. Steve's family was paying for the funeral and burial, so things were getting very complicated.

Shea was somewhat encouraged when the funeral director said, "I'll call the Findlays and tell them that protocol requires that I consider you to be Steve's next of kin. I'll also confront them about lying to me. I'll tell them that you're not looking to change anything, except to be mentioned in the obituary. And I'll tell them that you would like your pastor, Steve's pastor, to have a part in the service. Stevie is legally Steve's son. This obituary is already on our website, but I can easily change it. If the Findlays disagree, I can post an additional one with your input. We have till 5:00 p.m. to notify the newspaper. Hopefully, things will be settled by then. I'm sorry this happened."

When Brad read the obituary, he saw the name of the minister who was to officiate at the funeral. He knew Harry Ward. His church was a sister church to Souton Baptist. Both were in the same association of churches. He sat on committees with this man.

They reached the car, and before getting in, Brad took his phone from his pocket. He scrolled down his contacts, tapped a number, and in ten seconds was connected. "Harry. Brad Johnson here … So you've heard about that. Well, we know the Lord is moving. We've been praying for revival for a long time. Well, Harry, I have a situation here that is related to that guy. His name's Joe Parker. He's Jay Wilkes' nephew. The situation concerns the Findlays from your church."

Shea listened as Brad explained what had happened to date. She heard him say, "But they are married. They were married at Crossroads before Stevie was born. She's a sweet girl, Harry, and the amazing thing is that Steve and Shea are believers. When you do Steve's funeral, you can assure the people he is in Heaven." Shea listened a little longer, and then Brad said, "Shea's not out to get anything. She wants them to put in that she was Steve's wife, and that Stevie is Steve's son. Oh, and she'd like Jake Konrad to have a part in the service." Brad was smiling when he ended the call. "I think things are going to be okay, Shea."

• • •

BACK AT THE HOSPITAL, Shea met Joe's mom and liked her immediately. She'd never really had a mom. Her mom left her with her dad when she was three. She had visited with her sporadically until she was ten, but then her mom died. No one had ever told her how. She remembered some fun times with her dad, but he remarried when she was eight. She couldn't remember one nice thing about her stepmother. She moved out of the house at sixteen, and after two years of living with a few different friends, Shea found Steve's Place. She had Stevie when she had just turned twenty.

Shea had just returned to the waiting room after seeing Stevie when the doctor came in. Dr. Chambers looked from Shea to Joe, and Shea introduced Joe. "Dr. Chambers, this is Stevie's biological father, Joe Parker. He's never been involved in Stevie's life, but I think that it's important for him to be here."

Dr. Chambers looked down at her clipboard and spoke. "Well, Stevie is making good progress. The condition of his lungs has greatly improved. We'll try to take the ventilator out tomorrow morning. His brain scan from early this morning showed some swelling, but no bleeding. We'll have to watch that closely. The broken bones are set, and hopefully when he wakes up, they won't cause him too much pain. He'll have to spend most of his time in bed, or at least immobilized. Those ribs will be painful if he moves around too much. We want to go easy on the pain medication."

Shea spoke up, "Dr. Chambers, are you saying Stevie is going to be okay?"

"Well, he's still in serious condition, but he's improving daily. We'll watch the lungs and the brain injury closely. Hopefully tomorrow he'll be breathing on his own. We'll keep him sedated for a few more days and do what we need to do to control the pain as he comes out of it. If all goes well, he should be over on the ward by early next week."

With that good news, Shea left to go to Ronald McDonald House. Pastor Brad went back to Souton, and Joe and Joy spent the afternoon talking and reminiscing. Joy was able to see her grandson. She marvelled at the way Joe's story was unfolding. Shea returned at six o'clock. Joe had decided that he would return to Souton, and Shea said that she would stay in the waiting room till 9:00 p.m. and then return to Ronald McDonald House. She knew she would be notified if there was any problem with Stevie during the night.

• • •

JOY PULLED OUT OF Gramps' driveway at 8:00 p.m. It had been a long day. She had called Seth earlier. He was relieved to hear that their grandson's prognosis had greatly improved from what they thought that morning. She'd spent some precious time with Joey. It was real. He really had come home. She had been praising the Lord for that ever since the phone call they'd received back in April. She was excited that the Lord had already used him.

This whole situation with Stevie was frightening, but at the same time, she knew it was going to be okay. Look at how things had worked out with Steve's family. She and Joe had been with Shea when Pastor Brad's call came through. They watched the relief flood over her face as he said that the obituary would be changed, and Pastor Konrad would take part in the service on Friday. Joe would not attend but would stay at the hospital during the funeral. Joy hadn't planned to attend either, but she changed her mind when Shea looked at her and said, "Joy, I'd like you to be there. And Joe's dad too.

People don't have to know who you are. You'll fit right in with the folks from our church."

Yes, it had been a long day, and she still had the two-hour trip home. But she and Seth would be back on Friday.

Chapter Fourteen

THE CHURCH WAS PACKED. SHEA HAD ONLY BEEN TO ONE FUNERAL IN HER LIFE, AND SHE didn't remember much about that day. At ten years old, she knew that her mother had died and that she would never see her again. This morning she had broken down. Alone in her room at the hospital, the sorrow and loneliness that flooded her was overwhelming. Then there was a knock on her door. The staff told her Mrs. Griffin was there and wanted to visit. Shea went to the entryway to be there when they let her in. Mrs. Griffin looked at her tear-stained face and said, "I thought you might need someone here with you this morning." They sat together on the bed in her room, Mrs. Griffin holding her. Shea cried until she ran out of tears.

Mrs. Griffin had not left her side since. *This is so hard.* The tears came as she remembered Steve. She prayed silently. *Oh Lord, I don't know what I'm going to do.* She looked around. She'd never been in a church this large. So fancy, so many people all dressed up. As Shea walked with the Griffins down the middle aisle, she saw some of her church friends. They smiled at her in a guarded way. When they reached the third row from the front, Mr. Griffin stopped and slid into the pew. His wife followed, and Shea sat down beside her. She was so glad these people were with her.

She looked across the aisle to where Steve's family filled the second and third rows. His mother was crying. His father sat beside her. Shea was sad for them. They had been so angry with Steve that they hadn't talked to him for three years. She shook her head. *What will I do without him?* She had to talk to them after the service. She had to tell them something important. She saw the two pastors climbing the stairs at the front and focused as the service began.

• • •

STEVE WAS BURIED. SHEA had whispered her goodbye to him. She believed what both the pastors had said—Steve was in Heaven. And Heaven was so good that she couldn't begin to imagine it. Harry Ward, the Findlays' minister, hadn't known Steve well, but he had taken the stories his family had shared and woven them into a wonderful tribute. Shea had smiled as he talked about Steve's childhood and teenage years, his recent graduation from college, and his brand-new job at the local radio station.

Pastor Konrad spoke of Steve's involvement in their church. He described Steve as a godly husband and father. He talked about Stevie. Then he stopped the flow of the service to give thanks for Stevie's progress and to ask the Lord to continue to heal him. Yes, it was a good service.

Now they were going back to the church in a limo. The Findlays were in a limo in front of them. Shea was pleased that the service and burial had gone well. Steve was being celebrated, and her heart was glad for that. Now the lunch. And then it would be finished.

• • •

STEVE'S PARENTS WERE SITTING alone at the table where the rest of his family had been earlier. Most of the people had left. Shea sat with Joy, Seth, and the Griffins, along with Pastor Konrad and his wife.

"Maybe now would be a good time, honey," Mrs. Griffin whispered in her ear.

The others heard her soft reply as she stood: "I'll go talk to them."

Shea wasn't afraid of Steve's parents. She was just wary of where this conversation would go. They greeted her as she walked to their table and sat down. She was silent for a minute, and Mr. Findlay surprised her by asking, "How are you holding up, Shea?"

Shea looked at him and then at his wife. She hadn't expected a welcome. She replied that she was doing okay and that she felt the service was good.

Mrs. Findlay spoke. Shea knew she was struggling for words. "Oh, wasn't it? So many people. So many people who loved and cared about him … who care about us." She closed her eyes, trying to hold back her tears. "I'm going to miss him so much." She was quiet and then spoke softly. "Shea, we're sorry for the way we treated you. We made our own plans and left you out." Shea looked at her, wondering what brought on this unexpected apology. "I guess I should say how *I* went about it. I should have taken a lesson from my son, instead of pushing him away. After our pastor had a rather stern talk with us, I did some soul searching."

"I did too," Mr. Findlay cut in.

His wife continued. "We both know that Steve loved us, but I'm ashamed of our behaviour. And now he's gone. I can't even tell him I'm sorry." With tears in her eyes, she paused for a moment. Her husband reached over and took her hand as she continued. "Can you forgive us? Can we be friends?"

Shea thought for a moment. She knew that this couple had loved their son. She didn't know what had caused them to push Steve away. He'd only said that they were rather staunch in their beliefs and had a hard time accepting that he needed to live his own life. "I do forgive you. And Steve did too. He wanted very much to reconcile with you. And about the funeral and stuff, I'm okay with the way things turned out. This is just a hard time. I know you're hurting, and it's because you loved him."

Shea looked at Steve's parents and sighed. "I know you have a hard time with Stevie being your grandson, but Steve loved him. He couldn't have loved him more. And if … I guess I should say when … Stevie gets better, you should get to know him." She paused, unable to read their feelings. "I bet you'll see Steve in him. They were best friends, and all our friends say Stevie is a little Steve for sure."

Shea studied the Findlays again, then continued. "There's something really important I need to tell you, though. I'm pregnant." Shea paused as both Steve's parents looked at her, surprised. "Steve and I just found out two weeks ago. You're the first to know, except for Mrs. Griffin over there. She's a pretty wise lady. She said a child needs as many grandparents as they can get. This baby will need you to be in its life, and I want you to be there too."

Shea looked at Steve's mom and saw the tears forming again in her eyes. "Oh Shea," she said with a look of wonder on her face. "I think this is a great blessing for us all." Shea heard Steve's father whisper "Amen."

● ● ●

JOE HAD JUST RETURNED from the coffee shop when Shea entered the waiting room with his mom and dad. "How did it go?" he asked.

"It was hard, but it was good. How's Stevie?"

"I haven't seen him since just after lunch. They've started weaning him off the sedative. They figure he'll start to wake up soon, and they want you to be there when he does. I told them you were on your way." As Joe finished his sentence, a nurse appeared at the door.

"Hi, Mrs. Findlay. When you're ready, you can come in. We've got a chair set up where you'll be comfortable holding Stevie. We think he'll be awake any time now, and hopefully he'll lay quietly in your arms as he comes to. He seems comfortable, so we don't think the pain is severe. We don't know what he'll remember, but you're the best person for him right now."

Shea looked at the others. "I'll stay," Joe said.

"And we'll be going," Seth added. Shea thanked them for being there.

Joe smiled as his mom gave Shea a big hug and said, "Remember, if you need anything, just call." With that, Shea headed off to hold her son. Joe said goodbye to his mom and dad and settled into a chair with his coffee.

After Shea had washed up, the nurse took her to Stevie. They had moved him to a small room in the unit. Shea settled into a recliner in the corner. Stevie's colour was good, and he was breathing on his own without the ventilator. It had done its job well as it provided life-giving oxygen to his damaged lung. He still had his IV. In her report, the doctor said that the ribs he had broken would take about six weeks to heal. Hopefully, they'd be able to control his pain. Shea sat in the recliner, and the nurse put Stevie in her lap, positioning him so as to not put any pressure on his injuries.

Shea was tired, but her mind was racing. She went back over the funeral and what had happened there. She knew that many people hated funerals, but today had been good. Steve would have been pleased to see so many of his friends there, old ones and new ones. The pastors had described him well. Tears started falling as she thought about him. She had been young and so shy when she met him. From the beginning, he'd treated her like a queen. She never thought she would find a husband like him. She held Stevie a little tighter and felt him stir. She pressed the buzzer to call the nurse and looked down at him.

"Mom's here, Stevie. Mommy's right here."

The nurse was beside her. Minutes later, Stevie opened his eyes.

"I'm thirsty, Mommy."

The nurse picked up the water cup that sat on the tray and handed it to Shea with a straw. Stevie took a drink. "Thanks, Mommy," he whispered as he went back to sleep. Shea looked to the nurse. She was smiling.

"That was promising. He remembered you. He can drink on his own. He seemed lucid. If you're comfortable there, we can leave you with him. It's good if he drinks. Just ring the buzzer if he wakes up more fully."

"Can his father come in?"

"That should be fine, but just for fifteen minutes."

Minutes later, Joe was standing at the door of the room.

"How's he doing?"

"He woke up a bit. Drank some water. Talked to me."

"That's great, Shea. He looks a lot better too." Joe stood looking at the two of them. Neither said a word. After five minutes, Joe broke the silence. "I'm going to go back to Souton tonight. I've missed a lot of work, and I want to be there tomorrow ... unless you think I need to be here. Shea, I'm not sure how much you want me to be around."

"I'm glad you were here, Joe. I understand that you need to get back to work. I think I can handle things with Stevie on my own. The Griffins will come often when he gets over on the ward. Dr. Chambers said that will be soon."

"Do you know what you're going to do? I hear you moved from Steve's Place."

"We have a two-bedroom apartment up on College. Your mom might not have told you, but I worked things out with Steve's parents today. I think they'll help me out in the long run. I do have my license, but the car was totalled. I hope the insurance will pay something. It was older, but it was in good shape."

"If you're going to buy one, let me talk to my uncle first. He manages a car dealership in Foxhill. Shea, if I can help, I will. I have a job. I'm off drugs, and I don't drink. The Lord has changed me. I want to be part of Stevie's life."

"I can see you've changed, Joe. It's really unbelievable. You will be part of Stevie's life. Thank you for not barrelling in and claiming him, like so many guys would. We'll have to work out some kind of visiting arrangement." Shea paused, thinking about how she was going to word what she was about to say. "Do you mind if we keep it informal and take it slow? At first just meet together at a park or something, till he gets used to you? He's so little." Shea looked down at her son and started to cry again. "He'll probably forget Steve, but I don't want him to."

Joe moved closer to her, and she looked up at him. "Shea, I'll do whatever you say. You decide when, where, and how often I visit with him. When I first looked at him, I knew he was my son, but I also knew that Steve was his dad. I really believe that the Lord has His hand in all of this."

"I do too, Joe. It's hard to believe we're the same people we were back then. I never could figure out the part in the Bible where it says that God takes everything that happens—all our hurts and rejection, our messed-up lives, even unplanned babies—and works it together for good. If I hadn't seen that clearly to this point, I don't know how I could get through Steve's death, or Stevie being in such bad shape. It's still hard, but I'm okay. I know God's got us."

She felt Joe's hand on her shoulder. He started to pray, just as Steve would have, and asked the Lord to keep working in their lives. Then he moved his hand to Stevie and begged the Lord to heal him and let him grow up big and strong. Shea looked at Joe. There were tears in his eyes too.

A few minutes later, Shea felt Stevie move in her arms. She looked down, and he was staring at her, his big grey eyes wide open. "Mommy." He wiggled to change his position and she saw him flinch. She pulled him closer, trying to keep his arm and leg steady.

"It probably hurts, buddy. You need to try to stay still." She turned to Joe and whispered, "Can you press the buzzer?"

Joe quickly pressed it, and two nurses arrived. One spoke to Stevie, who said he was thirsty. She took the plastic cup from the small table and had him drink. Then they took him from Shea and settled him back in his bed. Apart from an occasional whimper, he settled without complaint as they efficiently positioned him with small pillows and rolls. Joe watched Stevie as he looked around the room.

"Where's my daddy?" was his first question.

"Stevie, Daddy isn't here."

His eyes took in Joe. "You came to the old house." He said in a sleepy voice.

Joe smiled at him. "Do you ever have a good memory. That was a long time ago. My name is Joe."

"I remember. Daddy said you are a good guy."

"Do you know any bad guys?"

"No. No bad guys. Only in the movie. The little dog's man. You know, he tried to shoot Copper. What his name, Mommy?"

"I don't remember his name, honey. You liked that movie, didn't you?"

Stevie shook his head. "My eyes are tired, Mommy."

"Well, it's okay to close them," Shea whispered.

As Stevie dozed off, he said softly, "Yup. Tod and Copper. We watched it last night."

The nurses looked from Stevie to Shea. Shea was crying.

"When did you watch the movie?" one of them asked.

"Sunday night. We watched it together. Stevie and his daddy and I. We watched it together."

The nurses looked at each other and smiled through their tears. The other nurse spoke. "Well, that precious conversation just confirmed that the brain injury doesn't seem to have affected his short-term memory. Everything is progressing very well."

Chapter Fifteen

JOE SETTLED INTO A BUSY ROUTINE. HE WAS EXCITED TO GET BACK TO WORK, AND THE ride to the farm always gave him time to think. The weekend had gone by quickly. It was good to be in church yesterday, and he'd had the chance to stand up and thank people for praying. Brad prayed for Shea and Stevie during the service. After church, Joe and Gramps ate at Jay and Michelle's. His Aunt Marge, Uncle Dave, and their daughter, Faith, had been there as well. Joe was sure the reason they had come was to show him support, and he was glad of that.

When Joe reached the farm, Carl was already in the building, loading the cart to take vegetables out to the stand. Joe started helping him. The cart filled quickly, and Joe marvelled at the excellent yield and variety of produce. He joked with Carl, "I don't know, Carl. A year ago I wouldn't have imagined I could do this. You're going to have to start calling me Farmer Joe."

• • •

JOE ATTENDED HIS MEETING as usual that night. He was sometimes tempted to skip the meetings and argued back and forth with himself because he knew he was doing well. Then he'd remember the others in the meeting. Some had been sober for years and years. He thought he better take a lesson from them and continue in the group. In it he received support and encouragement, and he could give those things as well.

• • •

A HIGHLIGHT OF JOE'S week was his men's group meeting on Tuesday nights. He didn't ride with Rob anymore because Kevin had begun to attend too. Everyone teased Kevin that he was the baby of the group and asked him why he was hanging out with a bunch of old men. Kevin would laugh and give a smart answer like, "Somebody has to keep you guys in line." Joe knew that Kevin attended for the same reason he did. It felt good to be with other guys—learning, talking, and sharing. He had never experienced friendships like those formed in that group.

One of the most significant things Joe had started doing was speaking to men's groups. He would rather call it sharing. He had never heard of a men's breakfast before he went to the one at the Foxhill church. He began to get invitations to speak, and by the end of the summer, he had spoken at six different churches. He still felt totally inadequate to be telling his story, but each time he did, he knew that the Lord was working through him. He began to realize that his story had an impact on others. He was always thankful that the Lord was using him.

One Sunday morning in August, Joe sat nervously in the front pew, ready to share, at Harper Baptist Church. Harper was a village about forty kilometres east of Toronto. When Joe had left there twenty years previous, it was beginning to grow. In the years since, the regional government had swallowed it into the next town. Toronto had grown outward and closer to Harper. The town was very different from what Joe remembered. He hadn't forgotten this sanctuary, though. As he and his grandfather entered the church that morning, people welcomed him by name.

Mrs. Grace, who was celebrating her eighty-fifth birthday that week, greeted him at the door. "Joe, it is so good to see you. I have prayed for you for years."

Joe believed her. His mom had once told him in a letter that Mrs. Grace prayed for their family every day.

Joe didn't know the pastor. His dad had introduced the young man as Pastor Owen. The order of service was almost identical to what it had been twenty years ago. After the announcements, everyone sang "Happy Birthday" to Mrs. Grace as she was presented with a bouquet of flowers. The songs they sang were more modern than he remembered, but he easily followed the words on the screen at the front.

When it was time for family prayer and share, a man stood up. Joe recognized the voice as Mr. Reggie's, his Grade Six Sunday school teacher. He stood up, and with a catch in his voice said, "We've been praying for Joe Parker for a lot of years. And I just want us to thank God that Joe is here today and that he's going to share with us how he came to the Lord." Mr. Reggie sat down as the congregation started clapping. Joe looked over at his mom and saw that she was crying. Then he was crying because he was thankful that her tears were tears of joy.

Joe made his way to the front. After Pastor Owen introduced him, he prayed that the Lord would speak through Joe. Once again, Joe's nervousness disappeared as he started to speak and tell his story. He had started including a description of his early abuse, and now he added the recent event of Steve's death and Stevie's injuries. He looked out at the people who had known him as a child—at men his own age who had been his childhood friends, and at strangers he had never met.

"Why do I tell my story? Well, it needed to be told to you folks today. You see, I want you to know and recognize God's grace and faithfulness. All these years I have been doing it my way. I was selfish and did things that hurt others. I turned my back on the Lord and did what pleased me. Yes, I went to jail. Yes, I was punished. But I was still a guilty sinner. Many of you folks have prayed and stood with that amazing couple sitting down there. They're sitting in the same place where all of us Parkers sat when I was young. That man beside my dad is my gramps. He and his family were praying for me too, the same way they prayed for their son, my bio dad. And God answers prayer. He is faithful, my friends. He loves us, and His grace is enough to change any life that needs changing.

Pastor Owen joined Joe on the platform. He stepped to the side as Pastor Owen spoke.

"Thanks, Joe. Your dad told us that the Lord has touched you in a mighty way." He looked out at the congregation. "You can see this young man. He's giving all the glory to the Lord for his changed life. Joe knows what it's like to be in prison, but he also knows there's a worse prison than any he spent time in. Jesus breaks us out of that prison. He sets us free from the chains of sin and death. If you have never come to Him, or if you've wandered far from Him, you need to come today. Usually we have a closing hymn, but today a song is going to play. You've probably heard "Chain Breaker" on the radio. The first few times Joe gave his testimony, this song was sung or played at the end of his message, without any request or planning on his part. Seth Parker tells me this song has become Joe's favourite.

"So let's sing. The words are on the screen … or just listen, which is fine too. Maybe you want to pray for a loved one who doesn't know the Lord. Maybe it's time for you to come to Him. If you'd like to come forward for prayer, someone will be here at the front to pray alongside you. Joe listened as the song played. He watched as people came to the front. Pastor Owen prayed and gave the benediction.

Joe made his way to where his family was sitting. The pew in front of them was empty, so he slid into it and turned to them. He looked at his parents and Gramps and down the row to his sister and brother. Overcome with emotion, he bowed his head and started to cry. He felt a hand on his shoulder and looked up to see Seth. Sitting on the edge of the pew, he had reached over to Joe. Joe smiled as Seth asked the Lord to give his son wisdom and direction and to bless his ministry.

• • •

SUMMER WAS COMING TO an end. Joe had thought long and hard about his future. He often thought about Gramps and Carl's suggestion that he attend Bible school. Joe had talked to Pastor Brad about the possibility, and Brad challenged him to develop some goals for his future. Joe found himself with more questions than answers. What about being a pastor? He couldn't see himself in that role. He asked Brad what he thought about his being some kind of counsellor. Brad looked at Joe and said, "You know, Joe, if you pursue a career in counselling, your schooling will entail a course that has you looking at your own life. It might be hard."

Joe's reply made Brad smile. "That couldn't be a bad thing, could it?"

Together he and Brad had discussed his taking a one-year leadership course. Many schools offered a year of in-depth Bible teaching and experience working in a variety of ministry settings. Brad was most familiar with one at a camp and conference centre called Clear Springs, which was affiliated with a nearby Bible college. Credits earned at the camp could be counted toward a diploma. Joe decided to apply to that program, knowing that because it was late in the summer, it could already be filled. He hoped to have enough money for the tuition and residence fees.

When Joe mentioned his criminal record, Brad offered some advice. "I've thought about that too. Rather than just send off an application, I think we should call and ask for a meeting with the director of the school. We're running out of time. Most likely you'll have to meet with the board of directors and have some specific references." So it was decided that Brad would talk to the director and make arrangements for a meeting.

When discussing goals, Brad asked Joe another question. "Joe, do you see yourself getting married someday?"

Joe was quick to reply. Lately he'd been thinking about just that. "You think I'd ever find someone to marry me?"

"That didn't answer my question, Joe."

"Well, as a matter of fact, yes. I want that to be in my future, and I've got a crazy idea."

Brad looked at him. "Bring it on, Joe. What's your idea?"

"I want to marry Shea."

"Does Shea know this?"

"Of course not."

"Do you love her?"

Joe hesitated before he answered. *At least he isn't asking hard questions.* "Yes, I love her. Not the crazy 'I've got to be with you' kind of love, or the 'I can't live without you' kind of love. I love her because of who she is. Because she loves the Lord. It would just depend on whether or not she could love me that way. I know what marriage is supposed to look like, Brad. I know it's not easy. Look at my life. A year ago this would be the farthest thing from my mind, but now I want to love a wife the way Christ loves His church."

"So do you have a plan?" Brad was shaking his head. He'd never heard of anything quite like this. But who was he to judge? His relationship with Jen hadn't been very traditional. When they decided to marry, it happened quickly. Both he and Jen believed that there are three important things in marriage: that you marry in the Lord, are sure of His leading, and make a lasting commitment to each other.

"Kind of. It can't happen right away. I was thinking I could approach her about it at Thanksgiving. She'll tell me what she thinks. If she wants to plan toward marriage with me, I think we'd be looking at next summer. She's not the shy young girl I took advantage of three years ago, and I'm not the man I was then. She'll send me running if she thinks I'm out of line. But I can't run too far because I'll need to see Stevie.

● ● ●

GRAMPS SAT IN HIS chair waiting for Joe to get home from work. The director of the college program had called. When Gramps told him Joe was working, he asked if it would be okay to call him on his cellphone. Gramps said to try. They were baling hay at the farm today, their third cut of the season. Gramps wondered what the decision was.

Pastor Brad had been with Joe when he met with Ray Hurst, the director of the program. After that, he was interviewed by the program's admissions team. The biggest challenge was to discuss all his charges and incarcerations in an informal meeting with the school's board of directors. He had shared his story and given excellent references. Two police officers and three pastors who knew him well had spoken to the fact that Joe was a changed man.

Joe hurried through the door with a smile on his face. "Gramps, they accepted me! I start the week after Labour Day. You should have heard what Mr. Hurst told me. To start off, right until the day I applied, they had no positions. Then someone backed out, and Gramps, three people … all three people on the waiting list decided on other programs, so there was room for me.

"The board was really concerned about my criminal record, even with the interview and my references. They had pretty well decided they couldn't take a chance on me. Then they went over my application again. They noticed the speaking engagements in the 'Experience in Ministry' section. One of the ladies said to wait a minute and pulled out her cell phone. She called her son and asked the name of *that guy* who'd shared his testimony at her church's last men's breakfast. She hung up the phone, Gramps, looked at the others, and said that she thought they better consider accepting me. She said that when I was at the breakfast, it was evident the Lord was using me. And she told them I have a *reputation* for that happening all over the place. Oh Gramps, all this worked out. Can you believe it?"

Gramps just smiled.

• • •

THERE WAS NO TIME off on Labour Day at the farm. Joe was busy harvesting the garden. When Joe talked to Jeff that morning, he apologized again that he was deserting them with some of their busiest days in the fields ahead.

Jeff brushed him off. "Will you stop it? You've worked hard all spring and summer. We'll manage just fine. The fellow I had last summer is back in the area and said he'll be glad to work again if we need him."

Joe finished off the week, and when he fell into bed Friday night, he looked forward to Saturday. Carl and Jeff had planned a big barbeque to send him off to school. Everyone was welcome, and a crowd was expected. Joe looked forward to the potluck salads and desserts that would compliment hamburgers and hot dogs. Most of all, he looked forward to gathering with his friends.

• • •

AS HE SAT IN CHURCH Sunday morning, Joe thought back to the evening before. This town, this church, never ceased to amaze him. Last night at the end of the evening, some had gathered around a bonfire, and others sat in groups just talking. Carl had blown a whistle to get everyone's attention.

"Everybody, listen up." Joe was surprised that Carl's voice carried. He turned to Joe. "Joe, I could see when I first met you that you're a special guy. It must be those grey eyes that are so much like Joe Senior's." Everyone laughed. "In just a short time, you've become part of us. Besides the good work you've done on the farm, you're an asset to our whole community. Between the church here in Souton and the one in Foxhill, you've brought great blessing. You've also shown us how the Lord can change a man. We've taken up a collection, Joe. We call it a love offering, and we're giving it to you because we know you'll use it wisely as you keep following the Lord." When he handed the basket to Joe, everyone broke into cheers and applause. Joe stood in amazement, trying to take in all that was happening.

• • •

JOE FELT GRAMPS POKE him to bring him back to the present. He looked to the pulpit where Brad was speaking. "And so, Joe, if you don't mind, we're just going to say a special prayer for you. Tomorrow's a big day. You're heading off to school for the first time in what ... fifteen years?" Joe was once again overwhelmed by what the Lord was doing in his life.

Chapter Sixteen

JOE SLOWED THE CAR AS HE TURNED INTO THE DRIVEWAY JUST PAST THE SIGN THAT READ, "Clear Springs Camp and Conference Centre." Both he and Gramps took deep breaths as they rolled down their windows and entered what looked like a wooded paradise. The trees formed an arch above them, and the light from the morning sun danced through the leaves. After about two hundred metres, the road opened to a large grassy field. Joe followed the signs to the office and stopped as a man approached them.

"You must be Joe. I'm Bill. Your group meets up at Riverside Hall. The first large building on your left. You'll see the cars parked alongside of it."

Joe continued up the road and then stopped to pull in beside a row of cars. He turned off the engine and sat for a moment. "Well, here we are, Gramps. A new experience for me."

"Are you scared, Joey?"

Joe laughed. "No, Gramps. I've been escorted into about a dozen different institutions in my life. I'll never forget how scared I was the first couple of times, and maybe again the first time I went to prison. This, my dear gramps, will be a piece of cake. See how young some of those kids look?" They looked at the group of young adults milling around in front of the building.

"Well, I'll be praying. Some of them might be struggling, and you can help them."

"Thanks, Gramps. I hope so ... I mean, not that they're struggling, but that I might be able to help them."

Joe popped the trunk and got out of the car. He handed the keys to Gramps as he pulled out his duffle bag. Joe felt like he was going to camp. He had everything on the list of things they said to bring. He picked up the plastic suit bag that held his dress clothes and shut the trunk. Last night, his uncle had discussed Joe's need for a car. He said he had spoken for one at the dealership that he thought Joe would like. It would be waiting for him when he got home in a month. He told Joe to schedule his driver's test online. Kevin would drive him to Coverton when he came home at Thanksgiving.

A group of guys made their way over to the car. "You must be Joe," one of them said.

Joe introduced himself. "Joe Parker." The others nodded and said their names. Joe turned and gave Gramps a hug. "Thanks, Gramps. For everything."

"You're welcome, Joey. Take care." Gramps climbed into his car and drove slowly away.

"Well, Joe-y"—the guy who introduced himself as Dillon was talking—"I hope you don't mind a roommate, because it's you and me for the next eight months. The rooms are upstairs. I'll show you which one is ours. This morning we meet in Riverside Hall, right through those doors, at 10:00."

As they reached the room, Dillon spoke again. "Have you ever seen a room this small for two people?"

Joe smiled as he entered the room. It was twice as big as some of the small cells he'd lived in. Sometimes they held three people. "Matter of fact, I have."

"There are all kinds of stories going around about you. The rest of us spent some time together for orientation last weekend. Pete Grant's father is on the board, and he overheard his parents talking about you." Dillon didn't seem able to take his eyes off the tattoos on Joe's hand. "How old are you anyway? Did you really spend time in jail?"

Joe was quiet for a minute. Dillon kept looking at him. "I have a past, Dillon, and that's what it is. My Bible says, "... *if anyone is in Christ, the new creation has come: The old has gone, the new is here!*" (2 Corinthians 5:17). I'm not proud of my past. I'm glad to share my story, but only to show people that God takes guilty sinners, proud and arrogant people who care only for themselves, and changes their lives. I'm thirty-three. I guess I'll be the old man around here. But I consider myself to be a baby Christian."

Dillon wasn't sure what to say at that point. He told Joe that the washrooms were down the hall on the left and disappeared.

• • •

JOE COUNTED EIGHTEEN OTHERS sitting around tables in the large meeting room. This was Riverside Hall, according to the sign over the entry. He sat at a round table with Dillon and two other guys he'd met outside. He saw a set of double doors in the middle of the wall on the far side of the room. He had watched as ladies came through that doorway, singly or in groups of two or three. *Their dorm must be over that way,* he thought.

Joe looked around the room and smiled. Such a variety of students. Some looked very young, but there were a couple who could be closer to his age. What was he ...

fourteen, fifteen years older than the youngest of them? Well, at least he wasn't thirty-five yet. When he was young, he thought that thirty-five was ancient. Joe turned to the door as he heard it open. Mr. Hurst, dressed in jeans and a t-shirt, hurried through the door, apologizing for his tardiness. Joe noted that he was in fact five minutes early, according to the clock. *I guess I'll have to make sure I'm on time for things around here.*

Mr. Hurst sat on a stool at the front, behind a simple wooden lectern. He looked around. "Twenty students. The biggest group in our four-year history. One more young lady will be joining us this evening. You met Liz last weekend. She had a family gathering in Kingston yesterday and is travelling back today." He pointed to Joe and said, "I'll introduce you to Joe Parker." Joe noticed that a man and a woman came through the doors and sat at a table at the back. "And here are the remaining two members of our faculty: Claire Simpson and Logan Hall. Welcome. I'll introduce myself. I'm Ray. I've heard a few "Mr. Hursts" here today, and I'd like you to call me Ray. I expect respect as the director. I in turn will respect you, and very importantly I expect you to respect each other. Let's begin our time together with prayer."

Claire Simpson led the group in an ice breaker. "We call this *pick your question*. There are twenty-two of us here, so please, no long answers. I have three questions, and you choose which one you want to answer. Before you answer the question, you have to say your name and where you're from."

Claire wrote the questions on the board and read them when she was finished.

1. Why are you here at Clear Springs today?
2. What was your best day of this past summer and why?
3. Tell about a bad experience that you came through, one you wish had never happened.

Joe looked at the list. He could answer the first one, but he would like to tackle one of the others. He listened as Claire answered question one. She then called on Ray, and then on her colleague Logan. They were part of the ice breaker too. And then one by one she called names from a list. Joe tried to remember the names and listened carefully to each person's answer. He wondered if he had been forgotten when Claire missed his name alphabetically.

With a few exceptions, most of the others answered question one. Joe realized it was hard sometimes to talk about personal things, but he was glad to get to know the others better. Finally, Claire called his name. He had been added to the end of list after his late registration. Everyone had stayed seated as they answered their question, and he did too.

"My name is Joe." Joe paused and almost laughed. He had been about to add, "and I'm an alcoholic." His thought was *Thanks, Lord. That would have been interesting*. "Where am I from? Well, I'm originally from Toronto. I grew up in Harper, which is a small town up that way. I've lived in quite a few other places, but today I came here from Souton. It's a small town over by Coverton. I guess I'll answer question two. I'd like to answer them all, but that's against the rules.

"My best day this past summer happened a couple of weeks ago. I told my story at the church I went to from the time I was adopted at six to when I started running away at thirteen. My family still goes there. My Gramps, who some of you guys saw today, brought me there that Sunday. I only reunited with my Gramps five months ago. He's my bio dad's father, and I hadn't seen him since I was six. As soon as I entered the church, I remembered the past. The smell. The colours. The smiles on all these people's faces. My family was all around me, with my gramps right in there with them. All of us believers. It was amazing. I shared my story. I like to share my story, not that it's much of a story, but I looked out at those people and knew that many of them had been praying for me for years and years with no good news coming in. Well, I was just overwhelmed. I thanked them.

"Before I sat down, the pastor came to the front and reminded everyone that they needed the Lord. They played my favourite song, and then he gave an invitation. People came to the front. I left the platform and sat down facing my family in the pew in front of them. I looked down the row and saw my dad, my mom, the rest of my family, and my gramps. I just bowed my head, thanking God that I was there. And, of course, I was bawling my eyes out." Everyone laughed. "And then my dad, who had prayed for years for me to come to Jesus, put his hand on my shoulder and prayed for me. I had lots of great days this past summer, but that was the best." Joe looked at Claire. "Oh! I'm sorry I took so long."

Claire laughed and said, "Thanks, Joe. You kind of made us all wish we'd been there."

The rest of the morning was filled with handing out papers and discussion. There was a list of rules and regulations, which Ray assured them would be posted in each dorm room. Joe studied the daily schedule and daily chore list. The general upkeep at the school was, for the most part, the responsibility of the students. They were assigned to cleaning and kitchen duties on a rotating basis.

The daily schedule began at 7:00 a.m. with an optional prayer meeting. It showed meal times and a compulsory chapel at 9:00 a.m. On weekdays, the only free time would be from 3:30 p.m., after classes, to 10:00 p.m., when everyone should be settled in their rooms. Students were allowed to leave the grounds after 3:30. A student was to notify the kitchen if they were missing supper. If it was their night for kitchen duty, the student must arrange for a substitute. Students asked questions, and the faculty answered them. At 12:30, when everyone was ready for a break, a bell rang outside to signify that lunch was ready.

Joe followed the others out the door and across the road to a long, low building. There were four eight-foot tables set up close to the kitchen. Everyone served themselves from the pots, pans, and trays placed on a counter that stretched across the front. It was a good meal. The cook appeared, and Logan introduced her as Millie Spark. She read five names from the chore list—the same list they had each been given. "Thank you, folks, for joining me in the kitchen." The other four groaned, but Joe was glad his name was on the list. When he went into the kitchen, he noticed the big industrial dishwasher.

"Anyone else want to tackle that monster?" Joe asked. The other four chosen ones shook their heads as Joe laughed. He thoroughly enjoyed his time in the kitchen.

By 4:00 p.m., Joe felt that he was experiencing information overload. The courses offered at Clear Springs were standard. Twenty new students would have classes together, eat together, and work together. That afternoon, they had received course outlines, textbooks, and class schedules. He was assigned to a prayer group. He and three other men would meet for prayer and support every evening before bed. Joe was looking forward to everything that was on the schedule.

After supper, Joe manned the dishwasher again. Millie came over to him as he was unloading the last tray. "You've done this before?" Joe noted the question in her voice.

"Yes, I have."

"At a camp?"

"No. At a detention centre. I worked in the kitchen during one of my longer sentences. But I got fired. It was a really good job."

Millie looked at him. "How on earth do you get fired when you're working in a prison kitchen?"

Joe couldn't believe it. He was blushing. He swallowed and answered. "Well, I was stealing garbage bags."

"What were you doing with garbage bags? Tying them together to go over the wall."

Joe laughed. "No, we filled them with water and used them as weights. Got to build those muscles up you know."

Millie just shook her head and walked away. Joe called after her. "Aren't you afraid I'll steal your garbage bags, Millie?"

It was Millie's turn to laugh. "No, Joe. There's gym equipment in the rec room downstairs."

At 8:30 p.m., Joe met with Dillon and the two guys in the room next to theirs. This time together was optional, but these guys seemed eager to take part. They were all in Joe and Dillon's room. Joe sat on his bed, and Dillon sat on his. Syd and Jason took the chairs from the desks at the end of the room and turned them around. Joe had never done anything like this before. He asked the others if they had.

Syd said a group of guys had met like this in one of the dorm rooms when they stayed in residence at a university down in the States. It had been a three-day mission conference. Dillon said at camp they had devotions at night. Jason said he went with his dad to a group on Wednesday nights for prayer and support. That put it in perspective for Joe. *I guess I have had an experience like this.* As Joe led their time together that night, he thought about his Tuesday night group. He would miss that group of men.

Here at Clear Springs, they would take turns leading. They talked about things they needed to pray about. They all prayed, and Joe couldn't contain his excitement. At the end, he closed off. "Oh Lord, I'm so excited to be here. Thank you that you worked miracles so I could come. Lord, we don't know each other well, but we are brothers in you. Bind us together, Lord, with your great love. You know our hearts. Keep them true to you. In Jesus' name. Amen."

● ● ●

RAY HURST SAT TALKING to his wife at the kitchen table. The kids were all in bed. Ray had stayed over at the school for supper. He didn't often, but today he wanted to make sure the students were settling in as expected. For the past four years, he and Heidi had lived in this three-bedroom house on the grounds at Clear Springs. It was a great place to raise kids. Heidi realized Ray's need to be at the school, but it had been a rough day for her. She home schooled the kids, who were twelve, eleven, six, and three. After a summer of practically living outdoors, they weren't impressed with getting back on schedule. She smiled at Ray. Just having him there made things much easier.

Thinking back over the day, Ray reflected on the group coming in this year. He wanted all these students to leave in April firmly rooted in their faith. He wanted them to see that the Lord is real and experience Him working undeniably in their lives. "Heidi, remember that guy Joe I told you about? Who we prayed about?"

"Oh! I do. Did he come?" She saw Ray nod his head. "How did he do today?"

"Heidi, he's hard to describe. Even after having met him for the interview, I was afraid he was going to come barrelling in. You know, we've met people like that. They tell their testimony and seem almost proud of their past sins. I knew his references all described him as humble, like he doesn't even realize the effect he has on people. You should see him. This tall, skinny guy with prison tattoos on his hands. He's only thirty-three, but he looks over forty. He goes to recovery meetings, Heidi. He was deep into drugs and alcohol. After he was finished in the kitchen tonight"—Ray stopped speaking, thinking back to what he had seen— "you should have seen him in there. Totally efficient. He even had Millie laughing. After he was finished, I asked him to come into my office for a bit.

"You know how we have testimonies after the singing and devotions during chapel? We usually wait until week two to start them, but I asked him to share his story tomorrow morning. I asked him, and he said yes. He said it's easy to tell his story. He always starts out nervous, but he says as soon as he opens his mouth, he isn't nervous anymore." Ray paused and shook his head. "You have to meet him. He says he loves to tell his story because he knows it's the Lord who changed him. And he always mentions the people who love him and prayed for him for years. And he wants us to sing "Chain Breaker" at the end of chapel.

"That wasn't all. He shared something else with me tonight. When I told him I was coming home to put the little kids to bed, he asked how old they are. I told him, starting at Sam and Angie and giving their ages. I told him that they stay up a little later, but Rosie and Eddy are only six and three, and I really hear about it in the morning if I'm not here to tuck them in at night. He said to me, 'Even Eddy?'

"I admitted that Eddy usually goes along with what Rosie says. Joe got really quiet, looked at me, and said, 'I have a three year old son.' He didn't go into details. When I asked him if he visited with him, he told me, 'I just met him five months ago. There was a bad accident, and his dad was killed. Stevie was hurt badly, but now he's doing okay. I'm just giving him and his mom time to heal. At Thanksgiving, I want to visit her and see if she'll consider marrying me.' He walked out at that point. If I hadn't seen him in action all day, I would have thought he had a problem or something. But Heidi, I think that young man is seeking the Lord every step he takes."

● ● ●

THE SMALL CHAPEL WAS packed on Tuesday morning. *Compulsory Attendance*—that's what the rules said. Ray led the first part of the service. When they finished a second song, he explained that part of the chapel services in the future would be the sharing of their testimonies. "I talked to Joe last evening and asked him if he would share his testimony this morning. He calls it his story. He agreed. I think you all have some questions about him and how he came to be at Clear Springs. Joe, the pulpit is yours."

Joe smiled as he looked out at his fellow students. "Please pray with me." The prayer was simple. "Lord, thank you for putting us here, in this specific moment, at this specific place. Thank you for saving me. For giving me a new life full of peace, joy, love, and all the wonderful things your Holy Spirit gives. Father, I ask that we might be sensitive to you this morning. Open our hearts. I pray that we will experience you in all of your majesty. And Lord, if by chance there is anyone here who has not put their trust in you, we pray that today may be the day of salvation for them."

Joe told his story. He told of his childhood and teenage years. He told about the abuse and neglect, his fear and uncertainty, his temper and lack of both self control and remorse. He never gave excuses for the things he had done. Into his story he wove the story of his redemption. He told how even when he was far from Him, the Lord was working. He couldn't explain how three years and five months ago he had decided to stop using drugs. He simply had decided that enough was enough. He told the other students about Easter Sunday and how he had exploded on JJ. He described his anger and the way he swore and punched JJ as the thoughts and feelings of his childhood came back. At that point, Joe said, "That scared me. I thought all that stuff was gone and settled in my life, but I was wrong."

Joe went on to tell of his experience at his men's group and how he picked up his Bible and came to Christ that night. He told of his baptism and of JJ's coming to Christ after so many years. Joe spoke about his excitement about being at Clear Springs, and as always, he challenged everyone who listened to fully embrace Christ as Lord of their lives. He smiled as he heard the music for his song come over the sound system and saw the words appear on the screen.

Chapter Seventeen

JOE HAD NEVER BEEN A SCHOLAR, AND BIBLE SCHOOL WAS A NEW EXPERIENCE FOR HIM. He was fascinated by a course he was taking: Christian Life and Discipleship.

GOD, YOU, AND OTHERS, Ray had written on the whiteboard the first day. Joe read all the required material. He listened to the lectures and was an active participant in class discussions. He'd never been good at relating to people, but as he learned more about God, he began to understand himself better, and in turn he could relate to others in a new way.

Late on a Friday afternoon, when most of the students were thinking about the coming weekend, Ray asked a question pertaining to growing in Christ. Joe remembered the song "I Will Make You Fishers of Men" from his Sunday school days. He couldn't stop himself as he suddenly started singing, "Read your Bible, pray every day, and you'll grow." Everyone turned to look at him. Joe smiled. "Sorry. I couldn't help myself. Man, I wish I had practised that advice sooner." Everyone laughed, and Syd asked if he knew the last verse of the song. It was Joe's turn to laugh. "We don't have to do the actions, do we?"

Syd started singing, and everyone joined in: "Don't read your Bible, forget to pray, and you'll shrink, shrink, shrink."

Ray smiled. He loved the way this group of young people were growing together. "Well, I guess we can end with that. I'm totally amazed at the amount of sound theology you all learned at young ages."

The pace at Clear Springs slowed considerably on the weekends. Many of the students left the campus. Some went home to their families, others to visit friends. Joe took advantage of the time to relax and study. When he was in jail, time had stood still.

Here, he experienced the feeling of time flying. His weekdays were packed full of activity, and he was very content.

Being the oldest student was sometimes hard. He was far removed from the present-day youth culture, not only because of his age, but also because of his time spent in jail. Joe often spent time with the faculty or other staff. Millie from the kitchen had become his friend. He enjoyed working in the kitchen and usually found himself there at least once a day. He remembered how he hated doing any kind of work in his late teens, so he really didn't mind filling in for the others. Millie appreciated his presence. He was an efficient worker who did things well. Joe also spent time with the maintenance man, Bill Manning. Bill was pleased when he discovered that Joe could drive a tractor. Whenever Bill needed an extra hand, Joe was glad to help out.

On Sundays, a local church met at Clear Springs. About a hundred people gathered in The Barn. It was a big old barn, nicely remodelled, that provided seating for two hundred and was used as a meeting hall during the summer Bible conferences. Clear Springs had been hosting Bible conferences for sixty years and was well known across the province. Joe attended the church services there. He also took part in one of their recovery groups that met on Saturday mornings.

● ● ●

JOE LOOKED AT HIS friends in the dorm room. It was Thursday evening, and everyone was looking forward to the long Thanksgiving weekend ahead. Joe had asked to be excused from Friday's classes. When he told the guys that his cousin was picking him up in the morning, it was only natural for them to ask why.

"The big day. I go for my road test. We're going straight to Coverton. My appointment is at 9:00 a.m."

"So we better pray about that. Anything else going on?" Dillon looked at Joe.

What will they think if I tell them my plans? What kind of honest relationship do we have if I don't tell them? Help me here, Lord. Joe took a deep breath. The other guys noticed his hesitation. "Guys, I never told you I have a son." He pulled out his cell phone and showed them some of the pictures Shea had sent. They listened as he told the story. As his friends read his emotions, Joe watched their reactions. Jason wiped a tear from his eye, and he was sure that Dillon was praying for him as he spoke.

When he finished telling them about Stevie, everyone was quiet. Joe prayed silently. *Look at us, Lord. In a month you've given me precious friends. They're so young, but you use them to teach me every day. Lord, thank you for this.*

"Will you see him this weekend?" Syd broke the silence.

"That's another story." Joe looked at them.

Jason and Dillon spoke at the same time.

"Spill it, brother."

"Come on, just tell us already."

"I don't think I'll see Stevie. He's only been home from the hospital for a few weeks. Shea has been gracious in giving me the chance to be in his life, but she wants to start things slowly, like having us all go together to the park, or out for a walk. But I do hope to talk to Shea. I want to ask her if she'd consider marrying me." He heard one of the guys gasp. He thought it was Syd.

"Would that be smart?" Dillon was trying to put this together in his mind.

"Oh. No. I don't mean now. She's still reeling from Steve's death. I just want her to think about it. I know it sounds kind of unconventional, but neither of our lives have been conventional. We're both very different people from who we were four years ago. Shea loves the Lord now. I know she's praying about her future. I'll tell her what I think the Lord is showing me. She can think and pray about it. I hope she thinks it's a good plan. Maybe by the end of next summer, I'll be a married man."

Syd spoke next. "Joe, do you love her."

"I've had a long time to think about that one, Syd. There was no love in my relationship with Shea. She was a sweet girl who was insecure and wanted to please everyone. I took advantage of that. I was a selfish, self pleasing, self centred pig." Joe stopped, shaking his head. "Yes, I love her. It's not the kind of love that makes me weak in the knees or think I can't live without her. The night I accepted the Lord, I had tried desperately to leave our men's group meeting. The topic of discussion was men loving their wives. I couldn't get out of it. After the video, I decided I would tell them about Stevie. I felt so worthless and filthy. I guess I realized no matter how much I had tried to mellow out in the past three years, I was still a sinner, deep in my sin. At that point, I was glad Shea had a good husband, and Stevie had a good dad. And then, all this happened. Shea is still sweet, but she's no pushover. I belong to Christ. If she'll have me, I'll strive to be a godly husband. I'll try to love her just like Jesus loves His church. No love can be better than that."

• • •

JOE HEARD THE GRAVEL crunch in the driveway below his window. He had cracked the window open last night, taking advantage of the mild October weather. He opened it a bit more and yelled, "I'll be right down, Kev." He looked at the clock over his door as he hurried to meet his cousin.

Joe greeted Kevin with a hug. "Thanks for coming to get me. You're a half hour early, you know."

Kevin answered, "There wasn't any traffic, and I thought I needed all that time."

"I just need to get a quick breakfast. Come with me." The dining hall was already busy. Joe caught Millie's eye. "Can you find us something easy to eat on the way, Millie?"

He turned to Kevin. "You are hungry, aren't you, Kev?" Joe smiled. *Of course he's hungry; he always is.*

Five minutes later, Millie came out of the kitchen with a big paper bag and two coffees in travel mugs.

"Oh look, Joe's getting special treats from the cook," somebody yelled out.

Millie looked at Joe and smiled. "This is just some payment … for the way he fills in when you slouchers don't show up for your chores. I'll be praying for you, Joe. Pass that test."

Everyone had heard Millie. Joe shook his head and smiled as someone started chanting, "Pass that test. Pass that test." They stopped chanting as Joe and Kevin left the building. They both laughed as someone behind them said, "What test?"

Kevin had driven Gramps' car to Clear Springs. "Thanks for bringing Gramps' car, Kev." Joe said as he slid behind the wheel.

"My dad thought it would be the easiest for you to drive. You've driven it the most. Are you nervous?"

"Not at all. I had lots of experience behind the wheel that I had to unlearn, but I think I know every word in the handbook. And thanks to you and Gramps, I've had lots of practise driving the right way."

The drive to Coverton took two hours. Ten minutes before the appointment time, Joe parked in the area designated for road tests. Inside, Joe took a number and sat beside Kevin in the waiting room. Joe was called to the desk as the clock switched to 9:03. After signing some papers, he was sent to wait in the car.

Joe didn't have to wait long. A door opened on the side of the building, and two people with clipboards exited. They walked toward Gramps' car and the car parked beside it. Joe sent up a prayer: *Please, Lord. The lady, not the man.* He smiled as a big guy approached. He looked like he would be more comfortable riding a Harley down the highway than squeezing into Gramps' mid-size car. He circled the car, asking Joe to test his blinkers, brake lights, and emergency flashers. Joe did well with that … after he remembered he had to turn the key to turn the power on. The man opened the door and sat beside him. His road test began.

Kevin had been waiting fifteen minutes when he saw Gramps' car turn into the parking lot. Joe came through the front door three minutes later. He gave Kevin a thumbs up, then went to the counter. Kevin heard snatches of what was being said. The woman told Joe to read the paper carefully, because there were still restrictions on a G2 license.

Joe's next stop was the probation office. Kevin chose to wait in the car. "I brought my book. I'm not worried about time," he said as he held up his Kindle. A half hour later, Joe was back in the car, and they were on their way.

Joe was excited to be in Coverton. So much had changed over the past six months. He believed that his police encounters were behind him, and he was comfortable driving in the city. He glanced at Kevin. "Do you mind if we stop at Mary's? We could get a coffee there. Maybe a piece of pie."

"Sounds good," Kevin replied.

Joe parked on the street in front of Mary's Diner. She smiled, greeting them as they came through the door. "Joe, Kevin, good to see you two. It's been a while. Can I get you breakfast?"

Joe thought of the breakfast sandwiches, muffins, and fruit they had eaten on the way. He wasn't hungry. "Have you got any pie?" He looked at Kevin, who answered Mary's question.

"I'll have the big breakfast. And a piece of pie too." Joe shook his head, and Kevin said, "What?"

Mary laughed. "A big breakfast and two pieces of banana cream pie coming up."

"Banana cream!" Joe couldn't stop smiling. "Oh Mary! I love you."

"Sorry, Joe." Mary was smiling too. "I'm taken." She held up her hand, and Joe saw the diamond ring on her finger.

"Congratulations. Have you two set a date?"

"We sure did. No stopping that man. Kyle's daughter and her family head back to Coverton for Christmas, so we're going to have a small wedding on December 23. It's coming up fast." She looked at Joe. "You're looking good. How's school going?"

"Really good. I can't believe how much stuff I'm learning. I'm headed home for Thanksgiving. And guess what … I got my license today."

"Congratulations! Now that we know you're home, I'll try to convince Kyle to ride out for church on Sunday. Your church is really special to us. Seeing you guys get baptized, hearing your testimony, Joe, meeting your moms and dads … the Lord used all those things to bring me to Him. Two weeks ago, I got baptized at our church."

• • •

JOE PUT THE SANDWICH he'd bought for Gramps on the back seat and slipped behind the wheel. It felt good to have his license. It was a beautiful day. He rolled down his window and put his arm on the door as he prepared to drive away. He turned his head to check for traffic, and a police car was slowly going past. He made eye contact with the officer in the passenger seat, and immediately the flashers came on. The car turned quickly into the space in front of them. Joe shook his head. "They've got to be kidding." He glanced over at Kevin, who looked scared. "Sorry, Kev. This might not be nice."

"Joe Parker." Joe didn't recognize this officer, but apparently he recognized Joe. "So you got out of jail. Up to no good in no time. ID. From both of you."

Joe started to speak "I've been—"

The officer pointed his finger at Joe and said, "Shut up. If you want to argue with me, how about a new plan? Keep your hands in my sight and get out of the car. Now." The officer opened the door, and Joe got out. "Let's do this without any lip. Put your hands behind your back." Kevin watched in horror as the officers cuffed Joe and roughly shoved him into the back of the police car. He sat immobilized, not knowing what to do. He put his head in his hands. He didn't notice the second officer return to the car. There was a tap on his window, and he jumped.

The officer reached and pulled the door open. "Step out of the car." When Kevin stood in front of him, he asked for ID. Kevin pulled out his wallet and handed the officer his driver's license. His hands were shaking. "So where did you two pick up this car?"

"I beg your pardon?" Kevin asked.

The officer looked at Kevin and said, "The car. Where did you steal it from?"

"Steal it? It's my grandfather's car. Joe's grandfather's car. Joe is my cousin."

"Can you produce the ownership."

"It's in the console."

"Get it."

Kevin reached across the passenger seat and retrieved a blue card case. Gramps always kept his ownership and insurance card there. As he turned back toward the officer, he noticed Mary, cell phone in hand, walking toward them. Kevin looked at her and said with relief, "Am I ever glad to see you."

The officer glanced her way. "This is police business ma'am. Please stand back."

Mary spoke, "Well, I think maybe it's my business too. These young men just left my restaurant. They're my friends. I know Joe messed up lots in the past, but I don't think you're going to find he did anything wrong recently." She looked at Kevin and tapped her cell phone. "Don't worry, Kevin. I reached Kyle just as he was leaving downtown. He wasn't going to come here for lunch, but he's on his way now."

In the police car, Joe was having a different conversation. He knew his name was being entered into the computer to search for outstanding charges and warrants. "It's my grandfather's car. It's not stolen."

"Says here the car is owned by a Joe Wilkes in Souton."

"My grandfather. If you'd given me time to pull out my license, you'd see that I live with him. The same address."

The officer smirked. "Well, Joe, it really doesn't matter who you live with, does it? I hope you have a good alibi for last night. A crime with your MO all over it. There's even a video. You're on your way to the station, and most likely back to jail. The other guy too. When are you going to learn, Parker? Crime does not pay."

"Thanks, Lord. They won't find me in any video," Joe whispered quietly. "Thanks that your compassions never fail. They are new every morning." The officer just shook his head, obviously thinking Joe had lost it. Joe didn't see or hear the unmarked car pull up behind them.

Kyle Waters got out of the car and walked toward Kevin and a young officer he recognized as Wyatt Clark. Officer Clark noticed that Kyle smiled at Mary. "Officer Clark, you aren't going to tell me this young man is in trouble, are you?"

Officer Clark was all business. "Well, sir, this is Kevin Wilkes, who is apparently Joe Parker's cousin. We noticed Parker driving this car. Officer Morrow pulled him over, thinking it was stolen. I see now that it belongs to their grandfather. This morning, during the briefing, we heard about the arson last night. We talked about that as we set out this morning. The captain told us Parker doesn't live in Coverton anymore, but he's here in town. Looks like he had opportunity to set that fire."

"And what did Joe have to say?"

Kevin answered. "They didn't give him a chance to say anything, Sarge."

Wyatt Clark was quiet. *Oh no. Someone is going down here, and I don't think it's Joe Parker.*

Kyle walked over to the cruiser as Terry Morrow stepped out of the car. "Sarge! What brings you here?"

"A phone call from my fiancée," Sarge replied. Terry looked confused. "I see you have Joe Parker in the car."

"Yes, sir."

"Can you explain why?"

"I'm going to take him downtown for questioning about the arson last night."

"Get Joe out of the car and get the cuffs off him. And let me do the talking."

Joe smiled at Kyle as he stood in front of him. "Joe Parker, what are you smiling about? You were just sitting in the back of a cop car."

"I'm smiling because I'm very glad to see you."

"I just have two questions for you, Joe. Where were you last night between 10:00 and 11:00 p.m., and why are you in Coverton today?"

Joe thought for a moment before he answered. "Last night I was in my dorm room. My roommate, Dillon, and I meet with the guys in the room next to us. It's not compulsory, but we thought it was a good idea when they suggested doing it. For prayer and support. You know, like my men's group in Foxhill. We went later than usual last night. It's really been great. I was in bed asleep by 11:00. I had an early start this morning. Kevin came and picked me up at 7:00. At 9:00, I was at the driver examination centre. I got my G2," Joe said with a smile. "Then I checked in at the probation office. I'm headed home for the long weekend, unless I have to go to jail. This officer here says I set a fire last night. There's apparently a video."

"Yes, there's a video, Joe, but I know for a fact that the video wasn't evaluated until this morning after briefing. There was no suggestion that you were involved." Sarge looked over at Terry. "Joe, Officer Morrow has detained you without reason. What are your thoughts about what went on here? Do you want to put in a complaint?"

"Well, Sarge, it wasn't nice, but I'm kind of used to being treated like that. He didn't listen to a word I said. He was really aggressive right from the start. I'm disappointed that I'm still paying for my past. It's not fair, but I understand that. It makes a big difference when I know I didn't do anything wrong. I think Kevin was scared. I hope that other guy was easier on him than this guy was on me."

Sarge turned to look at Kevin. "What about you, Kev? You okay?"

"I'm okay, Sarge. What would have happened if you hadn't showed up?"

Sarge looked at the two police officers. "Well, it sounds like you … well, maybe not you, but Joe for sure … would have been taken to the police station and questioned. And Officer Morrow would have been in trouble for the way he treated Joe today. As soon as you said he didn't give Joe a chance to talk, I knew something was wrong. The question is, do you or Joe want to take this any further? Like a complaint or something?"

Joe and Kevin looked at each other. Joe spoke. "I just want to get home to Souton. I don't want to file a complaint." He looked at Officer Morrow. "Probably you should listen before you push your weight around. I won't worry about this anymore. I'll just hope you choose to use a little compassion next time. My Bible says I have to forgive others, like Jesus forgave me. I'm up for that. What about you, Kev?"

"Sounds like a plan, Joe."

Kyle looked at the officers. "You two could learn some things from these guys." He turned to Joe and Kevin. "You can be on your way. Congrats on getting your license, Joe."

Kevin spoke. "Mary said she's going to try to convince you to come to our church on Sunday."

"She did, did she? That probably can be arranged."

● ● ●

WHEN JOE HAD DRIVEN OFF, Kyle turned to Officer Morrow, who spoke first. "What was that all about? That loser is getting away with—"

Kyle interrupted him. "With what, Terry? Joe Parker is not the man he was when he went into prison three-and-a-half years ago." He looked at Officer Clark. "Wyatt, apart from all of Terry's presuppositions, did Joe do anything wrong today?"

Officer Clark answered quietly. "No, sir. He actually was very respectful."

"If you had taken him down to the station, Terry, you would have looked like a fool. There was no evidence to link him to the arson. He's at a Bible school, for heaven's sake. Two hours away from here. He doesn't even have a car and couldn't drive alone until this morning. You were acting on information you had more than three years ago. You have to stop treating people like scum. Do your job, but don't set people up to fight you so you can be the big cop who comes down heavy on them. Joe and Kevin are okay leaving this situation as it is. Don't defend yourself. Learn the intended lesson."

Kyle turned and walked toward the diner. Terry and Wyatt watched him greet Mary. She had just come out of the door with a takeout box, which she handed to him. They watched him give her a hug before he turned back to his car, climbed in, and drove away.

Chapter Eighteen

GRAMPS SMILED AS HIS TWO GRANDSONS CAME THROUGH THE DOOR TOGETHER. HE was glad they were friends with each other. "How did it go?" he asked, trying to read their faces.

Joe looked at Kevin, who answered. "Well, how about you tell him the good news, and I'll tell him the bad."

Joe reached into his pocket and pulled out the paper that was his temporary license. "You must have been a good teacher, Gramps. The new one will come here in the mail within fourteen days."

Gramps looked at Kevin. "And?"

"Oh Gramps! You should see what happened." Kevin told the story. As he told it, Gramps remembered the day he'd been with Joe in Coverton. As Kevin ended his report, Gramps looked at Joe.

"Are they ever going to leave you alone?"

"I hope so. Let's face it, Gramps, some of those cops have a beef with the world. Today they took it out on me. I'm glad Sarge was there. After he lit into that Morrow guy, I think they both were convinced they were lucky Sarge came along. They were believing a lie, with no evidence, and would have looked pretty stupid showing up at headquarters bragging that they'd solved the arson case. I felt bad for Kevin, but I didn't even get mad at them."

"I was too scared to be mad." Kevin broke into the conversation. "I sure was glad when I saw Mary come out of the diner with her phone in her hand. And you should have seen the look on Morrow's face when Sarge answered his question. Morrow asked what had brought him there, and Sarge answered, 'A call from my fiancée.'"

"Fiancée?"

"Yeah, Gramps. He and Mary are getting married at Christmas. Cool or what?" Kevin smiled as he thought, *And did that ever work to our advantage today.*

• • •

"ARE YOU REALLY OKAY, Joey?" Gramps asked when they were alone.

"I really am, Gramps. Unbelievable, eh? It's not like it hasn't happened for years. I used to run, or make it hard for them to get the cuffs on me. I just remember being so angry. It didn't help that there was always something they had on me to justify the arrest. But this time, just like last time, I knew there was nothing they could pin on me, and I just chilled." Joe laughed. "Was Sarge ever great."

"Well, enough talk about that. Tell me how school's going."

Joe and Gramps spent an hour catching up on each other's news. Just after they'd eaten lunch, the phone rang. Gramps looked at it. "The car dealership. Must be for you, Joey." He handed Joe the phone.

Not sure what was going on, Joe pressed *talk*. "Hi, Uncle Jay."

Gramps smiled as he went to the living room, leaving Joe to talk to his uncle. Joe came to the living room a few minutes later.

"What did your uncle want?" Gramps asked.

"As if you didn't know. He wants you, or Kev, to drive me to Foxhill to pick up my car. There's an elaborate plan to go with it. I'm fine with him keeping it in his name and putting me on as the primary driver. That way he can just add it onto his insurance, which will cost a lot less, but will still cost a lot. It's to be paid, apparently, by an unknown benefactor." Joe paused, shaking his head. "Gramps, you don't have to do that."

"Joey, I want to do this. But I'm only paying half of the insurance. I was talking to JJ about the car. He's going to pay the other half, but only till you're done school and can get a job. JJ is changing too, Joey." Gramps looked at Joe with tears in his eyes. "It's just a miracle, Joey. I prayed for him for so long. First you showed up, and then JJ came home."

Joe sent off a text asking Kevin to come back to Gramps' house. Gramps had decided that Kevin should take Joe to Foxhill.

As they arrived at the dealership, Jay met them on the lot. Kevin led him over to the car. It was an Impala, ten years old, but in great shape with low mileage. Joe slipped behind the wheel.

"I made sure we got one with lots of legroom for you." Jay was beaming.

"Thanks, Uncle Jay. It's great."

"The ownership and the insurance papers are in the glove box. It's loaded. Even has heated seats."

"I'll pay you back, Uncle Jay."

Jay just shook his head. "We'll talk about that after you graduate and get some money saved. It will all work out."

Joe thanked his uncle again, and he thanked Kevin for driving him to Foxhill. He beeped the horn as he drove off in his new car.

Joe stopped at the farm on his way back to Souton. The first thing he noticed was that Annie's fruit stand was still loaded up with produce. He looked over to her garden; there were still things to harvest. He could see an abundance of pumpkins and squash. Annie and Carl greeted him on the porch. "Joe, come in." Annie was happy to see him. "How about a piece of pie? Apple, made with our own apples?"

"You talked me into it, Annie. Did I ever miss your baking. It's so good to see you."

Joe followed them into the house, and then into the kitchen. They talked for a while, then Joe asked how Jeff was doing.

Carl answered. "Right now he's trying to get the beans off. It's a big job. He'll stop for supper about 9:00 and then work long into the night. The fellow who took your place is good, but he was headed out of town this weekend. Jeff wants them off before the middle of the week. After that, we're supposed to get some heavy rainfall."

"Could I help? Maybe not out in the fields, but with all the other work. Switching, lining up the wagons, loading into the bins, filling the trucks? I've had some practice. If you're helping, I can be your muscle. I could work all day tomorrow."

"I'll ask Jeff if he can use you. He'll give you a call when he comes in for supper."

Joe was glad to help. He owed these people after all they had done for him.

Carl asked about school, and Joe was glad to catch him up on all his news. When Joe said he was going to head back to Gramps' house, Annie said, "Hold on a minute, Joe." She left the kitchen and returned a minute later with a frozen pie. "I have to get rid of some of my rhubarb to make way for the apple. I hope you and your gramps will enjoy this."

"Oh Annie, thanks so much."

As Joe went out the door, Carl told him to pull his car up to the large door of the building closest to the house. Joe did as he was told, wondering, *What is he up to now?* Joe followed Carl into the building.

Carl spoke as he approached the corner, where three rows of picking baskets stretched over a span of thirty feet. "We've had a great harvest this year, Joe. The garden was amazing. You did such a good job." He paused as he turned to Joe. "I wasn't afraid when we hired you, but I never imagined that things would turn out as they did. Jeff, Annie, and I feel like God gave us a precious gift this summer. Every once in a while, the Lord gives us glimpses of His working in a life. We really needed the encouragement that came along with you. This getting old thing is not fun. We've tried to be faithful through the years. Having you here, watching the Lord work through you both here and at our church, has been one of the biggest blessings in our life." He reached over and squeezed Joe's shoulder. "Thanks."

Joe smiled at Carl and said quietly, "I love you guys."

Carl began dragging baskets out of the lines. "I wish you had a truck. We take a lot of this over to the food bank in Coverton, but Annie thought you better share some of the crop with the kids at the school. You can impress them. But like you said before, they might start calling you, Farmer Joe."

"I'll be proud if they call me that," Joe said as he helped dump the contents of the baskets into banana boxes. He carried them to the car, and before long, four boxes filled his backseat and two occupied the trunk. Carrots and onions shared a box. Carl said that the tomatoes were the last from the garden. They'd been picked green but were starting to ripen up. There were also fall apples, sweet potatoes, potatoes, and squash. Carl pushed the boxes in the trunk forward a little and added three large cabbages to the load.

At home, Gramps greeted him outside to inspect the new car. "Very nice, Joe. What's with all the produce?"

"It's from our garden, Gramps. I planted that stuff and weeded and irrigated. There has been so much harvested since I left. I think I got out of the hardest job. I'm to deliver it to the school." Joe stopped and exclaimed, "Oh Gramps! I almost forgot." He ran around to the other side of the car and reached down to get the pie. "Special delivery. Rhubarb. We can eat it with supper." Joe smiled as he thought, *This will be my third piece of pie today.*

Joe grabbed the phone as he entered the kitchen and heard Gramps say, "Do you mind if we leave the pie till tomorrow, Joey. It'll take an hour to cook from frozen. I was thinking we should head down to the diner for supper."

"Sounds good, Gramps. I was going to tell you I might head into the city this evening. I just have to make a phone call, and I'll be ready to go." Joe went to his room and sat down on his bed.

Stevie had stayed in the hospital for a month after the accident. His little body healed quickly. Joe was thankful that Shea kept him informed of Stevie's progress. She sent him a picture of Stevie a couple times each week. Joe had purposely not visited them in that time. Stevie was getting to know Steve's parents, and together they were working through the tragedy of Steve's death. Joe was thankful that Shea had their support. Stevie had been told about his daddy's death. Shea had talked to the hospital social worker, and she was trusting that both she and Stevie would be okay. Joe knew that it was hard for them. Now that they were settled back into their apartment in Coverton, Shea thought, and Joe agreed, that Stevie needed time to adjust to not having a father. He shouldn't have another man just stepping in to take Steve's place.

Joe listened as the phone rang.

"Hello," Shea answered the phone. He could hear Stevie squealing in the background.

"Hi, Shea; it's me, Joe."

"Joe! Good to hear from you. How's school?"

"It's been great. I'm learning so much. The kids are quite a bit younger than me, but I've made some new friends."

"Younger than me?"

"Most of them. You're getting old, you know." Joe knew his comment would make her smile. "How are you doing?"

"Some days are rough, but Stevie keeps me busy. It would be a lot harder without him."

"He's feeling okay?"

"He's getting there. His breathing is good. No sign of a head injury, but we still have to keep him slowed down because of that. The broken bones seem to hurt him some, but the doctors say everything is healing well. He's missing his daddy." Joe knew she had started to cry.

"I know you miss him too. I'm so sorry, Shea. I hate to see you hurting like this."

"Yeah, but I know he's with the Lord. If I didn't totally believe that is true, I don't think I could make it. And the people the Lord put around us are always here for us. Joe, did you know your mom came down and took us to Storytime Village. We put Stevie in a stroller, and he had so much fun. Then we picked up some McDonalds for supper and ate it here at home."

Joe smiled. *Way to go, Mom.* "No, she didn't tell me, but she has a knack for knowing what people need. Shea, I need to talk to you. I'm here at Gramps' till Monday evening. I was hoping we could have coffee tomorrow sometime, but tomorrow I'm hoping to help the farmer I worked with all summer. If I leave for Coverton in an hour or so, do you think we could talk this evening? I can wait till Stevie goes to sleep and come to your apartment. Or, if you can find someone to stay with Stevie for an hour, we can go for coffee or something." Joe prayed as he waited for Shea to answer. *Lord, if the answer is no, please help me accept it.*

Shea took a moment to answer. "Sure, Joe. I can get my friend from the apartment next door to stay with Stevie. He'll be sleeping."

"Great, I'll see you at 7:30. Thanks, Shea." As Joe ended the call, he went to join Gramps in the living room. He wondered, *What's Gramps going to think of this crazy plan?*

• • •

"YOU WANT TO MARRY her?" Gramps had kept his voice low. Joe was glad of that. They both had ordered fish and chips and were waiting for them. Joe had told him that he was going to Coverton to talk to Shea about getting married.

"Yes, I want to marry her. I think she's part of God's plan for me, and that I'm part of God's plan for her."

Gramps actually scratched his head. He looked at Joe. "You've thought about this."

"Yes."

"And prayed about this?"

Joe nodded his head.

"Help me understand, Joey. Why?"

Joe thought for a moment. "I can think of a lot of reasons, Gramps. I want to get married and have a family. I never wanted that before. I hurt so many girls. They wanted my attention, and I'd give it gladly. They said they loved me, and for me it was purely physical. I never committed. I never even said I loved them back. I know what love is now, Gramps. It's not a warm, fuzzy feeling. I've seen lots of people *fall in love* and then eventually hate each other. I think of you and Grandma, Carl and Annie, my mom and dad, Uncle Jay and Aunt Michelle. Those are long marriages. That's what I want. I don't know much, Gramps, but I know I can love Shea the way I'm supposed to. She's the mother of my son. Besides that, she's a sweet girl."

"So you do love her, Joey?"

"Well, yes I do. I love her. I don't dream about her every night, or pine for her. I know that if she thinks I'm right out of line when we talk tonight, I won't die inside. I just have a real peace about all this. I've put it in the Lord's hands, and I believe things will work out. It can't happen soon. She and Stevie are still dealing with Steve's death. I just want to let her know my thoughts. If she needs a year to work things out, that's fine."

Gramps smiled at Joe. "You're really something, Joey. I'll be praying for you."

Their fish and chips arrived. As they ate, Gramps talked about his feelings when he married Joe's grandmother. "I guarantee you, Joey, if Shea doesn't think you're totally off base and says she'll consider marrying you, your love will grow, and you'll be having some sleepless nights over the next year.

Chapter Nineteen

JOE PULLED INTO THE PARKING LOT BESIDE SHEA'S EIGHT-UNIT BUILDING. IT WAS A modern structure but not elaborate like most of the new buildings in town. He pressed the buzzer and opened the door when he heard it click. He walked up to the second floor and stood before the door of apartment 201. As he lifted his hand to knock, it opened.

"Hi, Shea."

"Come on in, Joe. I'm just about ready. Stevie was a little late going down, but he's asleep now. Josie's here to babysit."

"Shea?" She paused to look at him. Waiting for a question. "Could I maybe just look at him for a minute."

"Sure. Follow me."

Joe followed her down the hall. She paused and opened a door, and they both slipped quietly in. The room was dark, but Joe could see Stevie's face in the light from the hall. He stood still, drinking in the sight, and even the smell, of his little boy. He turned and left the room. Shea followed, shutting the door quietly behind her. She had seen the look of joy on Joe's face as he gazed at Stevie. She smiled as she realized how much Joe loved her son—his son.

"Thanks." It was all Joe could say. *Lord, thank you for Stevie. Help me be a good father. A father just like you.*

Shea introduced him to her neighbour, Josie, who was sitting on the couch and working on her laptop. "Josie, this is Joe, Stevie's biological father." Joe thanked Josie for babysitting on such short notice.

Josie smiled and replied, "I can do my schoolwork here just as easy as next door. If you need to take a little more time than an hour, don't worry. This is no trouble at all."

"Anywhere you'd like to go?" Joe asked Shea as they reached the parking lot.

"There's a little coffee shop a couple blocks away. It usually isn't very busy this time of night. We can walk."

The coffee shop was well lit. There were only two tables occupied. Joe and Shea bought their coffees and sat at a table in the back corner.

"Shea, do you mind if we pray before we talk?"

"Good idea, Joe. I've been wondering what you wanted to talk about."

Shea bowed her head and listened as Joe asked the Lord to guide their conversation, and as he thanked the Lord for the privilege of belonging to Him.

"To start off, Shea, I want to apologize to you for taking advantage of you. You were young and insecure, and I was selfish and abusive. I am so sorry."

Shea looked at Joe. She knew he wasn't the same man he was those many years ago. "Joe, both of us sinned. I had no expectations from you. I forgive you for being, as you say, selfish and abusive. Most of all, though, I thank God that He has forgiven us both for what we did. He actually turned it into a blessing, in the little person of Stevie. What else is on your mind, Joe?"

"Well," Joe began, "I've talked to a few people about this. Nobody has told me I'm out of line, but even I admit this is a little unusual. What I'm proposing doesn't have a timeline. I just want you to listen and then tell me what you think." He stopped and looked at her.

"I'm listening," was all she said.

"We go way back, Shea. I hope you can see and believe that I'm not the man I used to be. And I know you're different too. And I know you love Steve, and that he and his memory are going to always be part of your life. This is what I'm thinking ..."

Joe was able to outline his plan quite quickly. Shea sat listening, showing little emotion. Joe continued talking, telling Shea everything he had told his grandfather two hours earlier. When he stopped talking, she looked long and hard at him and said: "And you think you could love me?"

"Well, Shea, what I said is, I do love you. I have a lot of people in my life who I love— love enough to want what's best for them. When I look at you, Shea, I see a beautiful woman who is a new person in Christ. You're not the girl I used to know, the same as I'm a new man too. I never knew anything about love before. I was out for me. Selfish and foolish. The Lord is working in my life. He teaches me new things every day. I know that if you say you'll marry me, I'll love you and be faithful to you always. I hope that you would do the same to me. I love Stevie, but I want what's best for both of you. If you say no, I'll keep trusting the Lord and seeking His plan for my life."

"Why are you wanting an answer now, Joe? If this won't be happening for a year, why talk to me now?"

"I don't need an answer right now. I'm asking you to consider this possibility. I realize there are reasons why you would say no. You're young and beautiful, and I'm nine years older than you. I have a bad history, and drugs and alcohol have taken a toll on my body. You wouldn't be wrong to consider me an old man. I'm young in the Lord, but I'm learning new things from Him every day."

Joe paused to make sure Shea was still following him. She nodded her head, looking confused. "I hear what you are saying, but I'm just not sure. I'd need some time to think about this."

"I get that," Joe continued. "I just want you to think about it. I know you need more time to grieve, and I want you to remember Steve and his love for you and Stevie. We already talked about how you want to introduce me gradually to Stevie, and that will take time. Shea, I do believe I could be a good husband and father. I could love you the way a Christian man is supposed to love his wife. If I'm right out of line here, if you don't think you could ever marry me, I'll give the whole situation to the Lord and move on. I'll still be your friend, and I'm still Stevie's biological father. But if we aren't meant to be together, it will be okay."

Shea was stuck in her thoughts. *He doesn't know. I haven't kept the baby a secret, but he doesn't know.* "I need to tell you something, Joe." She paused as Joe waited for her to continue. "Two weeks before Steve died, we found out I'm pregnant. Joe, I'm having a baby. I'm due the middle of April. What do you think of that?"

Joe answered immediately. "I guess I'm thinking, *Wow, what a great gift for you.* Congratulations! And I need to ask myself what you need to ask yourself: Could Joe Parker be a good dad to two kids? With the Lord's leading, I'd like to think I could be. I'd count it a great honour to raise Steve's child … actually, his children." Joe sat thinking for a moment and then looked at Shea.

Shea spoke first. "Joe, I know I meant nothing to you when you moved into Steve's Place. You were nice to me. You flirted with me. Unfortunately, you used me. I loved you, but I honestly didn't expect anything from you. I had stopped believing anyone could love me when my dad chose my stepmother over me when I was eight. My mom had already bailed on me.

"When I found out I was pregnant, I hadn't seen you for two months. It didn't bother me that you hadn't been around. It wasn't the first time you'd disappeared like that. I knew you wouldn't be good for the baby. I figured the longer you were away, the better. When I heard about your long sentence, I was glad. I'd decided the baby would be my priority, and I'd make sure he was safe. He'd know that I love him every minute of his life. I stopped drinking and using drugs. I decided to make something of myself. I met Steve at the coffee shop at the college when I was taking a night course there.

"After a coffee date with Steve, I was sure he was different from any guy I'd ever met. It wasn't long before I realized he was *the one.* He loved me. He loved Stevie before he was even born. He always wanted only what was best for us. It was phenomenal, and when we came to the Lord, we understood who we were in Christ. His love began to rule in both our lives. And that love ran deep. I'd never experienced anything like that. It's the Lord's love, Joe." Shea paused, her eyes filling with tears. "I won't marry a man unless I see the Lord using him and see the fruit of the Spirit in his life. Give me some time, Joe. If this is the Lord's will, we'll both know it."

"I believe that too, Shea. You're right, there is a lot to sort out." He paused and looked at her. "So you'll think about this and let me know when you come to a decision?"

"I will, Joe. Thanks for giving me time. There's a lot to work out. The Findlays are in Stevie's life now. They're very excited about the baby. Joe, I know you've gone over three years without drugs, but it's going to take time for some people to believe you're a different guy. I knew the old Joe. You are so different now. I know it's the Lord working in your life."

They walked back to the apartment. Joe glanced at his watch. They'd only been gone an hour and fifteen minutes. Joe stopped and looked at the bench not far from the door of the building. "Sit with me a moment?" They sat on the bench. "Let's pray?" It was a question, and Shea nodded her assent. They sat there for ten minutes, pouring their hearts out to their loving Father.

On the way back to Souton, Joe could think of nothing but Shea. *Why should I believe she'd even consider marrying me? Look how I used her.* He went over their conversation again and again. He smiled when he remembered Shea's comment, that she had once loved him. And then he shuddered at the thought that he had hurt her. *I knew nothing about her but her name. I still don't know much. She was pretty and she was there. Then she was alone and pregnant. What a jerk I was. I don't deserve a girl like her. My son deserves a better father than I'll ever be.*

Joe harboured those thoughts on the way back to Souton. He rolled down his window, welcoming the cool air blasting against his body. His mind was racing. He remembered watching his little boy sleep. He remembered Shea's beautiful smile and the tears that welled up in her eyes as she spoke of Steve. He remembered Steve that day back in April. If he had been Steve, he probably would have pounded the guy who hurt his girl into the ground. *What's different now?* Joe asked himself. *I'm still a loser. Who am I trying to kid?*

Joe noticed a police car parked just ahead on the far side of the road. He saw the radar gun as he went by. He looked down at his speedometer and gave a sigh of relief. *Only five clicks over, I should be fine.* Joe approached a traffic light, put on his blinker, and came to a stop because the light was red. The highway turned here. He knew the corner well. He would be home in five minutes. It was a busy corner. Across the road was a modern self-serve gas station with a variety store. At Joe's right, a building sat about forty metres from the road, surrounded by a parking lot. The lot was half filled with cars. Joe really hadn't paid much attention to the sign before. He knew it said, "Barney's Junction," but in small letters beneath the name he read, "Bar and Grill." The light turned green. Joe turned the corner quickly and then turned into the parking lot of Barney's Junction, Bar and Grill.

Joe didn't start to argue with himself until he was sitting at the bar inside. The bartender asked him what he wanted. As he scanned down the lists of the drinks, he realized he hadn't had much experience ordering in a place like this. He looked at the bartender. "Could I just have a double scotch on the rocks?"

"Sure. Coming right up."

"Well, actually," Joe spoke as the man turned away, "I don't need the rocks." The bartender laughed as he kept walking. There Joe sat, looking at the glass with two shots of whisky in the bottom. He picked it up and swirled the liquid around. *This should be enough to calm me down. Just what I need.* Joe's warring thoughts went on for fifteen minutes. He thought about Shea and Stevie. Maybe he could be somebody for them. He thought about the new baby. He kept coming back to his uselessness. His total failure as a human being. *I want this drink so bad. Just enough to calm me down.*

"Seems to me you don't want that drink too badly." Joe wondered if he had spoken out loud. He looked up to see the bartender looking at him.

"It's been three years. Sad thing is, I'd rather have a line of coke." The man glanced down at the tattoos across Joe's fingers.

"You've done time?"

"Most of my adult life. What about you?"

"Just once. I'm never going back." He watched as Joe hung his head. "You don't want to go back either, do you?"

The man's words had been spoken softly, but they hit Joe hard. *Oh Lord, no. I don't want that life back. How did I end up here? I'm so sorry.* Joe looked up at the man and shook his head. "You're right. No, I don't want to go back. I got out six months ago, and I've hardly craved a drink. Outside of a couple glitches, I had a great day and evening. Then within an hour, I'm throwing everything away. I was so stuck in myself, I forgot who I belong to. Thanks for reminding me. I'm never going back either." Joe stood up. His eyes met the bartender's. "I mean it, man, thank you so much." He dropped a twenty dollar bill on the bar and walked out the door.

The night had turned cold. As he walked toward his car, Joe couldn't miss the police cruiser parked beside it. *Oh no not again … but it's not a Coverton car. Maybe I'm okay,* he thought as he approached his car. As he reached it, the door to the cruiser opened.

"I was starting to worry about you, brother." Rob looked at him as he spoke. He wasn't smiling, but Joe could tell he wasn't angry. "Are you okay? I saw you fly by me back there and I wondered what was going on. You're the only person I've seen tonight driving with their window wide open. It's cold out. I thought I better check up on you."

Joe shrugged his shoulders. "I had a great day, and it went downhill from there."

"So what went on in there?" Rob nodded toward the building.

"Does that matter?"

"I ran the plates. Car belongs to your uncle. I ran you. Seems you've had your G2 since"—he paused—"today. Were you drinking in there? There's zero alcohol allowed with that license."

"No." Joe shook his head. "Thank God." Joe stopped, realizing what he had just said. "Yes … thanks, God, and thanks to that bartender in there. It was close."

"How close?"

"Well, I sat looking at two shots of scotch in the bottom of my glass all that time. Rob, that's the first time I've wanted it like that. But really it was drugs I wanted more."

"Joe, you know how we talk about the way the Lord takes our mistakes and turns them for good. To me it seems like maybe He was letting you go through some stuff today to show you that you're still an addict. Maybe He wants to show you that you can't be complacent and think you're above getting drunk. We're all just one fail away from sinning."

"I get what you're saying, Rob. I was really beating myself up tonight. I forgot who I am in Christ."

"Do we need to get together to talk?"

"Thanks, Rob, but I do have tons of support. I need to talk to Brad about something else. I'll work this through with him at the same time. It's kind of connected. I'm home till Monday, but I plan to help Jeff at the farm tomorrow. I'll catch you up eventually."

"Maybe you, Tina, and the baby can visit me at Clear Springs some weekend. Sundays I go to church right there. Not a very big congregation, but they have a nursery." He paused and looked at his friend. "Thanks for being here. And thanks for not thinking the worst of me."

"I was praying hard, Joe."

"That's what brothers are for, right? Thanks, Rob. I really mean it. Nice car, eh? Uncle Jay bought it for me, and Gramps and my bio dad paid the insurance. When I graduate, I'll work on paying them all back."

Joe got into his car. Before he drove away, he picked up his phone to send Brad a text. *Busy?*

He waited. A minute later his phone buzzed.

Not too. Need to talk? Come to my house? Jen went to the show in Coverton. Won't be home till close to midnight. Need a ride?

Joe was glad he hadn't touched that drink.

I've got some wheels. Be there in five.

Brad was standing on his porch when Joe pulled into the driveway. "Nice car," he said as Joe climbed out. "And somebody must have got his license."

"It was a productive day," Joe answered.

"But something went wrong?"

"Really wrong. Thanks for being here when I need you."

Joe followed Brad into the kitchen. Brad grabbed two bottles of water from the fridge, and they sat at the kitchen table. "It's been awhile. You've been going to meetings?"

"Yes, every Saturday morning. Right at the church that meets at Clear Springs. It's good."

"So what happened tonight, Joe? That's why you're here, right?"

"Yes. It was quite an evening. I need to talk to you about that, but I did end up at the bar down the road with a drink in my hands. A drink in my hands, wishing it was drugs instead of alcohol." Joe watched Brad's face as he finished his confession.

Brad closed his eyes. Joe thought he was about to cry, but he took a deep breath and opened his eyes. He looked at Joe and said, "And?"

"I'll start with the end, but I need to tell you the whole story. I sat there for fifteen minutes just looking at the drink. Then the bartender came and talked to me. The conversation was short, but I soon realized I couldn't drink it. I was so close. So close. I'm thinking back and asking myself how I could have gone so far. Why on earth would I do that?"

"Joe, do you want to tell me what else has been going on?"

"For sure. That's the other reason I'm here. I was planning to talk to you about Shea."

For the next forty minutes, Joe shared. He told Brad everything, all of the events of the night, in detail. He described his feelings right up until the time he pulled into the Barney's Junction parking lot.

Brad was quiet for a long time. "Sounds like you beat yourself up tonight. I don't know why it's so easy for us to do that. You went from high to low in thirty minutes. Look at the emotions you went through in that time. I can't imagine how you felt. You really got stuck on putting yourself down. You say you aren't deserving of a chance with Shea, and that she doesn't deserve you because you're so awful, or that you can't be a good dad. You were sure you needed drugs to settle down. If you couldn't have drugs, the drink would do. But you know different, Joe. You stopped listening to the lies, and it worked. You did not drink it." He stopped. "That's a success, Joe. Now you realize that urge can hit you anytime. Next time, call your friend here on the way into the bar, not on the way out."

"Thanks, Brad. I'm glad you were here for me."

Brad had listened as Joe described the conversation with Shea that evening. He was glad that Joe had told Shea that she should take as much time as she needed. He took Joe back to his thoughts of Shea.

"So how long are you willing to wait for her?"

Joe's answer came quickly. "I love her, Brad. I'll wait until she says she won't marry me, and then a little longer, hoping she changes her mind."

The two men prayed together and then discussed some specific things that Joe should pray about on his own. Joe wrote a list as they talked. They were still talking when Jen arrived home at 11:45. Joe greeted Jen and then picked up the list and folded it into his pocket.

"Thanks, Brad. I have to get home. I have to be at the farm at 7:00. See you both on Sunday."

Gramps was in bed when Joe arrived home. He went straight to his room. Before he climbed into bed, he went over the list he and Brad had made:

List: Concerns. Things to Pray About
1. People's reactions and trust of Joe: The Findlays, The Griffins
2. Stevie's health
3. The coming baby
4. Getting to know Shea better
5. Future plans, school, employment
6. Wisdom as we consider marriage

Joe looked over the list he held in his hands. He was tired, and his alarm would go off in six hours. He put the list on his nightstand and climbed into bed. He closed his eyes and started to pray. "Thank you, Lord, for all that happened today. Even the bad stuff. Help me to just trust you."

Chapter Twenty

ANNIE WAS ON THE PORCH WHEN JOE ARRIVED AT THE FARM IN THE MORNING. HE WAS excited to be there, wondering what he'd be working on today. Jeff was nowhere to be seen, so Joe wandered over to the house.

Annie greeted him with a smile. "Good morning, Joe. Have you had your breakfast?"

"I did have a good breakfast. Not much sleep, but Gramps had pancakes ready. What are you doing out here so early?"

Annie smiled again. "This is my favourite time of the day. I like to be out here to see the sun come up. The boys are inside eating if you want to join them. Jeff says they'll start at eight this morning. He was in the field until midnight."

Joe looked to the east. He noticed a narrow slip of gold beginning to show above the horizon. "I won't go inside, Annie. I'd rather share your sunrise with you."

Together they took in the beauty as the sun rose slowly and appeared through the darkness. The bright yellow light became a round white ball rimmed with gold. Joe had never seen the sun so big. There was a mist over the land, and it gave the effect of rippling water. They watched the landscape as the trees and farm buildings in the distance seemed to grow from the earth and then cast changing shadows.

They had watched amazed for fifteen minutes when Joe turned to Annie. "I haven't watched many sunrises, Annie, but this is phenomenal. Is it always so beautiful?"

Annie thought for a few seconds. "I love sunrises, Joe. Do you know the verse, *"From the rising of the sun unto the going down of the same the Lord's name is to be praised. The Lord is high above all nations, and his glory above the heavens"* (Psalm 113:3–4, KJV).

"I do know that verse, Annie. There's a song that goes like that."

"Really?" Annie smiled. "It must be a new one. I'd like to hear it. Joe, the sunrise reminds me of the Lord and His goodness. You asked if it's always so beautiful. Today it looks peaceful to me. Have you ever seen a sunrise with a storm on the way, with the light breaking through swirling clouds? I think it's even more beautiful than this, but maybe a little scary at the same time. And what about the days when the sun just doesn't shine at all? I used to hate those days. So dark and dreary. Like days when I hurt, or I get mixed up and can't remember things. Or when I think about the sad things in my past. The sun always rises, Joe. Sometimes the sun is hidden from us, but it always rises. It's just a reminder to me that even when it seems the Lord is distant, He's right here."

Joe looked at Annie. She was smiling, still staring at the horizon. Joe decided right then he would find the song she had mentioned, even if he had to tune up his singing voice in order for her to hear it.

"Joe, could you sing it for me?" She turned to look at him.

"You mean the song that goes with the verse?"

"Yes, that one." She nodded and smiled.

Joe smiled back. He didn't quite remember the tune, but he knew the words. He also knew that Annie would appreciate the song no matter how well he sang it. Joe sang the song and watched the smile on Annie's face as she listened, looking out across the farm. When he finished, she turned to him.

"Thanks, Joe, you have a lovely voice. Don't ever forget that verse. Never stop praising Him."

"Thanks for sharing your sunrise with me, Annie." Joe thought back to what had happened last night and silently prayed. *And thank you, Lord, for giving me this sunrise. And this lesson from Annie.*

• • •

JOE WOKE WITH A start. *What on earth? That buzzing? Oh, my clock.* Joe reached over to turn the alarm off. He realized he had accidentally set it to the buzzer last night when he had set the alarm for 9:00 a.m. He showered and dressed quickly, joining Gramps in the kitchen. The clock read 9:20.

"Wondered if you were going to come alive. What time did you get in last night? I don't usually hear your alarm."

Joe laughed. "That was some wake-up call. Usually my music wakes me up a little more gently. I think it was close to 1:00 when I got in. Did you have a good sleep, Gramps?"

"Slept fine."

Joe knew that's all he'd get out of Gramps. Gramps usually went to bed late and got up early. He often said, "Why stay in bed if I can't sleep?" Joe had talked to Gramps the morning before about his time at Barney's. There hadn't been time to tell him about his conversation with Shea. It seemed like there wouldn't be time this morning either.

"Gramps, I'm sorry I haven't been able to talk to you about what Shea said. There's not really time right now to do that; hopefully later this afternoon we can talk."

• • •

IT'S SO GOOD TO be here. Joe relaxed and enjoyed the service. He had greeted Sarge and Mary outside the building. He wasn't surprised to see JJ walk in just before the service started. Joe had nudged Gramps, and they slid over to make room for him.

Michelle and Jay were ready to host a family dinner, and they invited Sarge and Mary to join them. As Joe looked around the dining table, he saw that there was more room and less noise without Aunt Marge and her family—not that he minded the noise and lack of arm room. He thought about Easter. So much had happened since then. His eye caught JJ's, and they both smiled.

JJ, Gramps, and Joe didn't stay long after they finished the dishes. Kevin had asked Joe if he wanted to hang out, but Joe replied that he had to spend some time with Gramps. He did tell Kevin that he should visit him at school. He told him he was welcome to stay overnight if he wanted to. "There's lots to do. A bunch of sports stuff, canoes and kayaks, and some good fishing if you're interested."

Kevin said he'd come for sure, and Uncle Jay made everyone laugh by asking if he could come too. Joe took the question seriously. "I'll ask. Maybe we could have some of our Wilkes/Parker men's bonding time." This made Kevin and Gramps laugh. Joe said, "Don't worry, Uncle Jay, JJ, we'll fill you in on our private joke eventually."

Joe was glad that JJ came back to Gramps' house with them. They spent the afternoon talking. Joe told them what had happened in his meeting with Shea. He also talked about his time at Barney's Junction. Most of all, he stressed God's goodness in working out all that had gone on. It was a good afternoon.

As Joe went to bed that evening, he thought of Annie's sunrise yesterday. As he lay in bed, he went over the words to the song. He had learned it when he was about ten. He smiled as he remembered Annie's comment. *Must be a new one,* she had said.

Oh Annie, I will never stop praising Him. Joe drifted off to sleep with the words of the song settling his thoughts.

• • •

"WELCOME BACK. DID YOU have a good weekend?"

When Joe heard Ray's voice behind him, he ended his struggle to take the box of apples out of his trunk. He slipped it back into its place and turned toward Ray and Heidi, who had stopped to talk with him. Joe heard squeals and laughter coming from the other side of the dining hall. He could imagine their kids climbing all over the play equipment.

"I did have a good weekend. So much happened. All this produce is from the farm I work at. In fact, it's from my garden ... well, from my and Annie's garden. She was the brains behind it, and I was the muscle. Friday was a crazy day. Got my license. Got a car. Almost got arrested." Joe paused. "Come to think about it, I guess I better tell you about my Friday sometime.

"I came back early. When I found out my aunt was making dinner yesterday, I thought I might head to my folks' for dinner today. But I'm tired. I've got some studying to do and a book report to finish."

He looked at Ray and Heidi. "What about you two? How was your weekend?"

Heidi answered. "It's been great so far."

Right then, four kids came racing around the corner of the building. They stopped, panting, in front of their mom and dad.

"Okay, you guys," Ray spoke, smiling at their excitement. "We'll head down to the canoes as soon as we help Joe with these vegetables."

Joe smiled as he handed a big cabbage to Heidi and then one each to Sam and Angie. With those gone, he pulled the box of apples easily out of the trunk and handed it to Ray. When they piled the last box into the storeroom beside the kitchen, Ray turned to Joe. "I can talk after supper tomorrow, if you were serious about your Friday."

"I guess I better let you know what went on. I set myself up for a learning experience that was totally unexpected. I'm thankful God has a good hold on me."

Joe kept busy the rest of the day finishing up his schoolwork. Before supper, he gave his folks a call. Their reaction to his news about Shea was as he thought it would be. After the way he had messed up his life—and their lives too, to some extent—he was amazed that they still loved him. He could see that they trusted him now, and that was a relatively new thing. Joe was determined to never let them down.

His dad's advice was something he already planned to do: "Don't push things, Joey. She needs time to heal. I think she has more hurts weighing on her than Steve's death, as if that's not too much. It will all work out, Joe. The Lord's working it all out for good. For both of you."

"Love you, Dad. Thanks for the advice. Thanks for loving me." Joe ended the conversation.

Most of the students had returned to Clear Springs by supper time. It was a noisy meal as they caught each other up on their news from the long weekend. In a lull, someone asked, "Hey, Joe, did you get your license?"

Joe stood up, reached into his pocket for his wallet, and removed the temporary license. He waved it in the air and took a bow. Everyone applauded. His fame was short-lived, however, because in the next lull, Syd announced that he had an extra ticket to the Raptors' game next weekend.

• • •

"SO WHAT DID SHE say?" Dillon asked the question as the guys gathered to talk that evening.

Joe thought for a moment. "Well, I didn't ask her outright. I told her that I'd like to move in that direction, but I didn't ask her for an answer. She needs time without any pressure to think about it. If you guys don't mind, I'll keep you posted so you can pray, but I'd appreciate it if you keep what's said confidential."

"I already told my dad about you," Jason spoke up. Joe could tell he was hesitant. Jason didn't often speak up.

"Oh no!" Joe said. Then he laughed. "I hope you said good stuff."

"Well, I had to be honest, Joe," Jason smiled. "My dad asked me what's going on here at school. He has never heard me talk about the Lord like He mattered—ever, in my whole life. And this weekend we had some heavy conversations. So I blamed you, Joe. I told him about you and how the Lord has changed you. You challenged us all that first day in chapel, and in this past month I've grown. I do love the Lord, and I do want to serve Him. And I'm going to." He looked at Joe. "And Joe, my dad cried. And he gave me a hug. My dad isn't a hugger. And he asked me if I thought you would speak at his men's group sometime."

Two hours later, Joe was still wide awake. He'd been overwhelmed when Jason had told him about his weekend. *I'm still just Joe Parker, Lord. I don't know why or how you're using me. Look how I almost messed up this weekend. These kids are so young, Lord, and most are so innocent. Is this what you want of me, Lord? I'll do what you want. Don't let me do anything out of pride or selfishness. Remind me every day of what you brought me out of. Help me share you with others. Thank you for saving me.*

• • •

JOE ALMOST RAN INTO Jason in the hallway. They were both hurrying to get to breakfast on time.

"Hey, Jason, did you want to give your dad an answer about me speaking at the men's group?"

"Sure."

"Well, it's up to you. Tell him that I would count it a privilege to speak, and that you're going to be up front speaking with me." Joe was running down the stairs before Jason could protest.

The time between Thanksgiving and Christmas seemed to fly by for the students. In those ten weeks, everyone became involved in a community placement. First, they met individually with a faculty member. With their guidance, each student chose a placement where they would minister and learn new skills. Many of the students became involved in local churches, leading children's or youth ministries. Another had a position with the area foodbank, and two others with the local pregnancy resource centre.

When it came time for Joe's meeting with Ray, he had no idea what to present as options for his placement. He was relieved when he heard Ray's words as they sat together.

"Joe, I've been thinking. How would you like to consider a placement with Clear Springs? You already do so much extra work around here; I could just count what you already do as the required time served." He stopped as he saw Joe smile.

"Joe, I'm so glad you aren't serving that kind of time anymore. Right now, the required amount of service is four hours per week. After Christmas, with two afternoons off from classes each week, it will be ten hours. Keep doing all the extra that you do, and we'll log it.

"I know you've done a lot of speaking at men's groups and churches. I can see you're already doing direct ministry. I want you to count that time from now on too. I'm here for you. I'd like to go over your talks with you before and after you present them, but I certainly don't expect you to change your message. Joe, right now the Lord is using you and your testimony to do amazing things. We see it here at the school. Good reports are always filtering back to us from the places you've spoken at. I think you see it happening in the places where you fellowship and share.

"I do, Ray, but I don't want people to connect it to me. It's the Lord, Ray. He's doing it."

"Oh Joe, that is so true. Don't lose sight of that fact. Our job here at the school is to help you be more effective in ministry. Let me walk alongside you. We'll pray together. Right now I think you're just telling your testimony, and that is powerful. But I'm sure the Lord is showing you many new things that you may be wanting to share. My job will be to support you as you grow."

Joe thought Ray's plan sounded good, but he had an additional idea. "Sounds like a great plan. But could I do one other thing?" Joe thought back to the times he had invited Kevin and others to visit him at Clear Springs. This place was a great setting for fun and fellowship. "I'd like to plan a men's retreat. We could do it in the spring. It'll be a little warmer, and we could use the summer camp cabins."

"I should have known you'd make my proposition better. Great idea! To take it a step further, Jessica needs some additional hours for her placement. You could work together with her to plan two retreats—one for men and one for women. The gals could help Millie with food for the men's retreat, and the guys could help her during the women's retreat."

156

"That would be great. I know my mom would love that. Maybe Shea could come too."

Ray had never been so excited about a student placement plan. He was thankful that the Lord had clearly led the way, and that the board had allowed Joe Parker to come to Clear Springs.

• • •

FIVE WEEKS AFTER THANKSGIVING, with five weeks left before Christmas, Joe received a text from Shea. Two words—*Call me*—showed up on his screen. In the previous five weeks, Joe had continued to receive pictures of Stevie. He seemed to be growing and always hammed it up for the camera. Shea reported that he was doing well. After his classes that day, Joe found a quiet spot to make the phone call. He listened and thought that the call was about to go to voicemail when Shea answered. She seemed out of breath.

"Hi, Joe. Sorry it took so long to answer. Stevie just spilled a pitcher of juice all over the kitchen floor."

Joe couldn't help smiling as he pictured the mess. "Do you want me to call back?"

"No, we're good. I grabbed a bath towel from the cupboard in the hall, and it's soaking it up. Stevie is in his room playing with his cars. He's safe, and happy, and out of the mess."

"What's up? You wanted me to call."

Shea was quiet for a moment.

"Shea, are you still there?" Joe asked.

"Yes. Yes, I'm here. I've been thinking about what we talked about at Thanksgiving, and I've been praying. I talked to my pastor and Mrs. Griffin. And I talked to your mom, Joe. She called here first. After I talked to her, she actually came to visit. Have you thought anymore about it?"

Joe smiled to himself. "Pretty nonstop. But I still want you to be sure and to take all the time you need."

"Well, Joe, do you really love me?"

"Yes, I do."

"Joe, I had to sort out all my feelings about Steve. My pastor and Mrs. Griffin knew Steve, and they know me. Neither said they think it's a bad idea for us to plan toward marriage. They know how I'm struggling. They both said that people might talk, but there isn't a set time when it becomes *proper* to marry again after your spouse dies. I know how much I loved Steve, and so do you. I wouldn't be trying to replace him with you, and I know that you aren't barging in to take his place. The first time you met him, you showed him respect. I think Steve would be fine with this. Pastor Konrad said he knows Steve would be fine with this, because Steve is in Heaven, perfect and complete. He's not thinking much about the things of earth. Your mom encouraged me. She says she knows the change in you is real.

"Joe, my answer is yes. I do want to plan toward marrying you. I believe you're part of God's perfect plan for me, Stevie, and the new baby."

Joe could hardly speak. "Shea, I promise you, because I know the Lord is in control, that I will love, honour, and cherish you and your children. With God's help, I'll be the best husband and father I can be."

"Joe, thank you."

"Shea, we should talk. I don't like to talk about something this important on the phone. Can I come to town on Saturday? We could take Stevie to McDonald's or somewhere and then maybe get someone to watch him for a couple of hours."

"Sure, Joe. If Josie can't stay with Stevie, I'll talk to the Griffins."

"Great. I'll see you Saturday. About 11:00?"

"That sounds good. See you then."

• • •

SATURDAY MORNING, SHEA OPENED her apartment door and ushered Joe in. Stevie was watching a sing-along video on the television. He'd heard the door buzzer and now looked to the door as Joe entered. Joe watched as he turned his attention back to the screen and then sighed and turned the video off.

Shea gave him an encouraging smile. "Thanks for remembering your manners, Stevie. Do you remember Joe?"

"Yes," he replied. "I saw you. At the old house."

"It's good to see you again, Stevie. Did your mom tell you I was coming?"

"Yes." He looked at Shea. "We're going to Micadonalds. The new one. It's more fun."

"It's up to your mom. Are we going now?" Both he and Stevie looked at Shea.

"That's what we're doing," Shea replied. "Then Stevie is going to spend some time with Grandma. Right, Stevie?"

"Yes, Grandma's! She will read four books. Then we are going to make cookies." Stevie retrieved his coat and boots from the closet and put them on. Shea looked at Joe, shrugged her shoulders, and put on her coat as they both followed Stevie out the door.

Joe watched as Shea opened the car door, and Stevie climbed in the back seat. "Mommy, I can do it." Stevie was emphatic, climbing into his car seat and buckling himself in. Shea made sure the belts were tight. During the ride to McDonald's, Stevie talked non-stop. He pointed out every truck along the way. He knew all the colours. The bigger the truck he saw, the greater his joy.

As soon as they walked through the door, Joe realized why Shea had chosen this McDonald's. There was a playland with climbers to the ceiling. Three slides exited at the bottom, and plastic tunnels joined the sections at the top. They waited in a short line, received their food, and made their way to the playland. The area was sectioned off from the rest of the restaurant. Stevie found a table at the far side of the room, and they sat down to eat their meals.

"Don't rush, Stevie," Shea said. "We're going to eat slowly and finish everything, remember?"

"Okay, Mommy. Then I play, right?"

"That's the deal," Shea replied.

As they ate their meals, Stevie commented on everything that went on around him. When he finished his meal, he took the little book that came with his Happy Meal and handed it to Joe to unwrap.

"Franklin! We have a big Franklin at home. And a little one here. Read, Mommy?"

"How about we read it at home, Stevie. You can play if you want. Remember the rule."

"Up until I find a slide, then down. No going to the top. Slide down on my bottom."

Stevie knew the rules. Joe watched him play. He looked over to Shea and saw that she was studying him.

"What are you thinking, Joe Parker?"

"I'm thinking that I could get used to this."

● ● ●

THE AFTERNOON PASSED QUICKLY. After they dropped Stevie at the Griffins', Shea and Joe picked up two coffees at a drive thru and then parked in the lot at a nearby park. Shea turned off the car and looked to Joe. "Do you think it's too cold to walk?"

"I think we're above freezing. The sun has warmed things up a bit today. How about we drink our coffees and then we can walk for a while?"

As they talked, Joe and Shea both told their stories of growing up. They each could recall both good and bad experiences. Both had known the feelings of despair, helplessness, and sadness that came from losses experienced when they were very young. They also talked about life now.

Joe noticed that Shea seemed settled when she talked about Steve. That had changed since the last time they talked. When Steve died, she was devastated. Shea had no idea how she was going to live without him. As time passed, especially when Stevie came home from the hospital, she realized that she had to find a new normal. She was a good mom. The Griffins gave her lots of support, and Steve's parents had helped too. Shea was now at the point where she was glad that Joe wanted to be part of their lives.

They left the car and walked the trail for thirty minutes. For the most part, they were silent, but a few times one of them asked the other a question.

"Shea, did you ever contact your father after you left?"

She replied that she hadn't. Maybe one day she would, but it wouldn't be soon.

One of Shea's questions to Joe brought a longer answer. "Joe, what did you ever do that made your parents put you back into care? I know your mom and dad, but I can't figure out why they did that to you."

Joe thought for a minute. "I didn't want to live there. I didn't love them. It was like a game, a challenge to get away and not go back. I started running away when I was twelve, and for a year I was back and forth. I stole from them all the time. I set a couple little fires in the house and in the barn at the back of the property. I put the fires out ... I didn't want to hurt anyone. I guess they didn't know that. I was suspended from school for doing dangerous stuff, so I was home a lot.

"It was just too much for them. They signed me back into care for six months. It was always their plan that I would come home eventually. I ran away from my first placement, which was in the city. I went back to Harper and broke into their house. That was my first arrest. I was put in open custody. That was a group home too. My first night there I went out a window and went back to Harper again.

"I stole a friend's bike. His dad's best friend was a cop, so there was no talking them out of arresting me. They held me at the station. There I was, thirteen years old, sitting in a cell. The next day I went to a closed custody youth facility. Since then, I've spent more time in custody than out." Joe shook his head. "But my family never stopped loving me."

● ● ●

STEVIE WAS WATCHING FROM the window when Shea turned into the driveway at the Griffins'. A minute later, he came down the steps carrying two small bags. He was excited. "Cookies, Mommy. Some for us and some for Joe." Everyone was smiling as Shea made sure he was safely buckled in.

At the apartment building, Joe waved as Shea and Stevie stopped at the door and looked back. In seconds, the door had shut behind them. He climbed into his car and headed back to Clear Springs.

Chapter Twenty-One

"GRAMPS, I DON'T THINK IT'S EVER GOING TO STOP SNOWING." JOE PULLED BACK THE drapes in the living room. "Did you see the back door? We can't even open it. There has to be two feet of snow piled against it."

"Merry Christmas, Joey." Gramps was smiling.

"Same to you, Gramps. Sorry I'm such a grump. Looks like it's you and me today."

Joe had been looking forward to travelling to Harper. He and Gramps were going to drive up this morning, but they knew last night when the Christmas Eve service was cancelled that this storm was going to close things down. He had missed every Christmas with his family since he was thirteen years old. He wouldn't get there this year either.

Gramps was still in the Christmas spirit. "Worse things could happen. At least we know everyone is safe and warm. We've got lots of food, and look at that tree with a pile of presents for us under it. Don't worry, your aunt will make sure we have our turkey and the trimmings at dinner time. You'll see Kevin driving over on the snowmobile this afternoon. Some years that machine doesn't get used at all, but this is our second big snowfall of the season. Kev will be glad that I've got some added muscle around here today. Eventually that snow will have to be shovelled."

Joe spent a large part of the morning on the phone. He called his folks and talked to everyone there. He could tell his mom was disappointed that he couldn't get to Harper. He found out that the storm was worse there. Lisa and her family weren't going to be there for dinner either.

Next, he called Shea. In the weeks moving toward Christmas, he'd become more and more convinced that he and Shea were on the right track, but there had been a big challenge along the way.

• • •

TOGETHER JOE AND SHEA had decided that they would sit down and talk to Steve's parents. They had welcomed Shea as part of their family and embraced Stevie as their own. When Shea told them that she and Joe were planning to get married, they didn't get angry, but they weren't pleased. Joe talked with Brad about the situation, and in the end, the Findlays agreed to meet with their pastor, Shea, Joe, and Pastor Brad.

The meeting started with everyone on edge. Joe spoke first and honestly talked about his past. He spoke of his treatment of Shea and his most recent incarceration. He described seeing little Stevie in Steve's arms that first day out of jail. "Your son was holding him. I knew he was my son, but I also knew he would never be my son. I tried to leave, but Steve and Shea wouldn't let me. Steve told me firmly that he was Stevie's dad, and I agreed with him fully. I left there thinking I would never see Stevie again." Joe went on to tell them how the Lord had changed him.

Brad spoke next. He told how Joe's testimony had touched the lives of many people from Coverton to Toronto and how he'd worked hard all summer. He pointed out Joe's excellent reports from the Bible school.

When Shea spoke, she looked at Steve's parents and said, "Joe said it well. The night he first talked of marrying me, he said he knew I would always love Steve, and that he and his memory will always be part of my life. I really had never felt loved by anyone before I met Steve. It was easy to fall in love with him, and he loved Stevie too. Neither of us regretted that Stevie was coming, or that Stevie wasn't his biological son. We came to the Lord, and we learned how to love together.

"When Joe first met Steve, he didn't come barging in demanding his rights as a father. He acknowledged right away that Stevie was Steve's son. Actually, as Joe looked at the two of them together, I thought I could read his expression. He looked awestruck at Steve holding that little boy who looked so much like him. Joe was heartbroken, but he was also terrified. He wanted to get away from there as soon as he could, because he didn't want to hurt Stevie in any way. The last thing he said was, 'Maybe when he gets bigger and can understand, you can tell him that he has three parents who love him.'

"We don't pretend that Joe loved me when Stevie was conceived. But Joe is a different man now. When he proposed, if that's the word for it, I believed him when he said he loves me. He considers this baby a gift, and he wants to be a father to both of Steve's kids. I believe Steve would be pleased. It was more Joe's idea than mine that we're here. This is a really complicated, unique situation. We want you, as grandparents, to be with us in this."

William and Sharon looked at each other. Sharon did the talking. "Joe, we can see you are a changed man. We've done a lot of changing ourselves lately. But we"—she hesitated—"we just don't want Steve to be replaced. I guess what it comes down to is that we want him to be here. We miss him so much." She started to cry. "Oh, this is so hard."

No one said a word, so Joe spoke again. "Steve won't be replaced. Stevie and the baby will grow up knowing that Steve was their dad. But I'll be their dad too. You'll be their grandparents, and my parents will be their grandparents. Love is a crazy thing to start. I believe God is forming us all into an amazing family."

Everyone was quiet for a moment, taking in what Joe had said. William cleared his throat and spoke. "There is a concern. There will be a large amount of money when all the accident claims are settled. Steve's insurance policy also leaves a fairly large amount." He looked directly at Shea. "Shea, our first thought when we heard you were getting married to Joe was that he was after the money. What we just heard makes us feel better about that." He looked at his wife and she nodded. "But we're talking about a large amount. Things can change. What happens down the road if problems arise? What happens if you and Joe split up?"

"Mr. and Mrs. Findlay, I need to answer this one. I never really thought about the insurance money, or money from the accident. I can understand why you'd be wary of me. I've only been out of jail for seven months, and away from the drugs and alcohol for just over three years. All I can say is I never want to go back to that life. Never. I believe I can do this, but only by God's grace. In saying that, I want to tell you that I don't want access to any of that money. Ever."

Harry Ward spoke up. "William, what do you plan to do with the life insurance money? You need to decide that."

"Well, I know Shea needs money right now, and I've forwarded some to her already. The money is for Shea and the children. I can transfer it into her account. If she wants help managing it, I can do that. There has been some movement on the settlement too. That's going to be long and drawn out, though. Shea and I are already working together on that."

Shea interrupted. "William, I'm fine with you keeping the money in your account. You were the beneficiaries, and you paid the premiums. It's your money. I do need help right now, though. Thank you for helping up to now. You've given us all we've needed so far. I'd appreciate that continuing until we get the settlements. I can pay you back. I'll put money awarded to Stevie and the baby in trust funds for them. We'll talk to the lawyer to insure that the other settlement money is kept separate from our joint assets. Joe and I can have a legal document made up if necessary."

William spoke again. "Don't worry, Shea. The life insurance money is yours. We can put it in a joint account with me if you want, but that's not necessary. Then you can use it as needed. No offense I hope, Joe, but I think a prenuptial agreement would set our minds at ease." He watched Joe pause and then look over to Shea.

Shea nodded as she replied. "We both are fine with that. One thing we have talked a lot about is that we will ensure that Joe is legally both Stevie and the new baby's father. I'm sure a lawyer can figure all that out."

The Fidlays both stated that they could agree to that. It seemed that the meeting was winding down.

"I have a question." They all looked at Sharon. "What will the baby's name be?"

Joe and Shea looked at each other, and again Shea did the talking. "Joe and I talked a bit about this last week. If it's a boy, we're thinking Findlay. Did you know a lot of Steve's friends called him Finn? But we really don't know. We're still discussing that. We want to consider Steve, you folks, and Joe and I too."

William reached over and took his wife's hand. "There's lots of time to decide these things, Sharon. I think we can trust things will work out."

Joe and Shea were glad they had the meeting. Things were falling into place, and they knew the Lord was working, especially when the two pastors closed in prayer.

• • •

SHEA ANSWERED HER CELL phone on the first ring.

"Merry Christmas," Joe said.

"Merry Christmas to you too."

"Are you at the Findlays'?"

"Yes. We came yesterday before the storm got bad. Stevie is in his glory. So many presents."

"Was Santa good to you?"

"I got some really nice stuff." Shea sounded happy.

They talked for about fifteen minutes.

Just before they hung up, Joe said, "Shea, I love you. Give Stevie a hug from me."

"I will, Joe. I love you too."

• • •

AFTER HE TOLD GRAMPS it was his favourite Christmas movie, Joe found *Ernest Saves Christmas* on Netflix. As the credits scrolled at the end, Joe turned to Gramps. "Your turn to pick, Gramps. What's your favourite?"

Gramps laughed. "Well, my favourite is *It's a Wonderful Life,* but it sure feels good to laugh. How about you choose another?"

Joe thought for a moment.

"Do you like Michael Caine?"

"Well, he was a good actor. But I'm not sure I'd like most of the movies he was in. Didn't know he had a Christmas one." Gramps was wary.

"Don't worry, Gramps. This is a good one. Lots of laughs, guaranteed."

Joe smiled as he found *A Muppet's Christmas Carol* and pushed the play button. "The co-stars make the movie, but Michael Caine is fabulous!"

Joe watched Gramps' face as Gonzo and Rizzo came on the screen. Gramps looked at Joe, who winked, nodded, and pointed to the screen as he settled back in his chair.

Kevin arrived as the movie was finishing. He had carefully mounted the steps of the porch with a cooler full of food. Joe hurried to the door when he heard the doorbell. Wind and snow rushed in as Kevin pushed open the inside door and stumbled in. The aluminum door blew shut behind him. He struggled out of his snowsuit and boots and then smiled. "Merry Christmas! I hope you guys are hungry." He shook his head and scattered icy snow all over the floor.

Within ten minutes, the food was heated up, and all three men sat at the dining room table. As they ate, they exchanged stories of past Christmases. All the while the wind and snow continued its rampage outside.

Kevin stayed through the evening. As it got later, he decided to stay overnight. In the early hours of the morning, the snow stopped and the wind died down. Everyone slept in, waking up to a white world, with the sun shining brightly. After a typical Gramps' big breakfast, the two cousins shovelled Gramps driveway and then headed over to Jay's to do the same. Gramps was just contemplating what he wanted for lunch when Joe returned.

"Four turkey sandwiches and a whole pumpkin pie!" he exclaimed as he came through the door. He immediately started unpacking the backpack he carried. "Aunt Michelle is just like my mom, Gramps. If she can't find a great big turkey, she'll get two. Rule number one: you must have lots of turkey left over at Christmas."

• • •

THE ROADS WERE CLEAR by Friday morning. Joe's schedule had been revised by the storm. Today, he was on his way to visit Shea and Stevie. He had planned to be back at school to attend the recovery meeting on Saturday morning, but he also wanted to spend some time with his folks. Gramps was considering making the trip with him. His decision was finalized when he heard that Lisa and her family would be there too.

Joe's mom had promised a good meal. "What's your choice, Joe?"

Joe answered that it was a toss up between her shepherd's pie and macaroni and cheese. "Surprise me, Mom. We'll be there by noon on Saturday."

• • •

SHEA WAS WAITING FOR him at the door of her apartment. "Come on in, Joe. You can leave your boots on the boot tray here by the door."

He took off his coat and hung it on the coat rack. Stevie had heard the buzzer but didn't come out of his room until he heard Joe's voice. "Hi, Joe. MicaDonalds?"

"Maybe for lunch, big guy. How about I come in and visit for a while, and then we'll head out."

"Okay, Joe." Stevie went into his room and came out with a book. "My new book. Read, please."

Joe suddenly jumped up. "Oh, I have something in the car for you." He hurried to the door, slipped on his boots, and went out. He returned a few minutes later with a gift bag for Stevie. "Here you go, buddy. Merry Christmas. It's cold out there," Joe said as he looked at Shea.

Shea looked at him and shook her head. "Maybe that's why we're supposed to wear our coats in the wintertime."

Stevie squealed with excitement with every gift he pulled out of the bag. "Look, Mommy, a new book, cars … Marshall!" he yelled as he pulled out a pair of Paw Patrol pajamas. Shea had patiently coached Joe on who's who in the life of a three-year-old.

"He loves it all," Shea said as they watched him drive three very fancy cars up and down and over the furniture and across the floor. "Stevie, remember our manners."

Stevie looked at Joe and then ran toward him, jumping on his lap. "Thanks, Joe. Thanks for a book, a red car"—Stevie was thinking—"a blue car, a green car, and Marshall." He turned to look at Joe and then gave him a hug. "Marshall is my favouritest."

"You're welcome, little buddy. How about you grab one of your new books, and we'll read for a while?"

The morning sped by. Joe played with Stevie for two hours straight. Shea made soup and grilled cheese sandwiches for lunch, and they ate together at the small kitchen table. After lunch, Shea found *Raffi* on YouTube, and the three of them sat together on the couch watching. Joe started to tell Shea that he remembered Raffi from when he was little, but she put a finger to her lips. He looked down and saw Stevie nodding off to sleep. A few minutes later, Shea picked him up and took him to his bed.

"It works every time. Raffi puts kids to sleep. Ever since he's been little, it's a go-to. Sometimes he misses his nap, but he's really tired today. Not caught up from the holiday, I guess."

Joe pointed to the couch beside him, and Shea sat down. He put his arm around her and pulled her close. "It's a done deal, Shea."

"What are you talking about, Joe Parker?"

"I love you. That's what I'm talking about."

Over the past month Joe and Shea had been very careful in regard to their physical relationship. They hadn't spent much time together, and Stevie was always present when they did. They purposely didn't go farther than a quick hug or kiss. Joe had visited twice at the apartment—once to drop something off, and another time to take them all to the park. He had picked her up and returned her home the day they talked to the Findlays, picking Stevie up from the Griffins' and going to McDonald's along the way. Most days they had talked on the phone. At least once a day he sent her a text, or she would send him one: a smiley face, a row of hearts, and a *Thinking about you* or *I love you.* They each knew what the other meant. At first Joe had only kissed Shea on the forehead, but the last time he had taken her face in his hands and kissed her sweetly on the lips. Her heart had raced; she felt completely at peace with him.

"Shea, I got you a Christmas gift."

"You did? I thought we decided we weren't going to get each other gifts."

"Okay … it's not a Christmas gift." Joe smiled at her and then twisted away from her and stood up. He turned to her and got down on one knee. When he saw Shea's smile, he wiggled his eyebrows and whispered, "Just like in the movies." He reached into his pocket to lift out a ring and said, "Shea, I have never loved a woman the way I love you. I want you to be my wife. I will honour Steve's memory, and I will, by God's grace, love you and your children with His perfect love. Will you marry me, Shea?"

He watched as she took Steve's wedding ring from her finger and put it in her pocket. When she nodded her head, with tears in her eyes, he slid the ring onto her finger. It fit. Then he sat down again on the couch, gathering her into his arms. She turned to him, their faces inches apart. She reached up and traced her finger down his jaw to his chin.

"I love you too, Joe Parker. This is just … just perfect." She moved toward him, and their lips met. *What a kiss. Long and sweet. Perfect for sure.* Shea was content to sit close beside him. Just being with him gave her a settled feeling that was hard to describe. She picked up the remote and asked, "Favourite Christmas movie?"

Joe laughed as he answered. *Ernest Saves Christmas.*

Shea shook her head and replied, "You lose, Joe." She scrolled through Netflix, clicking on *A Charlie Brown Christmas.*

Stevie woke up from his nap. He was still a bit sleepy as he entered the living room. When he saw Shea and Joe sitting on the couch, he climbed onto Joe's lap. "We go outside?" He looked Joe in the eye as he asked.

"You betcha, bud. We need to dress nice and warm to play in the snow. I've got another surprise for you in the car. Right, Mom?" Joe looked at Shea.

"Right, Joe. First you need to use the bathroom, Stevie."

"Okay, Mom, I'll pee," Stevie yelled as he ran down the hall.

They had a great afternoon. Stevie was ecstatic when Joe pulled a snow sled out of his trunk. Jumping up and down, he yelled, "Mommy! Mommy, look! Marshall and Skye and Chase and Rocky." Joe was very proud of the fact that he was able to find a Paw Patrol snow sled.

At the park two blocks from the apartment, Stevie climbed onto the sled. Joe pulled him on the walking path that wound through the park. Every time they completed a lap, Stevie begged to go around again. Joe gladly obliged. After thirty minutes of pulling, Joe suggested they make some snow angels. Then Shea suggested they bury Joe in the snow. Stevie seemed to have endless energy. His next activity was continuously going up the slide and then down again. It was wide and low, so when Stevie rolled down it, he landed in a heap on the soft, deep snow below. It was getting late as they left the park. Shaking the snow off their coats and boots, they stopped at the coffee shop where Shea and Joe had talked at Thanksgiving. All three ordered hot chocolate, Stevie's cooled down with lots of chocolate milk.

Joe didn't take his coat off when he got back to the apartment. He said goodbye to Shea and Stevie at the door. It had been a remarkable day. Stevie watched as he gave Shea a hug and kissed her softly on the lips.

"Thanks, Joe," she said. "We had a great day."

Stevie looked up at Joe, who reached down to pick him up. "It was great having fun with you today, Stevie."

"Thanks, Joe. Great day," he said, copying his mother's words. Shea and Joe laughed, so Stevie did too. Joe hugged him, put him down, and was on his way.

Chapter Twenty-Two

JOE SAT IN CHURCH NEXT TO RAY'S FAMILY ON SUNDAY MORNING. IT WAS A GOOD SERVICE. He'd been in church here a week ago. They had sung carols and heard the Christmas Story. Joe was sorry that the Christmas Eve service in Souton had been cancelled. He loved Christmas, and he loved that this was all new to him. Every Bible verse, every song, shouted out to him that Jesus was born, that God came to the earth in the form of a little baby in order to redeem mankind.

Joe was invited to dinner at the Hursts'. He was able to update Ray about his week. Yesterday, he went to see his folks. He was pleased that Gramps had gone too. Lisa and her family welcomed him with open hearts. Little Seth left no mistake that he thought his Great Papa was the most wonderful person alive. Joy never stopped smiling. All her kids were home, and she couldn't be more content. Joe felt that he had robbed her of that for far too long.

Joe was glad to be back at Clear Springs. It would be a quiet week, and he was looking forward to that. He noticed that only the road to, and path around, Riverside Hall had been plowed. He looked forward to climbing on both the tractor and garden tractor to clear the rest of the paths and roads. He liked having the camp to himself. He had three commitments for the week. He would attend the church watchnight service on New Year's Eve, his recovery group on Saturday morning, and church again on Sunday. There was plenty of work to keep him occupied, but there would be plenty of quiet time too.

The other students arrived back to start the second semester on January 6. Schedules and classes changed, and workloads shifted. As promised, the students had Wednesday and Friday afternoons off as everyone became more involved in their community placements. Joe kept busy working and learning. He was more satisfied than he had ever been in his life. He missed Shea, but the time when he would marry her was quickly approaching.

Unlike the local colleges, there was no study week at Clear Springs. At the end of February, Joe received permission to take two days off classes. He would go home, intending to make some definite plans with Shea. The time had come to set a wedding date and discuss what would happen at the end of the school year.

After making the request, Joe sat in Ray's office. Ray seemed almost as excited about Joe's time off as he was. "Make sure you stay home on the weekend too, Joe. You've worked nonstop all year. You need to take time off from your volunteer jobs too."

● ● ●

JOE LOOKED AROUND THE dining hall. He was excited to leave for four days, but he was going to miss the joking and teasing that accompanied every meal. His friends knew that he was missing two days of classes. Today they were razzing him at breakfast for skipping out. "Give him a break; he's an old man. He needs a rest."

"Oh no, Joe's going to get to see his lady friend."

"Some nerve you've got, Joe, leaving us with all the work."

Joe smiled. He knew everyone appreciated the work he did. Joe's phone buzzed, and he checked the text that had come in from Ray.

Joe, can you come to my office? I need to talk to you.

OMW. Joe sent off a text in a hurry.

He turned to the others. "Oh no! Who squealed on me? I just got called to the office." Joe could still hear the laughter as he went out the door.

The door to Ray's office was open when Joe arrived. He could see that the chairman of the board was in the office with Ray.

"Come on in, Joe. You remember Dr. Bradley?"

"Yes, sir, I do. Nice to see you again, Dr. Bradley."

"Call me Peter, Joe. We don't have to be formal. Ray has asked me to sit in on this meeting. We have a proposal to make to you. It seems there are some interesting things happening in your life right now. Ray thought that a third person"—he motioned to himself—"might help in talking this through."

Ray began. "Joe, we've never met a young man quite like you. You have consistently and humbly shown the Lord to be working in your life, no matter what you're doing— leading the other students, cheering people up, plowing snow or cutting grass, or working in the kitchen. Your marks are the highest in this year's class. You constantly give your best, and you're a blessing to every staff member and student here. If I weren't here every day, seeing you in action, I wouldn't believe you're for real."

When Ray paused, Joe spoke. "Did you tell Dr. Bradley that I almost relapsed at Thanksgiving?"

Ray remembered sitting in his office that Tuesday, seeing the broken, humbled young man confess his shortcoming in tears. "Yes, Joe, I did. And the point is, you did not relapse. And you took no credit for stopping yourself. You knew the Lord had you, and when you recognized that, you ran with it. We're not worried that you'll relapse, Joe. Maybe next time you will, but we see who you are in Christ. Joe, we believe you belong on staff here at Clear Springs."

"Joe, tell me about your marriage plans." Dr. Bradley was looking intently at Joe.

"What do you know?"

"All Ray has said is that it's complicated."

Dr. Bradley had heard some of Joe's story when he was interviewed by the Clear Springs board. Today, Joe began his account from the time he had arrived at Steve's Place, when he met Steve and Stevie. He spoke of his heartache and his conviction that he would never interfere in Stevie's life. When Joe told of reading about Steve's death, and the things that happened afterward, he began to cry. "It was awful. Steve was dead. Shea was hurting, and Stevie was in bad shape. I felt helpless, but Shea let me be there."

Joe went on to tell Dr. Bradley of his growing conviction that he should marry Shea, and of her eventually reaching the same conclusion. Joe stressed that he believed he could love Shea the way the Lord said a man should love his wife. He mentioned the nine-year age difference and told him that Shea said that she had loved him, expecting nothing, when they first met. "We believe the Lord is in this, Dr. Bradley. Neither of us knew Him when we first met, but now we want to serve Him together."

Joe told Dr. Bradley about the baby coming, and that they had met with Steve's parents. "We just want to do things right. We want to honour Steve and consider his family. The baby is due the middle of April. We'd like to get married before that, but it wouldn't even be a year since Steve died."

Dr. Bradley looked at Ray. "I think we could present our plan to Joe. When he marries isn't an issue."

Ray began. "Joe, we'd like to make you a job offer. The camp has a parcel of land they bought three years ago. I think you've seen it. Right now, the fields are being rented out to a local farmer. There's an old house on the property. It needs some work, but we think our volunteers could have it fixed up in a few weeks. If you get married, the house would be yours to live in. We'll still provide accommodation if you don't get married. Here's what the job would entail. We'd like you to continue what you're doing in your community placement through the summer. As usual, we'll be hiring students to do maintenance and as kitchen helpers during the kids' camps and summer conference. You'd be supervising them. That could include the garden you wanted to plant but couldn't fit into the school year. You would also lead the camp staff devotions in the mornings.

"The new property has great potential. At this time, we're working on a new program. A prison ministry has approached us to work alongside them. They envision a place where guys who are coming out of prison can live with their families in a setting where they receive support."

"That really is a big problem coming out of prison." Ray knew Joe was speaking from experience. "No money, and no hope to get any honestly. No place to live. No one encouraging you to do better. What an excellent idea."

Ray continued. "The possibilities are endless. With online teaching, we see participants getting their high school and even post secondary diplomas and degrees. We could farm the land and teach new skills. We could pair up with tradesmen, so new skills could be learned as well.

"These would be men who are committed to changing their lives. Because we have the camp and conference grounds in such close proximity, we won't be able to serve any men who would be dangerous to others. Remember, though, that this is in the future. For the next year, you'd be doing much of what you're doing now. You'd be part of the leadership of the camp. We had to think and pray hard about that. Usually we'd never consider a guy as young in the Lord as you are for a leadership position, but already we've seen your influence on the young people here and on the people at the meetings and churches you've spoken at."

"We want you on our team, Joe." It was Dr. Bradley who spoke.

"It would be a dream come true for me. To be able to serve the Lord, to know He's using me. I'll talk to Shea about it and get back to you by Friday. I'll be praying.

"And we'll be praying along with you." Ray smiled at Joe.

"Joe, there's one more thing," Dr. Bradley said. "Is there a reason why you and Shea are waiting to get married. You've met with the Findlays. Seems to me waiting will just cause frustration. You must miss each other. I hope by now you're madly in love."

Dr. Bradley paused and Joe interrupted. "I'm afraid I am, sir," he said with a smile.

"Then I think you should get married as soon as possible. What do you think, Ray?"

"I know this young man, Peter. He'll talk to Shea, and they'll pray together about it. The Lord will show them what to do."

Joe left the meeting and thought about what had been said. It really seemed too good to be true. When Joe left Ray's office, he looked for a quiet place to call his dad. His mom answered the phone, and in less than a minute his dad greeted him. Joe explained the job offer to him, and his reaction was the same as Joe's. "Oh Joey, what a great opportunity!"

"My problem is that I'm not sure if we should wait till after the baby's born or not. Is it long enough after Steve's death?"

Seth didn't answer right away. He thought for a moment and then said, "Joe, I think that it's fine for you to get married now, but if Shea has any reservations, just be patient as you wait. You both have grown so much in a short time. Whenever you get married, Joe, you're going to be a blessing to her and the children."

As Joe ended the call, he thought, *Thanks, Dad. You always were one of my biggest fans.*

• • •

HE SAID HE'D BE here by 11:00. I hope he's okay. Shea walked around to the kitchen to read the time on the stove: 11:15. Five minutes later, she was startled by the door buzzer. She jumped up to let Joe in. The door was open when Joe reached it. He smiled at Shea, but the smile disappeared when he saw that she'd been crying. He reached to close the door behind him and took her hand.

"Honey, what's wrong?"

Shea's lip trembled, and she shook her head as she let go of his hand. She turned, went to the couch, and sat down. Joe watched as she put her head in her hands and quietly sobbed. Joe joined her on the couch, putting his arm around her and pulling her close.

"Mommy is sad." Stevie stood at the end of the hallway, watching Joe with a troubled look on his face. "Why's Mommy sad?"

Joe answered him honestly. "I don't know why Mommy's sad, Stevie. Right now she doesn't want to talk, but maybe it will help if we just sit close to her and show her that we love her very much."

Stevie slowly approached Shea. He put his head down on her lap and patted her leg. When she reached and put her hand on his head, he scrambled into her lap. She hugged him close.

"It's all right, Mommy. Stevie's here."

"That's what Mommy tells you when you're sad, isn't it? Thank you for being here. I love you and Joe so much. It's making Mommy feel better already."

They sat there together for a few minutes. Then Stevie wiggled out of Shea's hug. He bounced down the hall to his room and didn't look back.

"He's probably gone back to his new building blocks. We made a bridge earlier and used a little box to make a garage. Every car he has is parked back there. Joe, he is so creative."

"So is his mommy, and I don't think you've ever looked so beautiful, Shea." He went over to the table and came back with a tissue.

"Right, Joe. Seven months pregnant. Tears streaming down my face. I'm so tired."

"And something happened?"

"Just that you were late."

"I was?"

"Twenty minutes."

Joe knew he had said that he thought he'd be there by 11:00, but there was no promise. He realized that now was not the time to tell Shea that.

"I'm so sorry, Shea. I wasn't even thinking. I should have called you."

"I was so scared, Joe. I thought something had happened to you. Every time you leave, I just get an awful feeling. I don't want you to go. What if I lose you too, Joe?"

"Oh Shea." He sat down beside her again, took her hands, and bowed his head to pray.

"Lord, put your arms around Shea right now. She loves you so much. She's tired, and her and Steve's baby is reminding her of their love, and she misses him. And Stevie misses his daddy. But Lord, we know Steve is in Heaven, and we believe that Heaven is a real place, with none of the sin or death that causes so much sorrow here on earth. Lord, help her through this. Take our sorrow and our fear, Lord. We need your peace. Help us remember how good and perfect you are. Help Shea lean on you. In Jesus' name. Amen.

"I wish I could say I'll never leave you. I can only say that with God's help, I'll love you as long as I breathe." *We need some help here, Lord. We need to talk to someone older and wiser, like we said we would when we first decided to marry.* Joe had an idea. "Hungry, Shea?"

"I guess I am. I forgot about lunch with all this commotion going on. I'm surprised that Stevie hasn't been asking for food."

"Well, let's get ready, and we'll go out for lunch." Joe glanced over to the doorway and saw Stevie watching them with a smile on his face.

"Micadonalds!" he yelled as he ran to give Joe a hug.

"No way, buddy. I know a nice little diner downtown where you can get bugs and cheese, and maybe ice cream, if you finish your lunch." Everyone hurried to get out the door.

"Do they really have bugs and cheese, Joe?" Shea was smiling as she asked.

"Yup. Guaranteed. Stevie will love it."

Chapter Twenty-Three

SHEA REMEMBERED MARY'S DINER FROM WHEN SHE LIVED AT STEVE'S PLACE. SHE'D ONLY been there a few times for fries and a shake. Most of the tables in the diner were empty. Joe knew that the lunch crowd had headed back to the high school. They stopped to hang their coats on the rack at the door. When Mary saw Joe, she scooted around the other tables to give him a hug. "Joe, we were just talking about you yesterday. Here for a visit or for lunch?"

"Well, I was hoping to have a little of both." He turned to Shea. "Mary, this is my fiancée, Shea, and our boy, Stevie. Shea, Stevie, this is my good friend Mary." Joe paused. "Waters?"

"Yes, Joe. I took Kyle's name. Nice to meet you, Shea, and Stevie. You look really familiar, Shea. I think you lived nearby."

"A bunch of us lived in a house a couple blocks over," Shea explained.

"Aha. I thought so. Joe, Sarge will be here shortly. What can I get you?"

"What's the special?" Joe asked.

"Shepherd's pie with veggies or a side salad."

"Sounds good to me, with veggies," Joe replied and looked at Shea.

"I'll have the same."

Mary looked at Stevie. She hadn't meant to, but she looked to Joe and back to Stevie again. *There's a story here, Lord. Bless this little family.* "And what about you, young man? What do you want to eat?"

"Bugs, please."

"Bugs and cheese?" Mary asked.

"Yes. Joe said they are goodest. Right, Joe?"

"Sure are, buddy."

Sarge arrived just as their food was ready. When Mary saw him coming, she said, "Joe, pull that table next to you over. He'll sit with you so you can talk. We aren't very busy. I'll join you if I can."

"What a great surprise. Who is this lovely lady and this handsome little boy?"

"This handsome guy is Stevie, and this lovely lady is my fiancée, Shea," Joe answered, but he stopped as he noticed Shea and Sarge staring at each other. "Have you two met?"

Shea answered, "Your Sarge and his partner came to the house to tell me about the accident. He told me that Steve was gone and took me to the hospital to be with Stevie. Before we left the apartment, he asked me if I was a Christian and I said yes, and that Steve was too. He prayed, and he reminded me that Steve was with the Lord. He stayed with me until my pastor and the Griffins arrived. I thought he must be an angel in disguise."

Joe looked at Sarge and said to Shea, "Shea, Sarge is one of the best men I know. I'm glad he was with you that night." He turned to Sarge. "Thanks, Sarge. Thanks for being a man of God in a hard world."

As they began to eat, everyone was quiet at first. Stevie enjoyed his bugs and cheese and told Shea that she should make him some for supper. Joe knew from his silence that Sarge was praying. He felt confident that he would have some kind of advice or encouragement for them.

When Stevie was done eating, Sarge looked at him and said, "Stevie, how old are you?"

"Four," Stevie answered.

Joe looked at Shea.

"He always says he's four. Did you forget, Stevie, that you're still three?"

"Mommy, I'm four."

"Well, Stevie, there's something special over there in the corner for you. Mrs. Mary and I just went shopping last week. We picked up some toys in case some three- or four-year-olds came to play." He looked over and saw that Mary was available. "Mrs. Mary, can you show Stevie the toy box? He might like to play over there." The others watched as Mary pointed out some things in the box.

Stevie exclaimed, "Blocks like home!" as he pulled out a big bag of toddler-size blocks. He was also excited to find two little cars and a Spiderman action figure. Shea smiled. She knew that the toys would keep him busy for a while.

The last of the customers had left, and Mary had finished cleaning their table. She sat down with the others. "Do you want me in on this conversation? 'I'll need to take care of any customers that come in, but it's quiet right now."

"Sit down, sweetie." Kyle smiled at her. "They tell me they're looking to talk to an older, wiser couple." Everyone laughed.

"Shea, I'll talk, okay? Interrupt if I forget something or if you disagree with me." Joe quickly outlined the facts about his former relationship with Shea. He talked of meeting Steve, and how he dealt with the knowledge that Stevie was his biological son. Shea spoke up a few times. She told how Joe had respected Steve as Stevie's father, and how after Steve died, Joe had come to the hospital. Joe spoke of his growing conviction that he and Shea should marry, and he told of their talk at Thanksgiving and their relationship since. "We decided that we should get some input from a couple who might understand. I found Shea in quite a state today, and we just need to talk to someone."

Shea entered into the exchange. "He was late, and I panicked. I was terrified that something had happened to him. It's getting harder and harder for me to watch him leave when he visits."

"She's exhausted most of the time. The baby's due at the end of April, and Stevie is a very active three-year-old. Her feelings just overwhelm her sometimes. Is she just too tired? There's so much on her plate. I can't identify with losing someone like she lost Steve. Shea and I are getting married and want to do what's right. I think I can help her work through that grief. I just want to hold her and help her get through this."

"I take it you came to me because I lost my wife. I actually thought of that the night Steve died. Shea is young. I was married a long time, and my daughter is grown. I had another adult to go through it with. It was hard, though. I was glad that night when the people from the church showed up. I knew they would take care of Shea.

"Shea, I can identify with the broken heart. My heart is still broken, but I rejoice in knowing that Sarah is with the Lord. And I know that the Lord has taken care of me. The pain will get less and less, but it will be part of you always. You have Stevie, whom Steve loved. And I think you know that the new baby will be a very tangible reminder of your love for each other. When I met Mary and fell in love, I didn't forget what I had with Sarah. I just was thankful that God had blessed me again with a wonderful woman. In many second marriages there is comparison and jealousy, but that's not how it's supposed to be.

"Shea, I have never met a man like Joe. He lived his life selfishly and failed in many ways, but the Lord has changed him. It's not often you see such a visible difference in a new Christian. I think you will beautifully serve the Lord together. There are no guarantees in this life, except that God is in control. He knows the plans He has for us. Plans to prosper you and not harm you. Plans to give you …" Sarge paused.

Shea completed the verse in a whisper, "hope and a future."

Joe looked at her amazed. "I love it." He blinked. "I love you."

Sarge smiled at Shea. "I think, Joe, that you should marry this woman soon, if she'll have you. You just need to love her as a man is commanded to love his wife. And she will love you."

"That's what I want. To serve the Lord with Joe," Shea spoke quietly.

"And that's what I want too," Joe added.

"Miss Mary." Stevie was looking their way.

"Need something, Stevie?"

"Yes," Stevie answered. "Ice cream please." When everyone laughed, he looked at Joe.

"Well, you did eat your bugs and cheese, didn't you, Stevie? I guess we need a scoop of ice cream, Mary."

Stevie fell asleep on the way back to the apartment. Joe and Shea didn't talk at all in the car. After parking the car, Joe looked at Shea and smiled. "I love you so much. I'll carry this monkey in. Maybe he'll sleep for a while. I've got something else to talk about. It doesn't matter if he wakes up, though."

"I can't let him sleep too long or he won't go to sleep tonight."

Shea went ahead and unlocked the door of the building. Joe lifted Stevie and followed her to the apartment. He stopped to slip off his boots and then continued carrying Stevie to his room. After Joe laid him on the bed, Shea pulled off Stevie's boots and jacket. They both watched him sleep and smiled at the smile on his little face.

Joe sat down at the end of the couch, and Shea sat close to him.

"I love you too, Joe Parker."

"Well, we need to talk, but I'd rather do some kissing."

"You are such a smart man, Joe. You figured out exactly what I was thinking. And the baby agrees." Shea took Joe's hand and placed it far down on her stomach.

"I can feel him kicking!" Joe's excitement showed in his voice. He trailed his hand all the way up to Shea's face. He turned her face to him and whispered, "You are so beautiful." Then he kissed her. He shifted around so that she could lean on his chest. She wrapped her arms around him, and they held each other tight.

"I could get used to this," she said.

"Me too. But we do need to talk. Not as much fun, but kind of necessary. Actually, it's pretty exciting."

"So talk, and by the way, this baby might be a girl." She put her head on his chest, listening to his heartbeat.

Joe told Shea about his meeting with Ray Hurst and Dr. Bradley. He outlined the offer as it had been presented to him. As he talked, he became excited about all the possibilities it presented. Shea kept interrupting him, asking him to repeat and confirm what he was saying. When he was finished, she looked at him.

"Joe, it sounds great, but I don't want to wait till the end of April to get married. The baby should be born by then."

"Who said anything about waiting till the end of April?"

"You gave the date. After graduation. Was it the twenty-eighth?"

"Oh no, Shea, that was for the job. We can get married as fast as we can get a license. They said the house could be ready in a couple weeks. I could go back to school and come home on the weekends if the house takes a little longer. Or you could come and visit me at school. They probably would find a place for you and me and Stevie to be together there. You should have heard them, Shea. I'm so excited. I'd be on staff at Clear Springs, with you by my side."

"All right already. What time is it?"

Joe looked at his watch. "Just about three."

"We have lots to do."

"What?"

"To get married. There's lots to do. Starting with who should marry us?"

"Brad or your pastor. It doesn't matter to me."

"Witnesses?"

"I have no clue, Shea. What do you think?"

"I think there's a marriage license form on the City of Coverton website." She went straight to her computer. A few minutes later, she pointed to the screen. "See. We can copy it and fill it out. The offices at city hall close at 4:30. We need the right ID. Then we're all set. When we come back here, we can call either Brad or my pastor, depending on where we get married. We can pick our witnesses later. Here in Coverton could be the Griffins, and in Souton, maybe your aunt and uncle?"

"Oh Shea, you're so smart. This is going to happen. I guess we need to wake Stevie up?"

"No, just wait." Shea ran out the door and came back three minutes later with Josie.

• • •

SHEA AND JOE WAITED in the marriage license line at city hall for ten minutes. On the way back to Shea's, they stopped at the donut shop down the street from the apartment. Picking up donuts, lattes, and a hot chocolate for Stevie, they were back to the apartment by 4:30.

"Are you really getting married?" Josie picked up a latte and donut and sat on the couch.

Shea was excited. "Yes. Can you believe it?"

"When?"

Joe answered. "Not sure, but sometime this weekend."

The first phone call settled things. Joe called Brad, intending to ask his advice. He pushed the button to turn the speaker on. Early in the conversation, Brad said, "I can marry you tonight, Joe. All you need is two witnesses. Do you have people in mind?"

"Well, we were thinking that if it's here, we could have Mr. and Mrs. Griffin, and if it's Souton, maybe Uncle Jay and Aunt Michelle."

"If Shea wants to be at her church, I could marry you there. Want me to give Pastor Konrad a call?"

Joe looked at Shea. She nodded.

"Yes. Then get back to us. Thanks so much, Brad."

Brad called back ten minutes later. "It's all set up. Pastor Konrad will be leading a Bible study in their fellowship room, but we can use the sanctuary. I mentioned the Griffins. If you give them a call, they probably won't mind skipping out of Bible study. Oh! I've got a suggestion. How about we have coffee and sandwiches to celebrate after our Sunday service? We can introduce Shea and Stevie. You could invite your family. Then maybe you could do the same thing at Shea's church, and maybe at Clear Springs, at different times."

Shea was nodding her head. "That's a great idea, Brad. We've been feeling bad about not inviting the people close to us. This will give them at least a chance to congratulate us."

"See you at 8:00. Don't forget the marriage license."

Brad was gone. Ten minutes later he called back, "Can I bring Jen?"

"Sure, Brad." And Brad was gone again.

Shea called the Griffins. They said they would be honoured to be witnesses. Joe called his mom. She was excited and said she would be praying. "Joe, could we bring Sal on Sunday?"

"Sure, Mom. I've got some apologizing I need to do to her."

Gramps was excited. He would share the news with Uncle Jay and JJ.

When all the calls were made, Stevie, Shea, and Joe sat on the couch watching a Veggie Tales movie. In two-and-a-half hours, Shea and Joe would be standing before Brad, and he would pronounce them husband and wife.

Joe had his arm around Shea, and he whispered in her ear. "I didn't think these days off were going to start like this." He was perfectly content.

The sanctuary at the little church downtown was warm and welcoming. The Griffins, with Stevie between them, and Jen sat in the front row. There was no music. Brad opened by praying that God would be leading. He looked from Joe to Shea and put them at ease as he thanked them for the privilege of marrying them today. He solemnly reminded them that, in the presence of God, they were pledging themselves to each other. Shea knew that Steve would approve of this marriage. She looked up at Joe and thanked God for His love and grace. It had brought them together.

"Do you, Shea Lynn Findlay, take Joe to be your lawfully wedded husband? From this day forward, to have and to hold, for better, for worse, for richer and for poorer, in sickness and in health, to love and to cherish till death do you part?"

Shea said, "I do," looking into Joe's eyes.

Brad turned to Joe and said, "Do you, Joseph James Parker, take Shea to be your lawfully wedded wife? From this day forward, to have and to hold, for better, for worse, for richer and for poorer, in sickness and in health, to love and to cherish till death do you part?"

Joe said, "I do," smiling down at Shea.

Brad knew there were no rings. He pronounced them husband and wife and told Joe he could kiss his bride. They kissed for a long time and didn't stop until Stevie, who had wiggled away from the Griffins, tugged at Joe's shirt and said, "I want to kiss Mommy too." Joe picked him up laughing, and Stevie reached over to give Shea a hug and a kiss. Then he gave Joe a hug and a kiss.

Pastor Konrad had decided at 8:05 that he would leave the video running in the Bible study room and come to the sanctuary. Brad asked everyone to come to the front, and the five of them gathered around this new family and prayed for them. Both Joe and Shea felt that it was a holy moment, and even Stevie was still. Pastor Konrad ended his prayer with a loud amen, and Stevie gave out a loud amen too.

Chapter Twenty-Four

JOE WOKE WITH A START AND FOUND HIMSELF STARING INTO STEVIE'S GREY EYES. "GOOD morning, Stevie."

"Good morning, Joe." Stevie was whispering.

"Why are you whispering?"

"Mommy said *quiet. Joe is sleeping.*"

"Well, I'm awake now."

"Good!" Stevie yelled as he climbed on the bed. "Jump, jump, jump."

Joe laughed as Stevie jumped and fell. Joe caught him as he was about to tumble over the edge. He grabbed Stevie and gave him a hug.

"I think your next move is to tickle him, Joe." Shea was smiling in the doorway. Joe grabbed Stevie and rolled him around on the bed. Stevie howled with laughter. "Are you hungry, Stevie? Breakfast is ready."

Stevie looked from his mom to Joe, not wanting to end the game. "Yay! Pancakes." He scrambled off the bed and was off to the kitchen table.

"What time is it?"

"Seven," Shea answered. "He's been up for an hour. Are you hungry, Joe?"

Joe looked at her and answered. "Well, yes I am."

She turned around laughing. "Well, good. Because the pancakes are ready."

Joe and Shea had another busy day ahead of them. At 9:00 a.m., Joe called Ray. He answered on the first ring. "Hi, Ray."

"I didn't recognize the name on the phone. Oh, wait a minute … Findlay. You been there all night?"

"Yes, sir, I have been. And if your next question is did I sleep on the couch, the answer is no."

"Oh Joe, congratulations! And thanks for calling. Can I tell everyone here the good news?"

"Go ahead, Ray. But I called because we have an answer for you."

Ray knew what the answer was. "Great, because I already have the contractor who helps us out around here on notice. I'll get word out to the volunteers, and the house should be ready soon. Are you coming back for Monday?"

"That's my plan. I think ever since Brad pronounced us husband and wife, we're both pretty settled."

"No honeymoon?"

"Maybe this time next year. I'm perfectly content right here with Stevie, Shea, and that little baby kicking me when I'm holding its mother in my arms. Ray, I can't believe this is happening."

After Thursday's flurry of activity, Joe and Shea worked steadily on things that needed to be done. They purchased wedding bands. They talked to Shea's landlord, who said Shea would not be penalized for breaking her lease. He had a waiting list for apartments in her building. Joe was thankful that the man had been sensitive to Shea's troubles over the past months. Joe was content, and he didn't feel that he was under pressure. They began to pack up the apartment, confident they were moving soon.

● ● ●

ON SATURDAY, JOE ASKED Shea to go on an errand with him. It was time to start making some wrongs right. Shea was surprised when he drove back to their old neighbourhood. Joe sounded cautious as he made a request. "I'd like you and Stevie to come with me to the door." Shea looked at the old house. It needed a lot of work. Together they got out of the car and walked to the porch and up the steps. Joe knocked on the door, and it opened immediately. *Lord, please make this go better than it did last time.* Lilly stood there, glaring at him.

"Joe Parker, didn't I tell you to stay away from here? What do you want?"

"Lilly, thanks for talking to me. I'm here for a couple reasons. First, I want to say that I'm sorry. I treated you really badly and was right out of line. You were good to me, Lilly. You trusted me, and I stole from you." Joe didn't stop. He rushed on, saying, "Lilly, I want to pay you back. If you can try to figure out how much I owe you, I want to start paying you. I'm at school right now, but I'm starting a full-time job at the end of April."

Lilly looked at Shea and Stevie and said, "Who is this? I didn't know you have a little boy. He looks like you."

"This is my wife, Shea, and our little boy, Stevie. I didn't know I had a little boy either, Lilly, until I got out of jail. Lilly, I really am sorry. I don't drink or do drugs anymore. I'm trying to do what's right."

Lilly smiled at Stevie. "You are so cute."

Stevie smiled back. "Thank you." He turned to Shea. "Mommy, this a new friend."

"Only if you and Miss Lilly would like to be friends, Stevie."

Stevie looked at Lilly, who said, "Oh Stevie, of course we can be friends." She smiled at him and then turned to Joe. "I owe six hundred dollars to O-telecom. Forget the tablet. It came with the phone. And my cheque … what was it? About eight hundred? I guess you can pay me when you have it."

Joe reached into his pocket and took out his wallet. "Lilly, I've got three hundred today. I'll be back at the end of next month with more. The Lord seems to bring unexpected money my way these days."

Shea smiled. She knew that Joe was often able to do odd jobs for people, and most of the time they paid him. On top of that, he usually received an honorarium, or a love offering, when he spoke at men's groups and church services.

"You're really clean? Did you get religion or something?"

Joe laughed. "No, Lilly, not religion. I got Jesus, though, and He says I'm a new man in Him. Shea's a Christian too. Lilly, could we pray with you?"

"No way, Joe. I don't want none of that. I'm glad you're doin' good, though. Stevie is so cute." Lilly backed away and shut the door.

"That went well." Shea wished she knew the whole story. She was sure Joe had lots of stories to tell.

Joe replied, "Much better than last time." He smiled.

• • •

SUNDAY MORNING WAS FUN. Everyone at church greeted them and congratulated them on their marriage. They smiled at Stevie and talked to him, and he charmed them all. By the end of the day, he had a dozen new friends. Joe's family was there, and Aunt Marge and her family came. She cried when she met Lisa and was thrilled to see all Gramps' little great grandchildren together. With her two grandkids and Stevie, there were eight in all.

Joe watched as Sal stayed close to Joy's side. He picked up Stevie and took Shea's hand, leading her over to where they were standing. He smiled at Joy and turned to Sal. "Hi, Mom. I'm glad you could come."

"Thanks for inviting me. This boy looks so much like you."

"Those eyes kind of give him away. This is my wife, Shea."

• • •

MONDAY MORNING, JOE SPENT most of his first period class thinking about the events of the past five days. It had been a busy time, but he felt content. Thinking that Joe might want Shea and Stevie staying on site, Ray offered Joe the use of one of the winterized cabins. Because the cabin was small, Joe and Shea decided that Shea and Stevie should stay at the apartment. Shea would take her time packing and cleaning, and Stevie would be more settled in his familiar surroundings.

Joe easily caught up on the schoolwork he had missed. He did double duty in the kitchen, which for him wasn't a chore but a pleasure. Early Thursday morning he took a walk over to the farmhouse. He was surprised to see three cars and four trucks outside along the laneway. A group was gathered on the porch. Twelve people, most with steaming coffees in their hands, watched as Joe approached. *Who are all these people?* A man with a clipboard noticed him and shouted a greeting. Joe was relieved to see that he was one of the board members. Joe remembered that his name was Henry. Then he saw Syd's dad.

Henry spoke. "Guys … oh, and Emily and Cassie … this is Joe Parker." Henry had everyone say their name. All but a few mentioned a connection.

"Joe, I know your dad."

"I'm friends with Ray."

"I'm Hannah's dad."

"I saw you at our men's breakfast."

The list went on. Twelve people in all. Joe was amazed. For three days, people had come to prepare the house for his family.

Henry finished giving instructions, and everyone dispersed. He turned to Joe. "Would you like to look around?" Joe followed him for a tour. He started on the outside and pointed out that some boards on the porch had been replaced. A storage shed not far from the back porch had some new boards as well.

Henry described the updates that had been done as they meandered through the house. The house was old, but it seemed to Joe to be in excellent condition. They entered into a large living room where two men were replacing a light fixture, and another was putting caulking around some of the windows. Joe was glad to see the small woodstove off to the side in the living room. He noted the new fixtures in the small bathroom beside the kitchen. As they mounted the stairs, Henry turned to Joe and said, "We're pretty well finished up here." They came out on a landing, where three doors led to bedrooms. The flooring looked new, and Joe could smell paint. Windows were open, and when he looked in all three rooms, he saw people painting the trim around what looked to be freshly painted walls.

They stood again in the kitchen, and Joe could hear noise coming from what must be the basement.

"A crew is hauling a bunch of junk out of there," Henry spoke as Syd's dad came up the stairs, lifting a hand truck with another man balancing a big wooden box on it. "The basement isn't finished, but there's a hookup for the washer and dryer. There's also a nice cold room if anyone plans on canning. The gas furnace just needs a final check. That happens later today. And an electrician is coming tomorrow to put in a new breaker box. That will be an upgrade from the old fuses."

"Well, thank you. It looks like it's almost done."

"Joe, by tomorrow evening we will be done. Then it's just getting some good used appliances in here for you. Any other furniture you need?"

"Actually, between my folks, my gramps, and my uncle, I think we have a lot of furniture. We have the master bedroom furniture, Stevie's room, and the living room things from Shea's apartment."

"Well, you're probably wondering when you can move in. The house should be ready by Tuesday."

"Oh, that's great. But we'll have to wait until the weekend. I can't miss school. I've already missed too much." Joe stopped and looked at his watch. "Oh no, I've got five minutes to get over there to chapel. Thanks for everything. You guys are amazing," he called as he hurried out the door.

• • •

"YOU SHOULD SEE IT, Shea. Everything is so fresh and clean. And there's lots of room. Can you believe it? Next weekend we can move in." Joe didn't usually call Shea in the daytime, but today he couldn't resist. He still couldn't believe that everything had fallen into place so perfectly.

• • •

"JOE, YOU'VE BEEN BUSY. How did you get this assignment done early with all that's going on right now?" Logan shook his head and looked at Joe, expecting an answer. It was Friday afternoon, and Joe was on his way to Coverton to work with Shea, packing everything and cleaning up the apartment.

"Well, often when I do a paper, things come to me and I have to get them down right away. This paper was quite reflective, which was much easier for me than if I'd had to research it. I hope it's what you were expecting. I have to keep ahead of things; my life is just going to get busier."

The weekend was busy. By Saturday night, the only small things not packed were some of Stevie's toys and clothes, and the few things Shea and Stevie would need in the week. Shea had planned some simple meals. Stevie was looking forward to some necessary trips to *MicaDonalds*.

On Sunday at Shea's church there was a light lunch and fellowship after the service. The congregation was saying goodbye to Shea and Stevie and celebrating Shea and

Joe's marriage. Somehow the Findlays had heard about the get together. Shea and Joe were surprised as they came for the service and stayed afterward.

Stevie was excited to see them. He yelled, "Gramma, Gampa," and ran to them. He wouldn't leave them until it was time to go home.

Joe pulled into the laneway of the farmhouse when he got to Clear Springs Sunday evening. He had the house key in his pocket. The car was loaded with boxes, the first of many that would be unpacked there. He took the boxes out of the car and set them on the porch. He opened the door and turned on the lights and then took another tour through the house. *The appliances are here. Everything is bright and clean.* He prayed, "How blessed can one man be, Lord. Remind me always that these gifts are from you. Help Shea and I use them to your glory."

He went outside and one by one took the boxes into the house. When he finished, he locked the door behind him. He took in the clean air and the beauty all around. The sun had set, but it still glowed brilliant yellows and oranges in the west. *What a beautiful place to live. What a wonderful place to raise kids. Thank you, thank you, thank you, Lord. Just five more nights in the dorm room. I better get over there; the guys will be wondering where I am.*

Chapter Twenty-Five

"DADDY, LOOK!"

Joe smiled as Stevie took his hand and pulled him toward the window. A group of seven deer stood together beside the woodlot, just sixty feet from the house.

"Those are deer, Stevie. I don't think I've ever seen that many at a time around here. Nobody has lived here for a while. They must be wondering who we are."

Stevie had started calling Joe "Daddy" that afternoon. They had arrived ahead of the big moving truck that morning. Joe noticed that a few times since he and Shea had gotten married that people had referred to him as "your daddy" to Stevie. Stevie never seemed to question that, so they had decided to let Stevie bring the subject up. Today, a dozen men and women had shown up to help with the move, and Stevie heard the term often. The work was finished by suppertime, and the helpers gathered in the kitchen and living room for pizza. At one point, someone sent Stevie with a pop to give to *his daddy*.

Stevie took the pop to Joe and sat beside him with a puzzled look on his face. He turned to Joe and said, "Joe, are you my daddy?"

Joe looked around. Everyone had heard Stevie's question, and everyone was watching them. *Not how I was thinking this conversation would happen. Help me out here, Lord.*

"Lots of people are calling me that today, aren't they?" Stevie nodded. Joe continued. "Do you remember your daddy, Stevie?"

Stevie bit his bottom lip. "Yep. My daddy is Steve. Just like my name. Stevie, Steve. He is in Hebin. I did not see him for a long time."

"You're right, Stevie. Your daddy is in Heaven, and I know you miss him. Your mommy misses him too. Stevie, you'll see your daddy when you get to Heaven, but that might not be for a long, long time. Heaven is a good, good place. It's the place where

Jesus lives, and He's got lots of houses He's building there for us. I think your daddy is happy there. You know what, Stevie? Sometimes Jesus lets us have a new daddy. You have your daddy, Steve. But I could be your daddy too."

Joe could see that Stevie was thinking. *Not even four years old. This boy is so clever. Help him understand, Lord.* Joe gave Stevie a hug. "It's a little hard to understand, but I sure do love you."

Joe's heart exploded when Stevie looked at him with a big smile and said, "I love you too, Daddy." Joe looked around. He still had an audience, but he didn't mind. He saw a few tears to go along with big smiles, and then his eyes met Shea's. *Is there another man on earth right now who's as happy as I am?*

• • •

JOE DIDN'T THINK TIME could go any faster. Four weeks had passed since they moved into the farmhouse. Spring had arrived. He had seen his first robin. Buds were popping open on the trees, and the world was getting greener. He had plowed a plot of land over at the camp and had called Jeff to ask him to order seeds and plants. Joe had planned out a garden. It felt good to know what he was doing this time.

He was busy with Stevie. Shea was getting larger daily and was more than ready to have the baby two weeks before her due date. *She's tired and uncomfortable and*—Joe smiled as he thought about it—*a little bit cranky.*

There were only three weeks of school left. Joe had completed all his assignments and had three exams to write. He and Jessica had worked together planning two retreats. The men's retreat would be from May 8 to May 10, and the ladies' would be from May 15 to May 17. No one minded that the retreats were scheduled for after the school year ended. The organizers' marks would be determined ahead of the retreat, and all but four students were committed to attending the optional events. Joe was ready. He had found a speaker and planned a program. He made sure all of the sports equipment, including the equipment for archery and fishing, and the canoes and kayaks, were in perfect condition. Joe already had a good response to the printed flyers he'd sent out inviting the fathers, brothers, and grandfathers of this year's students. He had planned a menu with Millie. The only tasks remaining were determining the numbers as registrations came in, assigning accommodations, and ordering the food. The women students had committed to helping in the kitchen at the men's retreat, and the men had committed to helping in the kitchen for the ladies'.

• • •

JOE MET WITH RAY a week before graduation. "So the baby's due soon."

"Any day."

"Joe, are you confident that you'll do well on the exams?" Ray asked, sincerely concerned.

"I am. I think I know my stuff. It's quite unbelievable, isn't it? That the Lord could give me what I needed, after the way I abused my mind and body."

"It is, Joe. I think it fits our definition of a miracle."

Joe laughed. "Is this a quiz? I don't know about a definition, but I guess I'll just go with the verse: *'With man this is impossible, but with God all things are possible.'* I don't have a clue where it's found, but Jesus said it."

Ray smiled as he shook his head. "I don't know about you, Parker. But don't you worry about attending classes this week. Take care of that wife of yours and your sweet boy, and we'll all be praying as the new baby arrives."

• • •

THE NEXT MORNING AT 6:00 a.m., it wasn't Stevie's face Joe saw as he woke up. Shea was beside him, shaking his shoulder. "Out of bed, Daddy. We're going to have a baby today."

"What? Now?" he sputtered as he jumped out of bed.

"Oh, I think we have lots of time, but we better head to Coverton."

They'd decided to go to Coverton for the birth. It had been difficult getting Shea to her doctor in the city every week for the past month, but they'd done it. Stevie had been born at the bigger, more modern hospital in Coverton, and Shea was a little wary of the small hospital that was an hour closer. They would drop Stevie with the Griffins. If there were no complications, they'd be home by the end of the day. As they neared Coverton, Shea said, "The pains are regularly spaced, but they don't hurt much."

The Griffins were waiting for Stevie in the driveway. He waved goodbye with a smile. As they were entering the parking lot at the hospital, Joe heard Shea say, "Oh no!"

"What's wrong? What happened?" Joe looked over at Shea.

"My water broke."

"Oh no. Is that bad?"

"No, just messy. But it's good that we're here."

Joe parked at the front of the emergency door and got out to help Shea. A security guard was there immediately and said, "You can't park here, sir."

"But my wife, the baby. Her water broke!" He looked at Shea.

"Honey, go park the car. This fellow will make sure I get to where I need to be. Just check at the desk. You'll find me, don't worry."

As he left to park the car, Joe watched Shea enter the hospital with the security guard.

Twenty minutes later, Joe sat on the bed beside Shea, holding her hand. This was not like the movies. Shea was up and down and had even walked down the hall. The nurse monitoring her labour said the baby's heart rate was good. Everything was going well, but Shea was really hurting. Joe rubbed her back.

"Honey, you need to get my phone and call the Findlays." Shea sounded desperate.

"Why?"

"Because the baby is coming. Maybe they want to come up."

Joe grabbed Shea's phone from her purse and went to make the call. He was back a few minutes later.

"They'll be here in about an hour."

"Joe, I thought of a girl's name. How about Sharon Joy? After the two grandmas?"

"That's nice. I know my mom will be thrilled. And did you know that Jesus is called the Rose of Sharon in the Bible? What about the last name? We never really talked about that."

"How about we hyphenate both Stevie's and the baby's names. Findlay-Parker. Then we have to think of a boy's name, though."

"Seth William sounds good to me." Joe smiled.

"Ohhhhh!" Shea cried out in pain. When the contraction was gone, she whispered, "Joe, you're a genius."

After the first hour, Joe found the Findlays sitting in the waiting room. "The nurse says everything is progressing well. The baby and Shea are doing fine. She's hurting, though." Joe told them he would report in every half hour to keep them posted.

• • •

JOE LOOKED AT HIS watch. It had been three hours since they'd arrived at the hospital. He had just returned to Shea's bedside. The nurse was there. "The doctor's coming up from his rounds. I told him to hurry. This baby is on the way."

For the next twenty minutes, Joe spent most of the time watching Shea. He was fascinated but scared for her because she was in terrible pain. He felt helpless. When the doctor came in, Joe heard him say that the baby had crowned. Soon after that, he held up a screaming baby.

"It's a girl," he said and then he asked Joe if he wanted to cut the cord.

Joe shook his head quickly and said, "No. No, I don't." *Where did that question come from?* The doctor put the baby on Shea's chest, and she settled down.

Shea couldn't take her eyes off her. She was smiling through her tears. She looked at Joe. "You did good, Daddy."

A few minutes later, the nurse took the baby from Shea and put her on the scale. In no time she was wrapped in a pink blanket and handed back to Shea.

The doctor had been working on Shea. He looked up and said, "I had to put in a couple of stitches. Everything looks fine. Congratulations to you both. They'll give you a follow-up appointment when you're ready to leave. Any problems just call the office number. I'm on call this week, so if it's after hours, you'll talk to me."

Joe turned to the nurse. "Can I get the grandparents?"

"Sure. We leave you folks to yourselves. Not like the old days."

"When can we go home?' Shea asked.

"You can leave if everything is fine after two hours. But just rest, Shea. No one's going to rush you out of here."

Joe went to the waiting room and returned with the Findlays. They had heard the lullaby play on the PA system and hoped it indicated their grandchild's arrival. Shea looked at the nurse. "Joe needs to hold her."

Joe sat down and the nurse put the baby in his arms. He looked at Shea and smiled. "She's beautiful, like her mom."

Shea smiled, looking at Sharon and William. "We'd like to introduce you to Sharon Joy Findlay-Parker."

Sharon put her hand to her chest. She looked at her husband as she whispered, "Thank you so much, Shea. She is beautiful like her mother. But she does have Steve's eyes. He would have loved her so much."

It was a sad moment. No one spoke for a while. Joe stood up with the baby in his arms and motioned for Sharon to sit in the chair. He placed the baby in her arms as Sharon smiled. "Thank you, Joe. This means so much to us."

Joe had sent texts to Joy and Seth shortly after they had arrived at the hospital that morning. He sent off another in a hurry to say Sharon Joy Findlay-Parker had arrived. In his mother's reply, she asked if she should come, and that decided it. Joe knew that he had things to do before graduation, not the least being writing exams. He also had been chosen to be the valedictorian and had to prepare a speech. Shea was tired, and besides the baby, they had a rambunctious three-year-old to consider. It just made sense that his mom should come. Seth would come too to see his new granddaughter and get to know Stevie as well. A good friend of Joy's would stay with Chandra and Andrew.

• • •

JOE HAD BEEN GLAD to see his folks' van in the driveway when they arrived home two hours ago. Seth had come bounding down the steps as soon as he heard the car. He greeted Stevie first, and almost immediately Stevie let his new grandpa scoop him up and carry him into the house. As soon as the door was opened, Joe looked at Joy and smiled. Before she could ask if they were hungry, Joe could smell what was cooking. He looked at Shea. "Honey, my mom made us shepherd's pie."

Shea replied that she was starving. She hadn't felt like eating while they were at the hospital. At one point, Joe had grabbed a sub from the cafeteria, but now he was hungry too. Of course, he would always be able to eat his mom's shepherd's pie.

As the evening wore down, Joy helped Shea and the baby settle upstairs in bed. Stevie made it clear that he did not want to go to bed, but soon Seth convinced him that there was a story he needed to hear. They headed upstairs too. Joe went up to tuck Stevie in and to tell Shea he would join her soon.

• • •

"YOU HAD A LONG day." Joe looked up to see his mother looking at him from the armchair on the other side of the room. "You must be tired."

"Not too bad. I'm glad you're here."

"I'm glad I'm here too. Did you notice there's some food in the fridge? Millie sent over a big plate of sandwiches and a fruit and veggie tray. And Ray's wife …"

"Heidi," Joe filled in.

"Yes, Heidi dropped off a lasagna. You've made some good friends, Joe."

"Amazing friends. There are so many. And family. We are so blessed, Mom."

When Seth came down the stairs, he sat with them for a while. He told Joe that when they stopped at the camp on arrival, Ray had given him a key to Cabin Seven by the river.

"We'll head over there, but if Shea needs Mom in the night, just text us. We'll make sure the phones are on. We'll drive over there. Then we can get back in a hurry if need be. What time should we be back? Is 6:00 too early?"

"That's wake up time around here, Dad."

Chapter Twenty-Six

GRADUATION. THEY'RE GOING TO CALL ME UP THERE SOON. OH LORD, SO MUCH HAS happened this past year. Thank you for bringing me to this point in my life. Bless these people here today, especially my classmates. Remind each one of who they are in you.

Joe was a little nervous as he waited for his turn to go to the platform. The beautiful wide-open tent held up to three hundred people. Joe found it amazing that with only twenty graduates, most of the seats were full. There were board members, family members, community partners, pastors, and friends. Today's program had moved along quickly so far. It didn't look as if anyone was unhappy or bored. Of course, he could hear some laughter and squeals coming from the far end of the tent, where some little kids were running around. He suspected many of those little ones were his nieces and nephews, and probably even his son.

Ray was up at the front, looking at him, and Joe knew his time had come. "Ladies and gentlemen, I'd like to introduce you to this year's valedictorian, chosen by his classmates, Joe Parker."

Joe stood behind the podium waiting for the applause to stop. It gave him an opportunity to scan the crowd in front of him. He found Shea holding Sharon, and his mom with Sal beside her. His brother and sister both watched him carefully. His dad, holding Stevie, stood just beyond the chairs at the rear of the tent. Gramps sat with a group of people from Souton. The applause was over, and it was quiet. Joe took a deep breath and was about to speak when he heard, "Hi, Daddy." There was a chorus of laughter, and Joe watched Stevie hide his face in Seth's shoulder.

"Hi, Stevie. I'm glad you're here and being such a quiet boy." The whole crowd smiled with Joe. He began his speech.

"Distinguished members of the Board of Directors, faculty, staff, and volunteers. Our pastors and families and friends. Your support is what has made this day possible. I thank you on behalf of the fourth graduating class of Clear Springs Bible School. Today represents an end to a fantastic school year of learning and growth, as well as a springboard into new adventures for this year's graduates."

Joe stopped and looked deliberately at the graduates seated in the first row of seats. He smiled as he began his address to them.

"My fellow graduates, thank you for choosing me to be your spokesperson this day. Everyone knows that you chose me because I'm the old guy." *Yes, I was aiming for a laugh here, Lord.* "I certainly am the old guy, but as I told my dear friend and roommate, Dillon … just minutes after arriving … I came to this school as a baby Christian. I still have a lot of growing up to do, but the Lord has changed me over the past eight months. You, my friends, have taught me so much, and I count it a privilege to have shared this year with you. We are here to celebrate our graduation. Just a one-year program, but my purpose today is to drive home some of the things we have learned in this amazing place."

From here Joe had to use his notes. Actually, he had just put his fellow students' names down in a list. He began to share how each individual had brought blessing to others over the school year. Joe related some incidents that had brought them together as a student body. Some of his stories were amusing, and some so serious they brought tears to some eyes in the crowd.

"And so, my fellow graduates, we move on from here. Some plan to attend Bible college. Some have a call to missions. Some have applied to university or college. Some plan to stay right here at Clear Springs because they can't bear the thought of leaving." *Just what I figured, a few puzzled looks, but lots of laughs.*

"I want to leave a thought and a verse with you—not just for the graduates, but for everyone here. Just last week I met with our Director, Ray Hurst. All we students experienced a great deal of personal input from Mr. Hurst this year. We were talking about my life, and I said that all that's happened is kind of unbelievable. And this dear teacher, brother, friend, said to me that it really fits our definition of a miracle." Joe smiled and looked over at Ray. "I told Mr. Hurst then that I hoped it wasn't a quiz, because I really had never learned an exact definition of a miracle. I cannot give a definition, but I do know what I see over and over in my life. We've all seen it this school year. It is a promise to us as we leave this place.

"'*With men this is impossible; but with God all things are possible*' (Matthew 19:26b).

"Let's never forget this. It's not wishful thinking but a fact. What an opportunity we've had, learning and growing together this year. Let's purpose to pray for each other and practise the lessons we've learned in this place."

The rest of the ceremony went by quickly as certificates were received and awards were given. A prayer was said. People were encouraged to make their way over to the refreshment tables after the ceremony. The faculty and graduates filed out ahead of the others. Joe followed the other grads to the place where a group picture was to be taken. People began to come out of the tent, and most were congregating in groups around the field. As soon as the group picture was taken, Joe approached Shea, who stood holding Sharon. He hugged Shea and then turned to his dad, who was holding Stevie.

"Congratulations, Joe. You are an amazing young man."

"Thanks, Dad," Joe said as he scooped Stevie out of his arms and took Shea's hand. They walked together toward his mother, who watched him with a smile on her face. When Joe reached her, he gave her a hug and then looked around. He saw his family and his friends surrounding him. He had walked into what had become his place of welcome over the past year. *Thank you, Lord, for all these people. Thank you for bringing me home to you.*

Joe asked Joy if she would take a picture for him.

"Lead on, Joey" She followed him to where Gramps and JJ stood and said, "Joey needs a picture, guys. He wants all those beautiful grey eyes lined up together."

Even Stevie had a bright smile, and the picture was perfect.

• • •

JOE SAT WATCHING SHEA seated in the rocking chair across the living room. *It can't get much better than this. Lord, I love this woman.* Joe thought back over the day. Over the week. He was tired, but tired in the best way ever. That little doll in her mommy's arms over there woke him at regularly timed intervals in the night. It was his job to bring her to Shea to nurse.

Stevie had more energy than he did. Today his dad had done most of the chasing, and now his parents had gone home to Harper. *And here sits Joe Parker. A new creation in Christ. Prison, drugs, hopelessness, sin with its chains—all those old things have passed away. Now that's a miracle.*

P A I N. Joe flexed his fingers as he read the letters across his knuckles.

Shea's voice interrupted his thoughts. "What are you thinking, Joe Parker?"

"Well, I'm thinking I'm really tired, and I'm glad tomorrow's Sunday, because we can rest. Maybe Monday things will get back to normal. Except that Monday I have to make sure all the plans for the retreat are finalized. JJ heard Dad and Gramps talking about it, and he wants to come. Then Kevin asked if he could come. And Carl and Jeff want to come. And Sarge and Rob, and things are kind of getting out of hand. I'll have to talk to Ray about all that."

"Well, I'm thinking," Shea began, "that the Lord has good things planned for you here at Clear Springs. This men's retreat is just the start of something big. And I'm also thinking maybe it's time for you to do something about that tattoo on your knuckles. I love you, Joe." With that, Shea stood up and made for the stairs. She flicked off the light to the living room as she went up to bed.

Joe smiled in the darkened room. *Thanks, Lord, for that beautiful girl. And my two precious kids. So many friends. An excellent day. Thanks, Lord, that with you all things are possible.*

Joe couldn't see his fingers in the dark, but he flexed them and thought, *I guess Monday I need to find time to make an appointment with a tattoo artist.* He pictured the change on his hand. Two little words across the base of the two middle fingers: *NO* and *MORE. NO MORE PAIN.*

What had Gramps said about normal that day we met? I wouldn't worry about normal. I've been trying to figure out what that is all my life. Joe smiled. His life certainly wasn't normal, but he couldn't be more content as he made his way up the stairs.

The End

About the Author

JANET WEILER LIVES IN THE SOUTHERNMOST TOWN IN CANADA WITH HER HUSBAND OF thirty-eight years, Clarence. Both would say that they're retired, but they still have a busy household with many responsibilities. They wouldn't have it any other way! Determined to follow Christ together since they got married, they have opened their hearts, and often their home, to many.

Janet received a Bachelor of Social Work from the University of Windsor in 1976. Over a span of forty years, she gained valuable experience as she supported people of all ages in a variety of settings. She never had a job she didn't like.

With three sons and three daughters—and many foster children over the years— Janet concedes that parenting isn't easy, but it has been a joy from the start. Now that grandchildren are in the picture, the fun continues.

Janet is an avid reader who always wanted to write a novel. When the coronavirus pandemic began in 2020, she decided it was time. She has many stories in her head, and she hopes that this book will be the first of many.

janetweilerauthor@gmail.com

janetweiler.ca